WHEN HONOR DIES

A CRIME THRILLER

WHEN HONOR DIES
BOOK 1

ROBERT VAUGHAN

*ROUGH
EDGES
PRESS*

WHEN HONOR DIES

This book is dedicated to the memory of my brother, Special Agent Tom Vaughan, more courageous than we knew.

PROLOGUE

FRANCE, JULY, 1918

The heavy German bombardment that went on all night had, mercifully, been reduced to an occasional bursting shell. One shell would come in, swooshing like distant rolling thunder, then detonate in a fiery rose, sending deadly missiles of shrapnel whistling through the Meuse Argonne Forest. After each explosion, a plume of smoke would drift lazily up through the early morning bars of sunlight that were just now beginning to slash down through the trees.

Mike Kelly, lieutenant of infantry, American Expeditionary Force, and commander of the advanced listening post, tightened the bandage on his bleeding leg. It hurt terribly and in a war full of amputees, the thought that he might lose it weighed heavily upon him. He lay in a trench that was full of the dead from his little command and fought the nauseating waves of pain that threatened to make him pass out.

It was important that Mike remain conscious because he had to warn the main element when the Germans started their expected attack. That was the whole purpose of his being here, some one thousand yards in advance of his own lines.

When the shelling stopped altogether, Mike pulled himself up to the parapet of the trench so he could look over toward the German lines. There, moving en masse through the forest toward his position, he saw hundreds of dark, gray shapes. The attack had begun.

Mike slipped back down into the trench and twisted the crank on the field phone to call headquarters. When he got no response, he twisted it again. It was a useless gesture, however, because the artillery fire had chewed the telephone lines to pieces. His phone was dead and he was completely cut off.

Mike looked through the bodies until he found the soldier who had the flare pistol. Taking it from the soldier's holster, he pointed it up and pulled the trigger. There was a pop, then a hissing sound as the red flare arched high into the gray dawn sky. If he couldn't talk to his commander to tell him the size and direction of the attack, he could at least warn him that an attack was coming.

One of the German soldiers, seeing the source of the red flare, yelled something guttural and pointed at Mike. Several of the soldiers began firing at him. Mike slipped back down into the trench and covered up, listening to the drumming sound of their jackboots as they ran toward him. He realized that if he raised up and fired back at them he would be killed. His only chance was to wait for them, then surrender.

At first, Mike thought they were going to kill him anyway. Some of the soldiers may have but he was relieved to see that the German officers had no such intention. They wanted him for questioning so a German lieutenant signaled for Mike to climb out of the trench, and with his hands raised, Mike did as he was asked.

It was very late in the afternoon when a party of four soldiers was detailed to escort Mike farther to the rear of the German lines where their intelligence officers would question him about such things as the strength of the Americans across from them. There too, he was told, he would be given better medical treatment. Mike had already been given first aid at the German field hospital but his leg still hurt terribly and even with the makeshift crutch it was difficult for him to walk.

"How far do we have to go?" Mike asked, grunting with pain from the effort of trying to keep up with them.

One of the soldiers could speak English and he translated Mike's question to the others. They all laughed.

"What's so funny?" Mike wanted to know.

"Do not worry how far you have to go," the soldier explained. "You will not get there. You will try to run and...bang!" He and the others laughed again.

Mike knew then that they weren't taking him to the rear at all. They were just getting him away from their superiors so they could kill him.

Johnny Sangremano of the American 94th Aero Squadron was flying some five hundred feet above the road when he saw them. He banked his Nieuport Scout plane around to get a second look. From the distinctive shape of their helmets, Johnny knew that at least four of the men down there were German soldiers. The fifth man wasn't wearing a helmet and his red-blond hair shined brightly in the afternoon sun. From the cut of the uniform, however, Johnny was pretty sure the fifth man was an American. Also, he was unarmed, and walking with a crutch, while the four Germans were positioned around him, carrying rifles. It was obvious to Johnny that the German soldiers were escorting an American prisoner to the rear.

Johnny swung his little biplane around in a large circle to line up with the road, then he lowered the nose and swooped down to just a few feet above the ground. He flew directly at the little group of men and smiled when the four guards dived to the ditches on either side of the road, three on one side, one on the other. That opened up some distance between the guards and their prisoner and gave Johnny a clear shot at them. He touched the rudder bar just enough to line his guns up with the three Germans in the ditch to the right. He pulled the trigger and watched as the bullets from his twin Lewis machine guns kicked up puffs of dust from the road, then laced across the Germans themselves. As he flashed by overhead, he saw the German guard on the opposite side of the road throw down his rifle and get up to run toward the relative safety of a nearby clump of trees.

Johnny pulled the nose of his plane up hard, throttled back the engine, then kicked the rudder bar to wrench it over into a hammerhead stall. This allowed him to go right back down over the same path he had just flown, though he was now going in the opposite direction. With the engine still at idle, he landed on the road itself, bouncing to a stop some ninety feet away from the American prisoner. The red-gold hair and bright blue eyes of the American could be seen quite clearly now. There was also a spray of freckles across his nose and he smiled broadly as he hobbled on his crutch, moving toward the plane as quickly as he could. Johnny climbed out onto the lower wing and reached a hand down to help the American up.

"Taxi, mister?" Johnny joked.

"Yeah. How about taking me to Times Square?" the American shouted over the noise of the idling engine.

"You've got it," Johnny answered.

"The name's Kelly, Mike Kelly," the American said. "Boy, am I glad to see you!"

"Kelly? With red hair and blue eyes, what else could it be? I'm Johnny Sangremano. Get in, quick!"

"Where?" Mike asked. He had reached the wing now and was confused by the fact that there was only one seat in the airplane.

"There," Johnny said, pointing to the seat. "Where do you think?"

"But what about you?"

"Don't you worry about me. I'm going to be sitting on your lap!" Johnny replied with a bubbling laugh. He was holding a little brown sack in his hand and he held it out toward Mike. "Want one?"

"Want one? Want one what?" Mike asked, surprised by the offer.

"Lemon drops," Johnny replied. "I'm never without them."

Mike laughed. "Couldn't we go into this later? We aren't exactly taking a leisurely ride down Fifth Avenue, you know."

"Oh, well, if you were in such a hurry, you should have said so," Johnny teased.

Mike climbed into the seat, then Johnny got in on top of him. The weight of holding Johnny on his lap hurt Mike's leg, but he wasn't about to complain. He held on as Johnny gunned the engine, raced down the road, then lifted into the air just as a dozen or more German soldiers broke out of the tree line and began firing rifles at them. Mike could hear the bullets popping through the fabric but none of them did any damage. Then he felt a sickening lurch in his stomach as Johnny stood the Nieuport on its tail for a steep climb away from the road.

"Oh, shit!" Mike yelled. Involuntarily, he wrapped his arms around Johnny and squeezed hard as he held on for dear life.

"I know you're glad to see me, but don't squeeze so hard. I can't breathe!" Johnny said.

"Sorry," Mike replied, loosening his grip slightly. "I guess I got a little startled."

"A little?"

"A lot," Mike admitted.

Johnny laughed then and Mike began laughing as well. Both men laughed until they cried, laughing so hard that it could be heard even over the roar of the engine. And there, in the skies over the German lines in war-torn France, a friendship was born.

CHAPTER 1

NEW YORK, LATE SPRING, 1920

n New York City's Little Italy, people were standing eight deep on both sides of Mulberry Street, straining to see the funeral cortege as it passed. The first person to appear was an altar boy carrying the cross. Behind him was a drum draped in black crepe and behind the drum the red, white, and green flag of Italy, with black bunting at the tip of the staff. The drummer was beating upon the muffled drum, a very slow, measured cadence. The cross and flag bearer were marching to his time. As the crucifer passed in front of them, those who were standing on the curb crossed themselves. Many were weeping openly.

"Here he comes," someone yelled.

"Guiseppe Sangremano," another said. "Who could believe it?"

"God have mercy on him."

"May he rest in peace."

"Here comes his coffin!"

"Look how beautiful it is!"

The hearse was an automobile with glass side windows that would allow the coffin to be seen easily by those looking on. It drove very slowly behind the cross, drum, and flag.

The six pallbearers, all of whom were wearing tuxedos, walked with solemn faces alongside the hearse, three on each side of the car. They were there for more than ceremonial reasons, for occasionally a street-side mourner would get carried away by it all and rush out to throw himself against the side of the hearse. Whenever one of them did so, the pallbearers would firmly, but gently, move them away. This was not entirely new to them. Some of the pallbearers had been protecting Giuseppe for many years, because while he was alive, they had been Giuseppe's bodyguards. In fact, if the mourners had looked closely enough at the pallbearers, they would have been able to see the slight, telltale bulges under their jackets that indicated that, even now, these men were carrying guns.

Inside the hearse, the coffin lid was open and the body had been raised slightly so the viewers could see Giuseppe Sangremano nestled in the white satin lining of his expensive casket. Although there were no flowers in the hearse itself, three truckloads of flowers followed immediately behind, perfuming the air with their cloyingly sweet scent.

A big Cadillac limousine followed the truckloads of flowers and led the remaining cars of the funeral cortege. In this car were Giuseppe Sangremano's weeping widow, Sophia; their three sons, Tony, Vinnie, and Johnny, and their daughter, Katherine. Immediately behind that car was another carrying Tony's wife, Eva, and Vinnie's wife, Gina. Neither Johnny nor Katherine were married.

Also, riding with the wives was Al Provenzano, the *consigliore*, or chief counselor of the Sangremano Family.

Though not blood kin, Al Provenzano was the oldest and most trusted friend of the Sangremanos and on this sad occasion he was afforded a position of respect and honor equal to that of a member of the family.

With all the pomp and circumstance, as well as the public attention it caused, this procession was much more like a state funeral than a private burial. And in a way, it was a state funeral, for in life Giuseppe Sangremano had occupied a position of particular importance to each and every resident of the Lower East Side.

Although more of the area's residents were citizens than weren't citizens, even the native-born citizens didn't think in terms of U.S., state, or local government for functions and services. In their minds, the police, the city hall, the state house, and the federal government were all entities that were, at best, composed of confusing regulations and unfathomable mysteries. At worst, they were corrupt despots and organs of governmental bureaucracies whose only purpose was to oppress the people.

Therefore, when a local businessman wished to establish a grocery store, a laundry, a bakery, or a restaurant, he didn't go to the Chamber of Commerce. And when a woman wished to make arrangements to bring over her mother and father from the old country, she didn't go to Immigration. When seeking redress for a grievance, the injured party didn't go to the Justice Department. Where one went, on all these occasions, was to Giuseppe Sangremano. Giuseppe Sangremano, they knew, had the connections and the resources to cut through the red tape and get things done.

Giuseppe Sangremano was much more than the patriarch of a large Italian family. He was a man of such influence and power that what he did affected the lives of everyone who lived south of 38th Street. He was not only the one they came to when they needed help against some transgression, he was the one they feared when they were the transgressors. He was the final authority, the benevolent dictator, the godfather of them all, and when he was spoken to it was always with a respectful "Don" before his name. And just as Don Sangremano never turned down an earnest request, neither would anyone ever turn him down if he should happen to call upon them for a small favor.

The relationship between Giuseppe and the common people of Lower Manhattan and Queens was based not only upon fear and dominance, but also upon respect and honor. Honor was a very important thing to the Italians, more important than any other virtue. This was most evidenced by the code of Omerta, or code of silence. The code of Omerta specified that no Sicilian would tell the police anything, and in America, that honor dictated that even non-Sicilian Italians, and those who were subject to Sangremano's control, would follow the code. According to the code, they couldn't even identify the murderer of a member of their own family. That meant that if the killing was the result of an action sanctioned by Giuseppe Sangremano, the victim's family went without justice. If, however, Giuseppe Sangremano had nothing to do with the murder, the family could expect swift and sure justice. Sometimes, within twenty-four hours, the head of the murderer would be delivered in a package to the grieving family of the murderer's victim.

This code of honor was a part of the dependence upon family, kinship, and the Italian, particularly Sicilian, connection. A non-Italian could kill another non-Italian, but he could not kill an Italian, regardless of the justification. An Italian could kill a non-Italian, or another Italian, but he could not kill a Sicilian, regardless of the justification. On the other hand, if the killing was justified, a Sicilian could kill anyone.

Giuseppe Sangremano had been born in Sicily where membership in the Mafia was a way of life. The word "Mafia" was never used by its actual members, nor by those who were subject to its power. The members called it the Arm, the Clique, the Outfit, the Tradition, the Office, the Honored Society, the Combination, or La Cosa Nostra, but never the Mafia.

The Mafia had been founded for noble purposes in the seventeenth century as an underground army to fight against the oppressive rule of the Bourbons. When it began, the Mafia's aims were honorable and it thrived on strong kinship bonds, a code of ethics, and masculine honor. The individual groups were called "Families" and they were headed by "Dons," or men of respect. By the time the Bourbons left Sicily, the Mafia had grown too comfortable in their role of authority to share power with anyone else, and therefore, continued to operate. The Mafia was involved in all aspects of Sicilian life, not only controlling the criminal activities, but administrative services as well.

There were, however, too many people wanting a piece of the pie, and that led to disputes. Added to that was the rigid code of the "vendetta" that took literally "an eye for an eye" and "a life for a life," so that the death toll among the men mounted steadily. Giuseppe's father was murdered in a vendetta so by the time he was sixteen, Giuseppe found himself the male head of his family. When his eighteen-year-old sister was dishonored, Giuseppe killed the man who was responsible, and was forced to come to America, not fleeing the law, but fleeing the family of the man he had killed. That was in 1866.

Arriving in New Orleans shortly thereafter, Giuseppe got a job at a whorehouse, ejecting drunken patrons who were making trouble. Though some thought he was too young, he proved himself the very first week when one patron began brandishing a pistol, refusing Giuseppe's polite request that he leave. While the drunken patron was waving his pistol around, enjoying the sight of everyone in the house cowering before him, Giuseppe reached behind the bar to pick up a shotgun, called a *lupara* by his people, and used it to blow half the drunk's head off. In this way, Giuseppe "made his bones," and was accepted as a member of the Macheca Family in New Orleans.

Joe Macheca was the first Sicilian to bring to America the organization and discipline of the ancient order of the Mafia. It wasn't referred to as the Mafia. Joe Macheca's group, and other groups who modeled themselves after Joe's group, simply referred to themselves as the Family.

By the time Giuseppe was thirty, he was a *capo-regime*, or a lieutenant at the head of his own branch of the Macheca Family. When Joe Macheca died, Giuseppe believed he would take over the Family. Instead, the Family was taken over by Charles Matranga, one of the other *capo-regimes*. With no hard feelings, but an unrequited ambition, Giuseppe left New Orleans and moved to New York. New York was a big city and at the time of Giuseppe's arrival, not yet organized. Giuseppe, using the lessons he had learned from Macheca, gathered a handful of trusted Sicilians around him and put together his own Family. He ran it with an iron fist until he dropped dead of a heart attack at the age of sixty-nine.

Giuseppe's son Tony was now the heir apparent to the Sangremano Family organization. It was a big organization, with far-flung operations in all aspects of crime, from gambling and prostitution, to protection and organized labor unions. The Sangremano Family had an infrastructure as complex as that of a major business. Tony was fond of saying that the Sangremano Family was no different from any other successful business enterprise in America. Tony had trained his entire life to take over the operation and was ready for the leadership that had been thrust upon him.

With the advent of Prohibition, all the other Families in New York had gone into the bootlegging business. Giuseppe had not yet taken the Sangremano Family into the business, despite Vinnie's urging that he do so. The moment Giuseppe died, however, Vinnie began making plans, locating a source of supply, identifying which police officers and judges would have to be paid off, and determining where he would put the speakeasies.

Vinnie shared all his ideas with Tony because Tony was the one in whose hands the ultimate decision rested.

It was a decision that Tony agonized over, for the whiskey business was already proving to be extremely profitable for the other Families. However, there were other considerations involved, and on balance, Tony decided that, like his father, he would keep the Sangremano area dry. He announced his decision to Vinnie as they rode toward the cemetery.

For a moment Vinnie was stunned. He couldn't believe his ears and he looked at his brother as if he hadn't heard him properly. Then, when he realized that Tony was serious, he made an effort to change his mind.

"Tony, what are you saying?" he asked. "We can't afford to stay out of it, don't you see that? The Vaglichio Family is already in it in a big way and if we don't watch out, they'll move right in on our territory."

Vinnie was thirty-two but he looked younger. He had light brown, curly hair and a powerfully built physique that he frequently exercised by boxing—not professionally, though he did sometimes spar with professional fighters who trained at his gym. Vinnie could hold his own with the best of them and it was said that if he ever wanted to turn pro he could make it all the way to the top.

"You know Pop didn't want to do this," Tony replied. "And I think we should consider that. After all, he is the one who built the business into what it is today."

Tony was forty. He was short and bald and anyone who saw him in a restaurant somewhere might easily mistake him for an accountant.

"Yeah, well, Pop is gone now," Vinnie said. "It's up to us…" He amended his statement, "I mean it's up to you to make the decisions. Anyway, Pop never really believed Prohibition was going to happen. Well, it did happen. In January, Prohibition became the law of the land and that law is not going to go away overnight. There are millions of people out there wanting whiskey, with no way of getting it unless it is supplied to them by people with imagination and enterprise. You are a man of numbers, Tony. Just think about it. Why, if we only made one dollar per person, there would be more money in it than anyone could ever imagine."

"I don't know," Tony said. "My idea is to keep everything quiet. The less noise we make, the less interested the law will be in us. We've got several good operations going for us now, and all of them making money. Why not just let things go as they are? Maybe we will go into the liquor business someday, but for now, we need to just sit back and watch it for a while, to see how things are going before we jump in."

"If we sit back and watch before we jump in, there won't be anything left to jump in to," Vinnie warned. "Vaglichio is moving so fast that soon he will have everything all sewed up."

Tony chuckled. "It's a business, Vinnie, a business, that's all. What we may lose by not getting into it right now, we will more than make up for by not being too reckless."

"Tony, Vinnie, will you two listen to yourselves?" Katherine scolded. "Papa isn't even in his grave yet and here the two of you are, fighting over his business like vultures over a carcass." Katherine looked at her mother pleadingly. "Mama, won't you say something to them? It's disgraceful, the way they are acting."

Katherine was nineteen, tall, angular, and not at all pretty. However, as she was Giuseppe's only daughter, he had never realized that she wasn't beautiful, and when she announced that she wanted to be a movie star, Giuseppe, though having no understanding whatever of the business, vowed to make her wish come true. He died, however, before he was able to make good on his vow. Katherine had been her father's princess and she enjoyed a life of privilege in his house. She loved her father deeply and was thoroughly despondent over his death. She also couldn't help but wonder what was going to happen to her dreams of becoming a movie star now.

Sophia Sangremano, Giuseppe's widow, was a short, stout stack of black silk and lace, sitting all drawn up and veiled, way over in the corner of the Cadillac. She hadn't said a word since the funeral cortege left the church. Even her sobbing had been quiet, hidden behind the handkerchief she had kept clutched to her face throughout. Now she stuck a black-gloved hand out and touched her daughter lightly on the arm.

"Katherine, it is business they are talking," she said in her thick Italian accent. "You should know by now, the women do not interfere when the men discuss business."

"But, Mama, in the very car with..."

"Shh," Mama Sangremano said and, appropriately chastised, Katherine fell silent.

Johnny observed the byplay between his sister and

brothers, and between his sister and mother, with the bemused sense of an indifferent observer. Johnny hadn't made a sound since the funeral began. During the viewing of the body and at the funeral itself, all the people had thought Johnny's extreme silence was brought on by grief. Johnny did grieve for his father but his silence was more that of someone who felt a sense of detachment than that of someone who was being purposefully silent. Though the other two boys had always been intensely interested in "the business," Johnny's own interests had always been beyond that. He had at times wanted to be a professional baseball player, a merchant marine, a cowboy, and an aviator. From the time he was very young, all his dreams had taken him out of New York and away from the family enterprises. When the war began, Johnny was at just the right age to realize some of his dreams. He did become an aviator and he did leave New York. He was gone for three years, and because he was only eighteen years old when he left, he didn't know anything about what his two brothers were talking about. Therefore, it was impossible for him to be a participant in their conversation or to even have an opinion about the subject they were discussing.

Johnny was tall for a Sicilian, taller than either of his two brothers, though not as powerfully built as Vinnie. His hair was very dark and straight. He had flashing dark eyes and olive-complexioned skin. Women considered him very handsome, a point that the bistro girls in Paris had made, often, during the war.

Johnny not only had no interest in the family business, he wasn't even sure what all kinds of business, legitimate and illegitimate, they were in. After he returned from the war, Johnny finished college, then became reacquainted with a friend he had known in the army. The two of them bought a war-surplus airplane and that had occupied all his time.

The plane they bought was a De Havilland DH-4, a British-designed biplane built in America under contract. The plane was designed to be a single-engined bomber but it was built too late in the war for the airplane to ever see any action. As a result, there were literally thousands of DH-4s, many of which had never been flown, sitting ignominiously at airports all across the country. Most could be bought for a song, but if they had not been flown, that also meant that they had not been maintained. As they sat around, their rigging began to sag, the fabric sprouted holes, and the engine sprang leaks. That was the condition of the plane Johnny and his friend had bought and for the last several weeks he and his friend had been putting it back into flying shape. Now they were about to embark upon a barnstorming trip across the country. Johnny was looking forward to the adventure but it was not a prospect that had pleased his father and the two had argued over it just a few days before the old man was brought down by a heart attack.

Johnny had already made up his mind that he was going through with the barnstorming trip whether his father approved or not. Now, behind the legitimate grief he felt over his father's death, he also felt a sense of relief that he would be free to do whatever he wanted, without having to answer to anyone. And, though he shared this with no one, he was also experiencing some guilt feelings because of that sense of relief.

Standing in the crowd along the side of the street watching the funeral were Weasel, whose real name was Jimmy Pallota, Guido Fellini, and Dom Todaro. The three had managed to get a front-row position on the sidewalk and as the funeral procession passed, they dutifully, and respectfully, crossed themselves.

"We goin' down to the cemetery?" Guido asked.

"Yeah, sure," Dom answered. "I mean, ever'one'll be there. Come on, Weasel, what do you say? You want to go to the cemetery and see all the big guys?"

"No," Weasel said. "I'm goin' over to see Maxie Dunnigan."

"Maxie Dunnigan? What do you want to go see that mick for?"

" 'Cause he'll need numbers runners this afternoon but he won't have anyone, because everyone will be at the funeral. This is a good chance to pick up some money."

"Yeah," Guido said, rubbing his hands in excitement. "Yeah, hey, Dom, what do you think? That's a pretty good idea, isn't it?"

"Ah, he won't use us," Dom protested. "You prob'ly got to be at least eighteen to work for him."

"So, we'll tell him we're eighteen," Weasel said. "You think we'll be any smarter two years from now?"

"I don't know," Dom said. "I think we ought to go to the cemetery."

"Well, you go to the cemetery if you want to. I'm going to make some money."

"I'm goin' too," Guido said. "What about you, Dom?"

"What? Do you mean you aren't going to pay your respects? Your sister is married to one of the Sangremano soldiers, for chrissake," Dom said to Guido.

"So what? Who'll know I'm not there? Besides, if there's a chance to pick up some money like Weasel says, then I'm all for that. What about it, Dom? You with us?"

"Aw, I guess so," Dom agreed hesitantly. "I sure woulda liked to seen all the big boys out at the cemetery though."

"How do you think the big boys got to be big boys?" Weasel asked. He put his finger to his temple, then tapped it slowly. "They got to be big boys by using their heads, that's how. That's what we're goin' to do now. And our best bet is to see Dunnigan while we got the chance. Otherwise, someone else might beat us to it."

"All right, I'm goin'," Dom said. "Did I say I'm not goin'?"

The funeral procession continued as the Cadillac the Sangremanos were riding in made a sharp turn off the street. Tony leaned over to pull the black curtain aside so he could look out the window.

"We're here, Ma," he said. "We're at the cemetery."

Katherine began crying anew and Sophia put her arm around her daughter to comfort her.

"I'd better not see any of the Vaglichios here," Vinnie growled.

"Vinnie, we are under my leadership now, and I'm telling you that all that is over," Tony said. "The bad blood that existed between our families goes back to Papa's trouble before he left Sicily. But Papa is gone now and it is time we began working together, as businessmen should. The Vaglichios control Long Island and the Bronx. We have Lower Manhattan and Queens. The Nicolos have Brooklyn and Staten Island. There's no reason why we can't all live in peace and I intend to do so. As a matter of fact, Don Sam Vaglichio contacted me and asked if he could attend the funeral to show his respect and I told him yes. Furthermore, if Don Sam Vaglichio comes to us to offer his condolences, we will accept them graciously."

"You'd better watch out for him, Tony," Vinnie cautioned. "I'm warning you, he is just setting you up."

"It isn't like that now," Tony said. "The old ways are gone."

The car tires crunched through the gravel drive of the cemetery, then stopped alongside the grave that had already been opened. Doors slammed as people left their cars and came to stand around the grave, though by now there were so many mourners that the ones in the very back were so far away that they had no idea of what was going on. Up at the very front, a small tent had been erected and two rows of chairs were set up for the immediate family. Sophia, Katherine, Tony, and his wife, Eva, sat in the front row of chairs. Johnny sat in the second row with Al Provenzano, Vinnie, and Gina.

There were several uniformed policemen in the cemetery as well. Though some of them were there for crowd control, many were there as mourners for they had been on the Sangremano payroll for a long time. They couldn't help but wonder, now that the Godfather was gone, if Tony Sangremano would continue his father's practice of paying off the police.

One of the policemen present who was not on the payroll was Joe Provenzano. It wasn't because Joe had not been offered the opportunity to go on the roll. The offer had been made many times but Joe always turned it down. What made this particularly surprising was the fact that Joe Provenzano was the nephew of Al Provenzano.

Joe's uncle Al was a member of the Family, but Joe's father was not. Nevertheless, Joe's father had always studiously avoided doing anything that might displease the Family. The fact that Joe had become a policeman, an anomaly for a Sicilian, had caused his father some consternation and his uncle Al some difficulty. It was only because of the absolute trust enjoyed between the Sangremanos and their consigliore that there wasn't any trouble from the relationship.

Joe Provenzano was honest but he wasn't blind. He knew that the man his uncle worked for was a gangster and he knew that, by association, that made his uncle a gangster too. He told himself, however, that he was a policeman, not a judge, and though he studiously avoided any wrongdoing himself, he did not condemn his uncle for his actions.

Joe's sense of right and wrong was clearly recognized by his relatives and boyhood friends. However, that did not prevent Joe from attending all social functions. He was able to move easily and without fear among them. He would check his gun at the door, right alongside the Mafia soldiers who were also checking theirs.

Joe's presence at the funeral was duly noted and admired by all. Everyone knew that he wasn't on the payroll. The only reason he was present was to pay his respects. Joe stood in the very front row of mourners and crossed himself as the priest began the graveside service.

The priest, his alb glistening white in the bright sun, moved to the foot of the coffin and raised his hand to make the sign of the cross as he proclaimed a final absolution upon the remains of Giuseppe Sangremano.

"*Misereatur vestri omnipotens Deus, et dimissis peccatis vestris, perducat vos ad vitam aeternam.*"

Joe and the others who were close enough to hear the priest responded, "Amen."

"*Indulgentiam, absolutionem, et remissionem peccatorum nostrorum tribuat nobis omnipotens et misericors Dominus.*"

"Amen."

Sitting under the small canvas canopy, Johnny listened to the priest, crossed himself, and responded at the appropriate times. He couldn't help but wonder if God really was granting forgiveness for all of his father's sins. Were his father's sins measured according to the same standard by which other men's sins were measured? Johnny was ignorant of the details of his father's business, but he knew that it included many of the things that were in direct violation of the Ten

Commandments, from coveting to bearing false witness, even to killing. And yet, for all this, Johnny knew that Giuseppe was a man who had set certain standards of morality and honor that he expected everyone to follow and by which Giuseppe, himself, had abided.

As Johnny looked around the cemetery at the faces of the many who had come to mourn, he saw that for the greatest majority of them, the grief was sincere. That gave him pause for thought. A man who was truly evil could not elicit this much sincere grief, could he?

After the service was over, the mourners began returning to their cars. A few people remained, wanting to offer their condolences to Johnny's mother. The Nicolos came by first. Don Pietro and his two sons, Enrico and Roberto, bent over and kissed her hand, then spoke quietly. There had always been peace between the Nicolos and the Sangremanos. In the lower echelons, there had been a great deal of intermarriage between the two Families and that helped to cement relations.

But the Nicolos had also always gotten along with the Vaglichios, and there were several cases of intermarriage between their Families as well. As a result, the Nicolos had on occasion acted as peacekeepers, though peace-keeping was a nonproductive and often frustrating role so it wasn't one the Nicolos relished.

After the Nicolos paid their respects, the Vaglichios came by. Johnny watched dispassionately, but Vinnie stared at them with ill-concealed hatred. Tony thanked them for coming, and stood up and walked a few feet away with them. He began discussing something quietly, his face set in an expression of concentration and earnestness.

The oldest of the Vaglichio Family, the father, was Don Sam Vaglichio. Though some of the enmity between Don Vaglichio and Don Sangremano came from competing for territory in which to run their various businesses, much of it came from the old country. They had known each other in Sicily, not as friends but as enemies, and their enmity carried over to the United States. Don Vaglichio didn't look like an enemy though. Johnny thought he was a kindly, old, grandfatherly type of man, and if someone saw him in the park they might think he was there to feed the pigeons and enjoy the sun. There was nothing about his appearance to betray the fact that he was not only the head of a vast criminal empire but had, personally, been responsible for the murder of dozens of men.

Like Johnny, Joe Provenzano was also watching the Vaglichios. In particular, he was watching one of them, a girl, who was standing just behind Don Vaglichio and his sons as they spoke with Tony Sangremano. The girl had long, dark hair and oval-shaped eyes with naturally heavy lashes that highlighted an exquisitely lovely face. Joe did not think he had ever seen anyone so incredibly beautiful as this girl, and involuntarily, he drew in a short gasp of breath.

"Thank you for coming, Joe," Al said, coming over to stand beside his nephew. "The Sangremanos noticed it, and believe me, they appreciate it. I appreciate it."

"I never approved of the Don, nor of anything he did," Joe said. "You know that, Uncle Al. But I know that, for you, he was more than an employer. I know that you are grieved by his death and I grieve because you grieve."

"You are a good nephew," Al said.

"Uncle Al, that girl," Joe said, pointing to the girl. "The one standing over there. Who is she?"

"Don't you remember Maria, Joe?" Al asked. "Maria Vaglichio?"

"Maria? Yes, I remember her. She was a skinny little

girl, all arms and legs with buck teeth and big eyes and stringy hair."

"Ah, yes, but that was when she was fifteen, before she went off to that girls' finishing school down in Virginia," Al said. "She is twenty-one now. And as you can see, she's all grown up."

"Yes," Joe said. "All grown up."

Joe continued to look at Maria, staring unabashedly at her beauty. The girl made him a little dizzy and he could feel his heart pounding in his chest. Maria sensed his gaze and turned toward him. She smiled self-consciously and looked away.

Joe started toward her, but as he did, Al reached out to restrain him.

"No, Joe. She is a Vaglichio."

"I don't give a damn who she is," Joe said. "She is the most beautiful creature I have ever seen and I intend to talk to her."

"Now would not be a good time," Al said. "Not during Don Sangremano's funeral."

"I'm sorry," Joe said. "Of course you are right. This wouldn't be a good time."

"In your case," Al went on, "I'm not sure there would ever be a good time."

"Why not?"

"You're a cop, Joe."

"I'm not ashamed of who I am."

"No," Al agreed. "But the girl may be ashamed of who she is."

After Weasel, Guido, and Dom left Mulberry Street, they walked down a series of alleyways and slipped through the narrow spaces between buildings until they reached Maxie Dunnigan's place. Maxie Dunnigan was a midlevel hood who was able to stay in business because he was willing to recognize the Sangremanos' authority over him. He had a specified area in which he could run his numbers racket, and the Sangremanos allowed him to operate as long as he paid his percentages on time.

The numbers cards were put in grocery stores, butcher shops, candy shops, barbershops, and other such establishments all over the area. Customers would pay a dime to play a number. If their number hit, they could win a dollar. The take was ten dollars per card, which meant there was a profit of nine dollars per card. One dollar of each card went to the businessman who displayed the card and collected the money. Four dollars went to the Sangremanos as their take for allowing the action, and the remaining four dollars went to Maxie Dunnigan.

Dunnigan had over one hundred cards out and he collected the proceeds on them every day. Of course, he had more going for him than just the sporting instinct of the customers of the store. He had an arrangement with the storekeepers that guaranteed that the cards would be completely sold out each day. If they weren't sold out, accidents sometimes happened in the store.

Dunnigan operated his business out of a small tobacco store. A bell tinkled on the door as the three boys went in. The smell of tobacco was strong and pleasant. Weasel walked back to the rear counter where the clerk was reading a racing form.

"Is Maxie in?"

The clerk looked up.

"Who wants to know?"

"Tell him Weasel is here to see him."

The clerk looked back at the paper. "Never heard of you," he said.

"Tell him Uncle Tony sent us. You got that? Tony Sangremano. My uncle."

The clerk didn't respond.

"We're goin' to run Dunnigan's numbers for him today."

"You don't say." The clerk didn't bother to look up from his paper.

Suddenly, Weasel got angry at the clerk's snub. He swung his arm across the top of the counter and knocked over a display stand of pipes. They clattered loudly to the floor.

"Go get him, you mick bastard!" Weasel shouted. "Or Uncle Tony will come down on this place like stink on shit!"

The clerk stood up quickly, then looked at Weasel. At first, he thought the boy must be kidding. After all, he was nothing but a kid, and not even a particularly large one at that. However, there was a sense of cockiness about him that the clerk found intimidating. And even if he was just a kid, his eyes were old, very old, and there wasn't the slightest flicker of fear in them. He wouldn't dare do what he just did unless Tony Sangremano really was behind him.

"Yeah," the clerk said. "Yeah, all right, I'll get him. You stay here."

"Jeez, Weasel, what are you doin'? You're goin' to get us killed!" Dom said in a frightened voice.

"No, I won't," Weasel said. "I'm goin' to get us a job. You got to have balls to do this kind of work, Dom, so we may as well show them now."

"But you said you were Tony Sangremano's nephew," Dom said.

Weasel laughed. "No, I didn't. I just called him Uncle Tony. When my mama was alive I had lots of uncles, though none of them really were. What's the harm in calling one more man uncle?"

A moment later the clerk returned with Maxie Dunnigan, a short, fat man with a red face. Dunnigan was eating a sandwich, stuffing the dangling pieces of pastrami into his mouth with fat, sausagelike fingers.

"What the hell is goin' on out here?" he asked. "My man says you're tearin' up the place."

"Your man? Are you talkin' about this bum?" Weasel asked, indicating the clerk.

"He's been with me a long time."

"Yeah? Well, I hope you don't depend on him for too much, Mr. Dunnigan," Weasel said brashly.

"Maxie, you goin' to let this little punk talk like that?"

Maxie chuckled. "He hasn't said anything about me, Charley. It's you he's talkin' about."

"I don't like it," Charley said. He looked at Weasel, Guido, and Dom for a long moment, then he went back to his chair and picked up the racing form he had been reading.

Maxie finished his sandwich, then sucked on his fingers. "What can I do for you boys?"

"It's what we can do for you, Mr. Dunnigan," Weasel said. "We want to run numbers for you."

"I've got five runners now. I don't need any more."

"I know you've got five," Weasel said. "But I saw every one of them at Guiseppe Sangremano's funeral. And you know what happens when you don't pick up your cards on time, don't you, Mr. Dunnigan? Sometimes the shopkeepers get careless. You can't afford to wait. You got to pick them up now."

"I planned on sending Charley out to do that."

"That's this asshole you're talkin' about?" Weasel asked.

"Yes," Maxie said, laughing at Weasel's brashness.

"Yes, sir. Well, I tell you, Mr. Dunnigan, I don't think Charley can handle the job for you."

"And you can?"

"Yeah, sure," Weasel said. "Me and my boys can do it for you. Not only today, but anytime you ever need it done."

Maxie chuckled. "Your boys, huh? This is your gang?"

Weasel looked at the two with him. They had never referred to themselves in such a way, but he clearly was their leader.

"Yeah," he said. "Yeah, this is my gang."

"I generally pay fifteen dollars. You think you're worth that?"

"You don't pay fifteen, you pay twenty dollars," Weasel said. "And you have five runners. That's one hundred dollars. We'll do it for you today for seventy-five."

"So, you're a businessman too, eh, as well as a wise little punk?"

"You might say that," Weasel agreed.

"All right, you can work for me today." The smile left Maxie's face. "But I want to warn you right now, you try to skim so much as one dollar off the take and you three guys'll be wearin' cement boots at the bottom of the East River."

"Don't you worry none about that, Mr. Dunnigan," Weasel said. "If there's one thing people always say about me, it's that I'm dependable and trustworthy." Of course, no one had ever said anything like that before because Weasel had never done anything like this before. But he thought it would be a good thing to say.

"All right," Dunnigan said. "We pick up at two. It's time to get started."

"We're on our way," Weasel said.

"Do you know all the places to go?"

"Yes," Weasel said. "I know them."

When the three boys were about two blocks away from the tobacco shop they let out little whoops of joy.

"Oh, boy! Seventy-five dollars! Can you believe that? We're practically rich!" Dom exclaimed.

"My knees were knocking," Guido said. "I mean I was so scared I thought I was going to pee in my pants."

"Me too," Dom said.

"I wasn't scared," Weasel said.

"Oh, come on. Not even for a moment?" Dom asked.

"No."

"Well, that's because you're the leader," Guido teased. "And leaders never get scared."

"Who made you the leader?" Dom asked.

"I did."

"I think it should be put to a vote."

"I vote for him," Guido said.

"I vote for me too," Weasel said. "That makes it two to one."

Dom glared for a moment, then he smiled. "No, it don't," he said. "It makes it three to nothin'. I vote for you too."

"What are our orders, boss?" Guido asked.

"Your orders are to collect the cards."

"Okay."

"And the money," Weasel added with a broad smile.

———

Eight hundred feet above Long Island's Curtis Field, Mike Kelly chopped the throttle on the DH-4's Liberty engine. It popped and snapped and threw back a spray of hot oil to stain the fuselage and splash on the forward windscreen of the De Havilland biplane. Mike rolled it into a left turn, then came out of the turn perfectly lined up with the grass runway at the little airport. The plane slipped down out of the sky, losing altitude rapidly as its guy wires and bracing hummed at just the right pitch to indicate that Mike's final approach was at the proper angle and speed.

Like his friend Johnny Sangremano, Mike had come back from the army too restless to settle down. He had saved enough of his army pay to finish college, but after he graduated with a liberal arts degree, he still didn't know what he wanted to do. Then, at an air show, he ran into the young man who had landed on the road in France to save his life. The two of them became reacquainted and when Johnny offered to teach Mike to fly, Mike took him up on it. Mike was a quick learner and became a good flyer, though he was not as good at it as Johnny, and willingly admitted that he never would be. However, he discovered that flying was something that he very much enjoyed doing.

Johnny was the one who found the surplus DH-4 airplane, sitting disassembled out behind a hangar at Roosevelt Field. The two men were able to buy it with what little money they had. The barnstorming trip across the country, however, was Mike's idea. He had talked Johnny into it, and they were set to leave within a few days.

The DH-4 touched down so gently that it brought a smile of pride to Mike's lips and he wished Johnny were here to see how well he had done, particularly since Johnny had been so critical of him during his learning days. Mike let it roll out, then he taxied across the grass until he reached the hangar where the plane was being kept. He stopped the engine and was crawling down over the side as the field mechanic approached him.

"Well? How did she do, Mr. Kelly?" the mechanic asked.

"It's still throwing oil pretty bad," Mike complained.

The mechanic put his finger on Mike's cheek, then drew it away. When he held it up, his finger was wet with oil. He looked at it and smiled.

"Yeah, I can see that," he said, showing his finger to Mike. "But it won't really hurt anything. It's just coming from your rocker arms, that's all. I can't really tighten 'em any further. If you want the oil stopped, you're going to have to get a whole new set of lifters."

"No, I don't want to do that," Mike said. "We'll just have to live with it, that's all."

"Where's Johnny?" the mechanic asked. "I haven't seen him in nearly a week."

"His father died," Mike explained.

"Oh, I'm sorry to hear that. Did you know his ole man?"

"No, I've never met any of his family. I thought I might go to the funeral, but when I suggested it, I got the idea Johnny didn't want me to go."

"Really? I wonder why?"

"I don't know for sure. Johnny has always been pretty closemouthed about his family. Maybe it's because his mother and father both came from the old country and Johnny is a little self-conscious about them or something. I told him my mother and father both came from Ireland and their brogue is so thick you can cut it with a knife. Anyway, he didn't want me to go so I didn't. I did send some flowers though."

"When are you fellas leavin' on your trip?"

"I don't know. Two or three more days I guess. Soon as Johnny gets things all settled with his family. Listen, do what you can for those rocker arms, will you? I'd better be getting back into the city."

"Maybe I can put some shims in them," the mechanic suggested. "That ought to help a little."

Mike's mother had his supper simmering on the kitchen stove when he got home that evening. Mike's father was sitting at the table reading the evening newspaper. Tim Kelly was a big man, whose hair had turned the sandy gray color so common among those who had once been redheads. Tim was still wearing his police trousers though he had removed his uniform jacket. On the sleeves of the jacket were the stripes of a police sergeant. On the breast, in addition to his shield, was a medal of valor for Sergeant Tim Kelly had been cited four times for bravery.

"Sorry I'm late, Mom," Mike said, kissing her on the cheek and peeking into the pot of corned beef and cabbage. He pulled off a little piece of corned beef and stuck it in his mouth. "Uhmm, good," he said.

"And so we're to be graced with your presence are we?" Tim Kelly said. "Your mother had supper ready for you near to an hour ago."

"I'm sorry, Pop. I had some work to do on the airplane," Mike apologized. He pulled out his chair and sat at the table across from his father.

"Some work was it? There's little enough work with those contraptions. What are they good for besides being a waste of time? And you've been doing plenty of that lately when it's a job you should be looking for."

"I'll go to work, Pop, right after Johnny and I get back from our trip."

"Oh," Mike's mother said as she began dishing Mike's dinner onto a plate. "Those airplanes scare me so. I was hoping you wouldn't be taking the trip now that Johnny's poor father has died."

"We're still going," Mike said. "Just as soon as Johnny gets some of the family business taken care of. Thanks, Mom," he added as he took the plate and began eating.

"Sakes alive and would you look at this now?" Mike's

father asked, pointing to a picture in the paper. "They made a parade out of that dago mobster's funeral, what with all the fancy cars and flowers and the people linin' both sides of the street." The senior Kelly read the caption under the picture. "Giuseppe Sangremano, well-known mobster, was buried today in a gangland funeral." He looked up at Mike. "Sangremano. You know, I hadn't thought of it before, but Sangremano is the name of your friend, isn't it?"

"Sangremano? Yeah, it is. Johnny Sangremano."

"No matter, I suspect Sangremano is about as common a name among Italians as Kelly is for us Irish. I'm sure there's no connection or you would probably have known about it. Old Giuseppe has run things for several years now," the senior Kelly went on. "It'll be interestin' to see what happens now."

"What did you say the man's first name was?" Mike asked, looking up from his corned beef and cabbage in surprise.

"Giuseppe."

"That's funny. That's the name I sent the flowers to. May I see the paper for a minute, Pop?"

Mike took the paper from his father, then read through the story, noting the criminal allegations made by the paper against Giuseppe Sangremano. Then he came to the part of the story that spoke of those who survived him.

Most authorities believe that Sangremano's crime empire will now be taken over by his eldest son, Tony. Tony is said to be an astute businessman who has learned the crime business at his father's side. Another son, Vinnie, will also play an important role in the operation, possibly as an "enforcer," or one who sees to it that the ordinary people of Lower Manhattan and Queens are made to support the criminal operations of the gang.

The youngest son, Johnny, was an aviator with the American 94th Aero Squadron during the war.

He was a genuine war hero and is said not to be interested in following in his infamous father's nefarious footsteps. It is not known what role Johnny Sangremano will play in the family's crime empire, if any.

"Well, I'll be," Mike said in surprise. "It *is* the same family." Mike handed the paper back to his father. "Giuseppe Sangremano is Johnny's father. Johnny never told me that. In fact, he never talks about his family at all."

"Oh, Michael, do you mean to say you're taking off to who knows where with a...a gangster?" Mike's mother asked.

"Johnny's not a gangster, Mom. It even says in the paper that he has nothing to do with the business or the rest of them."

"He's Italian, isn't he?" Mike's father asked.

"Yes, of course he is."

"Then his time will come. No one has stronger family connections than the Italians. Mikey, 'tis a fine job you've done of pickin' your friends. You should've known with a name like that what business his father was likely to be in. They're all into somethin' crooked. It's just a matter of degree, that's all."

"When Johnny Sangremano landed on that road in France to pick me up, I never thought to ask him who his father was," Mike said dryly.

"There is that to be said for the lad, Tim," Mike's mother put in. "If he hadn't picked our boy up that time, we might not have him now." She walked over to stand behind Mike and put her hand on his neck. Mike took her hand, raised it to his lips, and kissed it.

"Yes, well, sometimes even the worst of men find a bit of good in them durin' wartime," Tim said gruffly, not willing to give in to the argument. "Mikey, I'll not be askin' you to stop bein' friends with this man but..."

"It's a good thing, for it would do you no good to ask," Mike interrupted.

Tim Kelly held up his hand. "But," he went on. "Just you be careful is all I'm sayin'. There may come a time when you'll be wantin' to come onto the police force and bein' a known associate with a gangster like Sangremano won't be winnin' you any friends down at the station house."

"You needn't worry about me ever coming onto the police force," Mike said.

"Why not? There've been many an Irishman before you and there'll be many after who put on the blue."

"Yeah, it's pretty well worked out, isn't it, Pop? The Italians all go into crime and the Irish all go into the police force. Only you can't always tell the difference, can you? Well, no thanks, Pop. I don't intend to be another Irish cop on the take."

"Michael, what are you saying?" Mike's mother gasped. "Why, my father was a policeman and my brother is one. Your father and your father's father were policemen. It's an honorable profession, one that has brought this family pride for many years."

Mike looked over at his father and saw his father's eyes dart away. Then Mike softened and he got up and walked over to put his hand on his father's shoulder.

"I'm sorry, Pop," he said. "I didn't mean anything by that. It's just that when I was in the war I promised myself that I'd make up for some of the time that was taken from me. I want to have a little fun, that's all. That's why I'm taking this trip with Johnny. But afterward, I'll come back and I'll find some honorable work to go into that you and Mom will both approve of, I promise."

The elder Kelly reached up and put his hand over Mike's hand.

"You're a grown man, Mikey," he said. "The only one who has to approve of what you go into is you. Go on the trip and have a good time. Your mama and I will be just fine here."

When Mike went to bed that night he lay with his hands behind his head, looking at the curtains at his window as they did a slow dance in the soft evening breeze. The wind carried with it the smells of his neighborhood: cabbage, whiskey, garbage from the alley, lye soap, and a dozen other intermingled scents that he had grown up with and that had become an inseparable part of his heritage.

There were sounds too, such as the steel-rimmed wheels of the night delivery wagons, the shriek of a policeman's whistle, and the rattle of an elevated train. He could hear a baby crying, and the fishwife, nagging voice of Mrs. Quinn, yelling at her husband as she had every night for over thirty years.

Mike had been born right here in this same fourth-floor walk-up apartment and his earliest memories were of this very room. Some of those early memories were pleasant and reassuring, such as his mother bathing his face when he had a fever, or the smell of her baking cookies at Christmas. He could also remember, fondly, the times his cousin Bill Carmack would come to spend the night with him. After everyone was in bed, the two boys would sneak out through the bedroom window and climb down the fire escape for some nocturnal adventure, always managing to return before anyone found out they were gone.

But some of those memories were unpleasant, and tonight, unbidden, one of the memories returned.

Mike had been ten years old when he went for a walk

with his father on his father's beat. Mike used to enjoy accompanying his father during those times. He remembered how tall and strong his father looked in his police uniform and he was very proud to be seen with him. Mike even had a small nightstick that he learned to swing with the same degree of swagger as his father.

Often when they passed grocery stores, the grocer would give Mike an apple. Mike always accepted it as his due. After all, he was a policeman's son.

Then one day he happened to see his father take a payoff from a local hood. The payoff amounted to only a few dollars and it arranged for Officer Kelly to "walk his beat a little slower between nine and ten." Mike learned the next day that an independent bookie joint on his father's beat had been robbed, sometime between nine and ten. He realized then what he had witnessed, and he was humiliated for his father, and for himself.

When Mike's father brought home an unexpected treat of ice cream for their supper that night, Mike left the table without eating it.

"Are you sick, Mikey?" Tim asked when he found Mike brooding in his bedroom.

"No."

"Then would you be for tellin' me what's troublin' you now?"

"Nothing."

"Nothing is it? Sure and you can't be savin' ice cream, lad. If you don't eat it, it'll be goin' to waste."

"You can get some more," Mike said.

"Aye, I've no doubt of that. But it comes dear and I've other things to do with the money."

"You can get more money," Mike said. "Just walk slower on your beat."

The color drained from the senior Kelly's face that night, and without saying another word, he got up and left Mike's room. They never mentioned that particular incident again, but it was always there, hanging between them, even now.

———

ON LONG ISLAND, AT THE HOME OF DON SAM VAGLICHIO

That evening the Vaglichio Family had an important meeting in the house of Don Sam Vaglichio. Present were Don Vaglichio, the head of the Vaglichio Family, his sons Luca and Mario, his chief enforcer, Sal Croce, and his Consigliori, Ben Costaconti.

Don Vaglichio sat in his big leather chair and puffed contentedly on a Havana cigar as his eldest son, Luca, conducted the meeting. Don Vaglichio was in his late sixties, a small man with a narrow face and hair that was still more brindled than white. He enjoyed painting and he had long, thin artist's hands.

Luca was about five feet seven, with a broad face, heavy brows, and high cheekbones. He tended to squint whenever he was discussing anything intently, which, because of the cheekbones and brows, turned his eyes into narrow slits.

"How are things going with our new venture?" Don Vaglichio asked.

"It's going fine, Papa. We have boats to bring the liquor in, trucks to transport it, and warehouses to store the goods."

"The only thing is, we need more joints where we can move the stuff," Mario interjected. Mario was good-looking, with a long, straight nose and dark eyes.

"What's holding you back?" Don Vaglichio wanted to know.

"What we need are the joints down in Lower Manhattan and over in Queens," Mario said. "Especially since Tony hasn't done anything with them yet. I mean, the territory is wide open, thousands of thirsty people over there, and nowhere for them to go get a drink."

Don Vaglichio took his cigar out and studied it for a moment. "Tony has asked for a meeting. I told him we would discuss it, then get back to him. Maybe we can work something out with him."

"From what I hear, the Sangremano Family won't have anything to do with the liquor business," Sal said. "I've got a cousin who is one of their button men. He tells me that Tony ain't interested in the booze."

"Maybe we can make a deal with him," Mario suggested. "If he doesn't want to handle it, we can handle it for him."

"What do think, Luca?" Don Vaglichio asked.

"It's certainly worth a try, Papa," Luca agreed.

"Ben?"

Ben, the Vaglichio consigliore, had been leaning against the bookcase with his arms folded across his chest, following the conversation. Now he moved out into the room with the others.

"I think it is a good idea," he said. "But you should know that Tony is the consummate businessman. He may go along with this, though I am sure he is going to want a percentage."

"No way," Luca said, shaking his head no. "We're buying the whiskey, financing the boats, running the trucks, and taking all the risks. That means we get all the profits. We aren't going to give the Sangremanos a percentage, just for letting us sell booze in their territory."

"I don't think Tony Sangremano is going to let us do it for nothing," Ben said. "And if you want my advice, it's worth a little percentage to have the territory all to ourselves."

"No," Luca insisted. "If the Sangremanos do no work and take no risk, they get no percentage."

Don Vaglichio took his cigar out and examined the tip of it for a while, then he looked up at Luca.

"You are running the show now, Luca," he said. "So whatever you decide, you decide. But I've never known Ben to give poor advice."

"Ben, this ain't a knock against you, you understand," Luca said. He looked back at his father. "And if Giuseppe..."

"Don Sangremano," Don Vaglichio corrected. "Luca, we must always pay honor and respect to such a man, even if he was our enemy."

"Don Sangremano," Luca said. "If Don Sangremano were still alive, maybe I would go along with what Ben suggests. But Don Sangremano isn't alive and that leaves Tony in charge. He doesn't have the power to demand a percentage from us. And I don't intend to pay it."

"Mario?" Ben asked.

Mario shook his head. "Ben, it's my brother's call," he said. "You know that."

"I'm sorry, Luca," Ben apologized. "I didn't mean to question your authority. I thought the subject was still being discussed. Of course, we will do whatever you say."

"When is the meeting?" Luca asked.

"Two days from now."

"Mama Tantinni's?"

"Yes."

"All right. Ben, you make the arrangements with Provenzano."

"Okay," Ben replied. "If you'll allow another suggestion? Don Vaglichio, if you really are turning everything over to Luca now, then I don't think you should go."

"Why not?" Mario asked.

"If Don Vaglichio isn't at the meeting, then Tony will understand that Luca is the one he has to deal with," Ben explained. "Otherwise, no matter what Luca says, Tony will always think he has an avenue of appeal."

"Ben's right," Luca said. "Papa, you don't mind?"

"No," Don Vaglichio said. "I don't mind."

Ben smiled. Whatever points he may have lost a moment earlier when he appealed to Mario, he had just regained by showing Luca that he had now accepted fully, and without question, Luca's authority.

"I'll make all the arrangements," Ben promised.

"Mama Tantinni's," Luca said. He smiled. "By meeting there, Tony will realize that we are serious."

Mama Tantinni's was a restaurant on Bleecker Street in the Village. Though not technically associated with any of the Families, and not directly involved in any criminal activities, Mama Tantinni and her four sons fulfilled a vital role. Mama Tantinni's Restaurant was the "Switzerland" of organized crime in New York. There had never been a kidnapping, double cross, or hit in her restaurant. The Tantinni word was bond, and if anyone violated an agreement guaranteed by the Tantinnis, or violated the neutral territory as established by them, all other Families would put aside their differences to punish the offending party.

That did not mean, however, that only the truth was told there. The meetings conducted there were as full of lies, subterfuge, and deception as meetings conducted anywhere else. The only guarantee one had in attending a meeting at Mama Tantinni's was that if they walked in, they could walk out.

CHAPTER 2

Spread out through six big rooms on the ground floor of a building on Bleecker Street, Mama Tantinni's Restaurant was just off 6th Avenue. The rooms were crowded with tables, statues of the Madonna, splashing fountains, figures of birds, potted plants, oversized paintings, and hanging tapestries. Christmas decorations hung from the yellowed ceiling throughout the year.

Mama Tantinni had not chosen the role of mediator, it was thrust upon her, ironically, by the popularity of her restaurant. Her restaurant had become a favorite spot due to the quality and the quantity of the food she served. As soon as a diner was seated, he would be brought a big hunk of cheese and a loaf of Italian bread, followed by artichokes, tomatoes, and peppers. Steaming plates of pasta were served, followed by the entree of veal parmigiana, or chicken cacciatore, or roast chicken, or filet of sole. After that came the deep-fried bugie, sugar-dipped and crunchy, and if one was still hungry, there was an entire assortment of pies, cakes, and ice creams.

When Tony, Vinnie, and Al Provenzano arrived, they were greeted at the front door by Juno, one of Mama Tantinni's sons. He, of course, knew that the restaurant was to be used as a meeting place tonight, for which the Tantinnis would be paid a five-thousand-dollar fee by each Family. Juno smiled and escorted the three men through the crowded dining rooms to a small waiting room. Another waiting room in another part of the restaurant had been set aside for the Vaglichios. At the proper moment, one of the Tantinni boys would escort the Sangremanos to the private dining room at the same time another Tantinni would escort the Vaglichios to the same private dining room. The Sangremanos and the Vaglichios would not see each other until then. In that way no one would ever know who arrived first and thus there could be no gamesmanship derived from deducing "who was the most anxious to conclude the deal." That practice helped to start every meeting on equal footing.

Once the participants were seated around the table, which was already set to prevent any unwanted interruptions by waiters, the meeting would begin. It could last as long as necessary with never an intrusion from the Tantinnis or any of their staff, unless something was specifically asked for. In the early days of establishing the Family territories, one meeting continued nonstop for thirty-six hours.

Tony, Vinnie, and Al were led into the dining room and seated at the table and at the same time Luca, Mario, and Ben were brought in. Tony, seeing that the table was set for only six people, spoke first.

"Where is Mr. Vaglichio?"

"Luca is head of the Family now," Ben answered. "Any deal he makes will be binding."

"Is that going to be a problem for you, Tony?" Luca asked.

"No," Tony answered. "Of course not. I'm very happy to be dealing with you, Luca." He reached across to shake Luca's hand, then the others, and Luca and the others did the same so that everyone shook hands with everyone. Finally, the greetings were completed and they all sat down.

"Okay, Tony, you asked for the meeting," Luca said after they were seated. "What's on your mind?"

"To begin with, I would like to extend my appreciation to you and the Vaglichio Family, and especially to your father, for your graciousness in attending my father's funeral and in offering your sympathy."

Luca nodded, and Tony took a deep breath and went on. The others began to eat. This wasn't a demonstration of rudeness on their part, nor did it indicate a lack of interest in the proceedings. It was just the way of things. When such meetings were conducted over the dinner table, eating the food was an expression of the goodwill of the participants.

"We are truly starting a new era now," Tony said. "The great war in Europe has been concluded, we are about to begin the third decade of the twentieth century...there are many wonderful new inventions and ideas. Everywhere we look we see that the old ways are behind us. And we have entered a new era in our own situation as well," he continued. "I have become the head of the Sangremano Family and you, Luca, are the head of the Vaglichio Family. Because of all this, it is time for some changes to be made, some very important changes."

"What kind of changes do you have in mind?" Luca asked.

"I feel that it is time we began operating more as a business, and less as a group of thugs."

"Hell, I thought we were a business."

"We are," Tony said. "But there are a few things we can do to become more businesslike. Let me tell you what I'm talking about."

As the men ate their meal, Tony continued talking about his ideas. During that time Vinnie was able to study Luca and the other Vaglichios. Vinnie believed he could see something in their eyes that Tony, in his eagerness to establish a businesslike atmosphere between the Families, was not able to see. Vinnie could see that the Vaglichios were construing Tony's request for peace in this new era as an admission of his own weakness and inability to handle the job he had just inherited. Vinnie didn't believe that was true, he had a great deal of love and respect for his older brother. But Vinnie understood that perception was as valuable as truth and if the Vaglichios believed Tony was weak, that could be dangerous.

"And so," Tony concluded. "In that spirit I would like to ask that we begin here, today, to explore new ways of developing cooperation, rather than extending the old ways of competition."

Luca touched the napkin to his lips, then leaned back in his chair and pressed the tips of his fingers together, studying Tony for a long moment before he answered. Al Provenzano smiled, for this was a gesture he had seen Luca's father make many times. He didn't know if it was something that came naturally to Luca, or if Luca was consciously mimicking his father.

"I'm glad you have called this meeting, Tony," Luca began. "You are right when you say things have changed, and I too would like to explore ways that we can work together." He leaned forward then and held up a finger as if he were just getting an idea. "And one such way has just come to me," he suggested. "As you know, Prohibition has provided many opportunities and a lot of money. It could also open up new areas of competition, but wise men could sit down and work out something. I believe we can work together in this new liquor business."

Tony shook his head no. He had just taken a forkful of spaghetti and he had to swallow before he could answer.

"There is no need for us to work together in that business," he said. "It is not my intention to get into bootlegging. If you wish to run liquor, then do it. You'll get no competition from us."

Luca smiled broadly. "Good, good. I think perhaps this new spirit of cooperation is really going to work after all. You say you will not participate in the business and I respect that. But, already, we have opened as many joints as can be accommodated on Long Island and in the Bronx. Since many of your people are coming to us to drink, would it not be better all around if you would allow us to set up liquor joints in Lower Manhattan and Queens?"

Vinnie looked at Tony, anxious to see how Tony was going to react to this request. Vinnie had already warned Tony that the Vaglichios would surely make such a request, but Tony had not said how he would answer. Vinnie hoped that Tony wasn't going to let them do what they asked. If he did, that would forever blur the territorial lines. Allowing the Vaglichios to cross over and sell their whiskey meant they could also cross over to operate a few numbers games. And if that, perhaps a bookie operation, then a little protection, and before anyone knew what was going on, there would no longer be an area designated as Sangremano territory. To Vinnie's relief, but not really to his surprise, Tony saw it as well.

"No, I don't think that would be a very good idea," Tony answered, using his own napkin before folding it carefully and laying it down beside his plate.

Luca looked surprised. "Tony, I don't understand," he complained. "You just said you weren't interested in going into the liquor business and you invited us to handle it ourselves. Yet you refuse to allow us to sell our product in your territory when you have clearly said you don't intend to go into the business yourselves. Since we are not competing, why are you making this unfriendly gesture toward the Vaglichio Family? Surely you can see that it does no good to bring whiskey into town if we don't have enough places to sell it?"

"You aren't a teetotaler, are you?" Mario interjected. "You have nothing against a man taking a little drink now and then?"

"No, of course not."

"Then why are you so dead set against our selling a little whiskey?"

"You don't understand," Tony said. "What I'm trying to do is run our Family like a business. I keep a good set of books on every operation, the numbers, the bookies, the banking, prostitution, all of it. I know how much money each enterprise brings in and I know how much money each enterprise costs us to operate. I also know which police officers work which beats, and how much it takes to keep them all quiet. I know which judges will turn their eyes aside and how much it costs to arrange that. Everything is going very smoothly now, like a well-oiled machine. Every month much more money comes in than goes out. We are making a good profit and we are not antagonizing the police."

"But wouldn't you like the profit to be larger?" Luca asked.

"Not if the risk is proportionately greater," Tony replied. "Consider this. If I allow liquor joints in our territory, people are going to get liquored up and do foolish things. There will be drunks turning up dead in the alleyways, there will be robberies and burglaries that I know nothing about. The police will become more interested in what's going on in my territory and the newspapers will decide that it is all the result of illegal liquor. There will be a great civil crusade to smash the liquor joints, but it won't stop there. As you well know, Luca, in organizations such as ours, everything is connected." Tony joined his fingers together to illustrate his point. "When you go after one operation, it is like pulling on a loose thread. Soon the others will begin to come unraveled as well. The profit looks good, I will admit. But the risk is greater and I do not consider it good business to take that risk."

Luca sat quietly, listening to Tony's explanation, then he sighed.

"Suppose I offered you points?" he suggested. "A percentage of the profit we make from any whiskey that is sold in your territory. That way we take all the risks but you still make a profit."

Tony shook his head. "You still don't understand. Any whiskey that is sold illegally in Sangremano territory puts the Sangremano Family at risk, no matter who is selling it. If I am not prepared to take that risk, then I will not allow anyone else to take it for us."

"You have called this meeting to ask that there be a new spirit of cooperation between us," Luca said. "And then you refuse to cooperate."

"Tony?" Vinnie said, raising his finger to ask permission from his brother to speak. Tony nodded and Vinnie pushed his empty plate aside, then leaned forward, resting his elbows on the table. He looked across the table at the Vaglichios and their consigliore for a moment before he spoke.

"Gentlemen," he said. "We have listened to your proposal and my brother has told you why he is not interested in allowing you to operate your whiskey business in our territory. I know that you do not agree with it, but that is the way it is. It has been discussed honestly. We have reasoned with you, and I think it is time you listened to reason."

Vinnie's voice was quiet and controlled. It was so quiet and so controlled that no one except Al Provenzano recognized the hidden danger in it. Al recognized it only because he had heard it before, in the old days, in the Don's voice, during the wars to establish territory. Then it generally meant that someone was about to die. It shocked Al somewhat to hear it today in Vinnie's voice. He had been looking for some sign of the old man in Tony and had found none. He did not realize until this moment that it had skipped over Tony to reach Vinnie.

"Of course we will listen to reason," Luca replied.

"Very well. My brother has offered you our hand in peace and he has told you that we will not compete with you in the liquor business. All we ask in return is that you honor that peace, and you honor our request. Does that not seem like a reasonable request?"

"What about you, Vinnie? Do you agree with your brother? Do you think the Sangremano Family should stay out of the liquor business?"

"My brother is the head of this Family," Vinnie said.

Vinnie did not say whether he agreed or disagreed, but Luca smiled, for he knew then that Vinnie disagreed.

"All right, if that is the way it is to be, that is the way it will be," Luca said. He extended his hand across the table toward Tony. "Let there be peace between us," he said.

Tony smiled broadly. "Thank you, Luca," he said, taking Luca's hand and shaking it. He extended his smile to the others. "Gentlemen, let this be the last peace conference between us. From now on there will be only business meetings."

Joe Provenzano stood at the call box on the corner of 156th Street and Courtland Avenue, watching a storekeeper sprinkle water from a watering can onto the fruits and vegetables he had displayed in front of his store. Three little girls were skipping rope on the sidewalk.

Though he was right in the middle of one of the largest cities in the world, there was a small-town atmosphere about each of the neighborhoods. Joe liked that. He liked that the grocer, Mr. Colandrea, could call each of the little girls by name, and that the little girls could refer to him as Officer Provenzano. Such an atmosphere made his job satisfying for his instructions to "protect and defend" took on more meaning when he knew, personally, the people he was protecting and defending.

"Joe," Mr. Colandrea said. "Did you hear about Julio?"

"Julio? You mean Julio Pizaro, the baker's son? What about him?"

"What about him? He's getting married, that's what about him," Mr. Colandrea replied. "He's marryin' Elsie Grinaldi. You know Elsie, don't you? She's Phillip Grinaldi's daughter."

"Yes, I know her," Joe said. "I know her father too." Phillip Grinaldi was one of Vaglichio's lieutenants, specializing in loan-sharking operations.

"So, you goin' to the weddin'?"

"I haven't been invited."

"Sure you have," Colandrea said. "What am I doin', talkin' to the birds here? I'm invitin' you."

"You're inviting me? How come you, are inviting me? Shouldn't that come from the family?"

"I am family. Julio is my cousin. Didn't you know

that? He told me, invite anyone I wanted. So I'm invitin'
you. Are you cornin' or what?"

"I don't know," Joe answered. "The truth is, I don't
know how welcome I would be at the wedding of one of
Vaglichio's men."

"Why not? You mean 'cause you ain't on the take?
Don't worry about that, they don't nobody hold it against
you. And if you don't come, you're goin' to miss a big
party. Lots of food, booze." Colandrea stopped and
squinted at Joe. "Wait a minute, you bein' such an honest
cop and all, you wouldn't come bustin' up the party for
the booze, would you? 'Cause if you did, that could mean
a lot of trouble."

"I may be honest," Joe said, "but I'm not dumb."

Colandrea smiled broadly. "No, I didn't think you
was. Well, there you are then. There ain't no reason why
you can't come. And there's goin' to be lots of good-
lookin' young women there too. That ought to attract a
young single man like you. Julio's sister Ellen is going to
be there. She's a very pretty young lady. You ever seen
her?"

"Yes, I have seen her and you're right, she is pretty,"
Joe agreed. She was all right, he thought, big brown eyes,
dark hair, high cheekbones, pretty but nothing to get
excited about. At least, not in Joe's opinion.

"She's going to be one of the bridesmaids. Maria
Vaglichio is too."

Maria Vaglichio? Joe thought. Now she was something
to get excited about. Joe remembered seeing her at the
cemetery at Giuseppe Sangremano's funeral. He would
like to see her again but he knew better than to show his
interest to Colandrea. People like Colandrea dealt in
information and it was best to give him as little as
possible.

"Okay," Joe said casually. "Maybe I will come. When is it?"

"It's next Friday night," Colandrea said. "Come on into the store, I'll give you one of the invites."

Smiling, Joe followed Colandrea into the little grocery store. The store was typical of the neighborhood grocery stores and it smelled of flour and deli meats and sorghum molasses. Colandrea walked around behind the long wooden counter, beyond the oversize roll of wrapping paper, all the way down to the cash register at the far end. He opened it and took out a little white card, then handed the card over to Joe.

"You've got to have one of these to get in," he said. "Don't lose it."

"I won't," Joe promised, putting the card in his jacket pocket.

"Stop, thief!" somebody shouted from somewhere outside the store. That was followed by the sound of two gunshots, then the crashing of a window. Joe had his pistol in his hand instantly, and he darted through the front door and onto the sidewalk. He looked up and down the street then, just two doors down he saw a man backing out of Harris's Drugstore. The man was brandishing a pistol, which he held pointed toward the front of Harris's store. The plate-glass window of the drugstore had been shattered and was now lying in shards on the sidewalk. Harris, the proprietor of the store, was down on the sidewalk in a sitting position. He was leaning against the front of his building holding his hand to his chest. Bright red blood spilled through his fingers and ran down to stain his shirt and form a little pool in his lap. Harris was looking up at the robber, not in fear or anger, but almost in detachment, as if this were all happening to someone else and he was just a bystander.

The gunman raised his pistol and took aim, about to shoot Mr. Harris a second time.

"Hold it right there, mister!" Joe yelled. "Police officer!"

The gunman was surprised to be challenged and he swung around toward Joe, bringing his gun to bear as he did so. He fired and Joe heard the bullet slam into the vegetable stand just alongside him. At the same moment the gunman fired, he started toward the three little girls who had been skipping rope, but were now just standing there watching, terrified.

"No, stop!" Joe shouted.

Joe realized at once what the gunman had in mind. He was going to use one or more of the girls as his shield. Joe knew that if he was going to get a shot at the gunman it would have to be right now. He could not afford to wait another second. Joe pulled the trigger and the gun boomed and kicked back in his hand. His bullet caught the gunman high in the chest, knocking him down and causing him to drop his pistol. Joe ran toward the pistol as the gunman was trying to retrieve it. He managed to kick it away, right from under the gunman's fingertips, then he turned and pointed his gun right at the gunman's head.

"Lie still!" Joe ordered.

"You shot me!" the gunman gasped. "I didn't think you'd take a chance with the little girls so close. What are you, crazy?"

Joe looked over toward the wounded druggist and saw that two or three people were bent down beside him, apparently giving him first aid.

"How is he?" Joe asked.

"He needs a doctor."

"Mr. Colandrea, call an ambulance for Mr. Harris," he ordered.

"What about me? I need a doctor too, you sono-fabitch," the gunman growled.

Joe put his pistol away now and leaned down to look at the man's wound. The bullet had hit high in the shoulder and though the shock of its impact had knocked the gunman down, Joe didn't believe it was a serious wound. He took the handcuffs off his belt and cuffed the man's hands behind him.

"You're wound isn't serious," Joe said. "We've got doctors down at the jail house. They'll take care of you." Joe walked over to the call box, took his key from his pocket, opened the little door, and called in his arrest.

The double shooting and all the excitement began gathering onlookers so that by the time of the arrival of the police car Joe had called, and the ambulance Colandrea summoned, a sizable crowd had gathered. They had to be separated so the police and ambulance attendants could get to the victims. A police lieutenant arrived with the patrol car and took Joe's statement, as well as the statement of half a dozen other witnesses. Finally, the two wounded men were loaded into the cars, the doors were slammed, and the vehicles drove off, the ambulance leaving with a wailing siren. With all the excitement over, the crowd began to disperse. Only one man hung back, standing in the shadows of the alley opening, and Joe didn't even see him until he called out.

"Provenzano?" Joe looked up to see a man standing just inside the corner of the alley. He was holding an envelope in his hand and he held it out toward Joe. "This is for you."

"What is it?" Joe asked.

The man grinned. "Look inside."

Joe took the envelope, peeked inside, and saw a big wad of bills. Without looking any further, he handed the envelope back.

"No," he said. "I can't take that."

"Go on, it's for you," the man insisted. "The little girls," he said. "The papa of one of them wants to reward you."

"I can't take a reward. I was just doing my duty, that's all."

"Come on," the man insisted. "The girl's papa, he wants to show his appreciation, that's all. And he ain't one to turn down, if you know what I mean."

"I can't take the money."

"It ain't like you're bein' paid for lookin' the other way or somethin' for chrissake," the man insisted. "What's the harm of takin' a little money for doin' somethin' that you was supposed to do in the first place?"

"If you can't see the harm, then there's no way I can explain it to you," Joe said. "Now get out of my sight and take that envelope with you."

"All right, all right, I'm goin'," the man growled. He took a couple of steps, then looked back with a greasy smile on his face. "But you want to know somethin', Provenzano. It's about time you learned not to turn your back on your own kind."

Pointedly, Joe turned his back and walked away.

After the meeting at Mama Tantinni's, the Vaglichios had another meeting that evening in Don Vaglichio's house. Although the Don was retired, he still liked to keep his finger on things and he listened with great interest as his sons and his consigliore filled him in on what happened at the sit-down with the Sangremanos.

"We were wrong about Tony wanting a percentage, Papa," Luca said. "Not even the offer of a percentage would bring him around."

Don Vaglichio pulled his cigar from his mouth. "Luca, as I told you it is your decision to make. But if you would like my suggestion..."

"Of course I would, Papa," Luca said quickly.

"Tony Sangremano is not going to be able to keep the liquor joints out of his territory. If the Sangremano Family doesn't operate them, someone else will, whether it's the Nicolos or a handful of people who think they can go into business for themselves. It may even be someone moving in from outside. I don't know who will do it, but there are going to be liquor joints in the Sangremano territory."

"So what you're saying is if there are going to be liquor joints in there, they should be ours," Luca said. "Is that it?"

Don Vaglichio closed his lips back over his cigar and nodded.

"Luca, did you notice the expression on Vinnie's face when you asked him if he agreed with his brother?" Mario asked.

"I noticed," Luca replied.

"I don't think he agrees with Tony at all," Mario said.

"What do you think, Ben?" Luca asked.

"I don't know. There's something about Vinnie Sangremano that makes me uneasy," Ben said. "Something in the tone of his voice."

"I think Mario's right. I think Vinnie knows Tony is wrong but there's nothing he can do about it," Luca suggested. 'That's all. I don't think Vinnie is the problem. I think it's Tony and his business ideas."

"What are you suggesting?" Ben asked.

"I'm suggesting that we get rid of Tony Sangremano," Luca said.

"What if it starts a war?" Ben asked.

"What if it does?"

"The Nicolos won't like it," Ben said. "You remember what happened two years ago when the police started cracking down all over the city because of what was going on between us and the Sangremanos. The Nicolos said then that if we went to war again, they would join with the other Families to put a stop to it."

"Yes, I remember," Luca said.

"If we get rid of Tony and deal with Vinnie, there won't be a war," Mario suggested. "Hell, we'd be doin' Vinnie a favor."

"Is that what you really think?" Ben asked.

"I think Tony has to be taken care of," Mario said. He looked at Luca. "Only it isn't my call."

"I guess it's my decision to make, isn't it?" Luca said.

"You're the head man, now," Mario said.

"Ben?"

"Your brother is right. It's your call," Ben said.

"Papa?" Luca was still looking for someone to help him with his decision and he got it with Sam's answer.

"Do it clean and do it quick," Don Vaglichio said. "If it is clean enough and quick enough, you can stop it before it gets into a war."

"What you are saying is that I need to hit Tony, then make peace with Vinnie?"

"That's what I'm saying," Don Vaglichio repeated.

"Right," Luca said: He let out a long sigh. "Okay. I guess all I have to do now is come up with a way to get the job done."

———

OHIO, A FEW DAYS LATER

Navigation across country had been easy. Mike and Johnny just followed the railroad tracks between the towns. Most of the time Mike rode in the front cockpit while Johnny flew from the rear, though sometimes they changed positions. The plane could be flown from the front cockpit as well as the rear so that if one of them wanted to sleep the other could fly. Both wore helmets, goggles, and leather jackets they had picked up from a war-surplus store. The rest of their belongings were thrown into a couple of canvas bags and stuffed down into the little cargo well between the front and rear cockpits.

They generally flew at about a thousand feet, always on the lookout for a town where they might be able to drum up a little business. When they did come across a place that looked good, they would drop down to a couple of hundred feet, make a low pass just over the main street, then repeat it, this time in full view of all the gawking eyes their first pass had brought out of the houses, stores, and office buildings. After that they would land in the nearest open field they could find. Then all they had to do was wait until the curious came flocking out to the plane where they would be offered rides for five dollars.

The biggest problem, they learned, was in finding enough people who weren't too frightened to fly. There were always several who would come out and stare curiously at the airplane. Some would even venture up to touch it. But few were adventurous enough to actually entrust their lives to some stranger who dropped down out of the sky just to offer them a chance to swoop back up into the air again. So far, they were barely earning enough money to keep the thirsty Liberty engine in fuel. That didn't matter, though. They were having a good time and they had no plans to go back to New York anytime soon.

The airplane had no gosport, or speaking tube, so when they were flying, the only way they could communicate was by hand signals, or by throttling back the engine and yelling at each other. As a result, they did all their talking at night while they lay in their bedrolls on the piece of canvas they would throw out. They slept alongside the plane if the weather was good. They slept under the wing if it was raining.

It was during one of these midnight conversations that Johnny, sucking on his ever-present lemon drop, discussed his family for the first time.

"What I don't understand," Mike said, responding to a comment Johnny had made about his father's funeral, "is how someone like your father could have so many people under his thumb. It sounds like a nobleman with his serfs. I mean, by your own admission he was a gangster. Yet there were thousands of people who came to his funeral. Why did they come? Was it out of fear, or curiosity?"

"If you had been there, if you had seen them, you wouldn't even have to ask. You would know that they came because they wanted to come," Johnny answered.

"But that's what I'm asking. Why would they want to come?"

"I don't know that I can answer that," Johnny replied. "Maybe you have to be Sicilian to understand the Mafia, and what it means to the people."

"To understand what?" Mike asked. "What was that word you used?"

"The Mafia."

"Mafia? I've never even heard of that word. What is it? Is it an Italian word?"

"It's the name of an organization, but the word is Sicilian."

"Sicilian, Italian, isn't that the same thing?"

Johnny raised up on one elbow and looked over at Mike. "You're Irish, aren't you?"

"Yes."

"Are the Irish and the English the same thing?"

"No," Mike replied with a little laugh. "I guess I see what you mean. Still, I've never heard the word 'Mafia'."

"Very few non-Sicilians have," Johnny admitted, lying back down. "The word itself is never used, though the Mafia exists."

"What is the Mafia? You said it is an organization. What kind?"

"A very secret organization. Most of the time it's called a Family, only, in this case, it's Family with a capital F. I guess the best way to explain it is to say that it's a little like a brotherhood, or maybe a fraternal order."

"A fraternal order? You aren't trying to tell me it's like the Masons or something, are you?"

"Well, in that there are secret rites and its members are ranked at different levels, I suppose I am."

"But the Masons help people, they build hospitals and provide for the poor."

"My father helped people," Johnny said. "Do you think ten thousand mourners would have shown up at his funeral if he hadn't helped people?"

"But your father was a criminal."

"Yes, he was a criminal. He ran bookie operations, numbers, and prostitution, I'll admit that. But he didn't rob banks, or grocery stores, or commit murder."

"He didn't? What about all the gangland killings?"

"That happens sometimes, when it is necessary to defend a territory. There have been shootings and bombings, but that's only when there is a war between rival Families. The Mafia does not make war against the ordinary people. At any rate, my brothers have taken over now and Tony has plans to change things, to get away from the ways of the past. He is going to run it like a business."

"An illegal business," Mike suggested.

"So what if it is? They are just providing what people want, anyway. I mean, nobody goes out onto the streets and brings someone in to make them bet, or to force them to spend the night with a whore. It is like selling liquor. Selling is only half the crime. The other half is in the buying and everyone, all the good people, buy the liquor. Where is the harm in this? Who is hurt by it?"

"The harm is in the policemen who have been corrupted," Mike replied with what seemed to Johnny to be a surprising amount of bitterness.

"A few dollars given to a cop on the beat so that he'll look the other way. No one is hurt," Johnny said.

"Do these policemen who get paid off know of the Mafia?" Mike asked.

"I don't know whether they do or not. Mike, this conversation is beginning to make me nervous now. What do you say we talk about something else for a while? Do you want me to tell you the truth? I could get killed for what I've already told you."

"But you haven't told me anything."

"I have told you that the Mafia exists," Johnny said. "I could be killed for that and if the wrong person found out that you now know about it, you could get killed as well."

"Just for knowing of its existence?"

"Yes, just for knowing of its existence."

"My God, Johnny, you must be joking with me," Mike said, laughing.

"No," Johnny replied. He folded his hands behind his head and looked up at the stars, then added quietly, "No, I wish I were joking, but I'm not." He sighed, then turned his head to look at Mike. "Why are you so concerned with it, anyway? You aren't Sicilian. You aren't even Italian. The Mafia doesn't have anything to do with your life."

"Oh, but it does," Mike answered. "You forget my father is a policeman. He is one of those who have been corrupted."

"And that bothers you?"

"Yes."

"All right, I guess I can understand that," Johnny said. "I am certainly not proud of the things my father has done. But, Mike, you are not your father and I am not mine. Their world is back there, on the streets and alleys of New York. Our world is out here, where it's fresh and clean."

"Fresh and clean?" Mike teased. "Take a deep breath, *paisano*. Do you recognize that smell? It is essence of pig shit. Do you like that?"

Mike was referring to the fact that the field where they had landed to spend the night was right next to a large pen of particularly malodorous pigs.

"Yeah, I like it." Johnny laughed. "You have obviously never gotten a whiff of my uncle Guido after a meal of garlic and sardines, have you? Compared to that, this pig shit smells like perfume."

———

27TH PRECINCT STATION

As Lieutenant Herbert Trapnell passed the open door of the night court he glanced over toward the judge. The judge was leaning back in his chair, his eyelids drooping heavily under bushy, white eyebrows. The prosecutor was making a point and he emphasized his statements by pounding his hand into his fist. The accused was at his table, looking properly contrite.

Trapnell walked on down the hall to the squad room, a large, stark-looking room with bare wooden benches and stained walls. On one wall was a large calendar with the year 1920 in bold black type just below the picture. The picture was an idealistic full-color drawing of a farm, with fields of corn, pumpkins, squash, melons, and tomatoes, all portrayed at the simultaneous and unrealistic peak of ripeness. Beside the calendar was a large, bold-faced clock. The time was 6:45 p.m. Several of the police who had the night watch had already arrived and they were milling around, waiting for the mount inspection. They were making last-minute checks of their shoes, shining their badges, and squaring away their hats.

A desk sergeant was writing in a ledger and when Lieutenant Trapnell stepped up to the desk, the sergeant looked up.

"What are you doing here, Lieutenant? I thought Sergeant Kelly had the watch tonight," the sergeant said conversationally.

"He does," Trapnell said. "That is, as far as I know he does. I have some paperwork to do, that's all. By the way, has Pendarrow come in yet?"

"No, I don't think so. At least I haven't seen him," the sergeant answered, looking out over the ones who had already arrived.

"When he does, ask him to step back to my office, would you? I need to talk to him."

"Sure thing, Lieutenant."

Trapnell was a heavyset man with close-cropped, gray hair and light blue eyes. He was in his late forties and might have been a distinguished-looking man had it not been for the fish-hook-shaped scar on his face, the result of a run-in with a man who tried to hold up a grocery store with a butcher knife. Trapnell had caught him red-handed and attempted to take the man in peaceably. The robber had other ideas, however, and he cut Trapnell's face. Trapnell put his .38 Special to the man's stomach and pulled the trigger. Trapnell would be scarred forever, but the robber would be dead forever.

Trapnell had been a good cop then. Of course, in his own mind, he was a good cop now. He would still hunt down robbers and purse snatchers, and all the other riffraff who scummed up the streets of his precinct.

And that was the real reason he had begun working with the Vaglichios. In effect the Vaglichios were his allies, for they would not allow panhandlers, pimps, muggers, or hold-up men in the neighborhoods they controlled. The way Trapnell saw it, he and the Vaglichios were just working together to maintain the peace. If the Vaglichios were violating the law, what was the real harm? The people seemed to want to play the numbers and bet the horses and baseball games. And since the new law of prohibition had come in, the simple act of having a beer was illegal. What was wrong with having a beer, for chrissake?

Trapnell earned his first payment from the Vaglichios when, as a favor, he warned them that a raid was going to be made on one of their bookie joints. A bookie joint raid was particularly devastating to a gambling organization. It wasn't that the punishment was so bad, the punishment itself was generally no more than a short stay in jail, or probation and a fine. The real damage came from the confiscation of all the gambling slips. Without the slips, the bettors could claim that they had backed the winner and demand to be paid. Trapnell's timely warning saved the Vaglichios fifty thousand dollars and they rewarded him with an envelope containing fifteen hundred dollars.

That had been the first payment. Now they came on a regular basis, not so much for services performed as for having Trapnell's loyalty whenever they might need him.

Luca had contacted Lieutenant Trapnell earlier in the day to suggest that that time had come.

A knock on his office door pulled Trapnell out of his musing. When he looked up he saw Officer Pendarrow standing there.

"You asked for me, Lieutenant?"

"Yeah, come in, Pendarrow. Come in," Trapnell said. He pointed to a chair. "Have a seat."

Pendarrow was a beat cop. Trapnell was a lieutenant and a watch commander, though he was not the commander of Pendarrow's watch.

"Your beat is down on Spring Street, isn't it?" Trapnell asked.

"Yes, sir."

"Sangremano territory."

Pendarrow cleared his throat. "Uh, yes, sir," he said.

"They take care of you pretty well, do they?"

"Beg your pardon, sir?"

"Come on, Pendarrow. You think I was born with these lieutenant's bars? I was a beat cop for a long time. I know the things you have to do to survive out on the streets, especially if you're walking a beat that's controlled by the mobs. They do you a favor here, fingering a hold-up man, or giving you a tip on some job that's planned, and you do them a favor there. Sometimes a little money changes hands, hell, it's all a part of operational procedure. Nobody thinks anything of it. Now, are the Sangremanos paying you anything or not?"

"Uh, yes, sir," Pendarrow said. "They give me a few bucks a week for providing security."

"Well, there you go. They aren't paying you to do anything you wouldn't be doing anyway, right? So what's the harm?"

Pendarrow smiled, more relaxed now that he knew he wasn't the subject of any internal investigation.

"Yes, sir," Pendarrow said. "That's sort of what I thought."

"What sort of security do you provide for them?"

"Oh, the usual thing," Trapnell said. "For example, if I see anyone who doesn't belong there, I'm supposed to let the Sangremanos know."

"Uh-huh. By that, you mean any of Vaglichio's men?"

"Yes, sir," Pendarrow said. "Anyone else too, if they don't belong, but, chiefly, I'm supposed to keep Vaglichio's men out of there."

"Yeah, well, it's probably a pretty good idea anyway, to keep these dago bastards separated. Otherwise they'll start shooting each other and the next thing you know, we've got a war in the streets. I don't see anything wrong with what you are doing."

"Thanks," Pendarrow said. "I didn't know how the department would feel about it."

"Officially? Officially, they'd probably fire any policeman they thought was on the take. But, unofficially, most of the guys up there have been on the street themselves and they know what it takes to survive down here. The best thing to do is just to keep your eyes open, your mouth shut, and your pockets full."

"Yes, sir, that's just what I was thinking," Pendarrow said.

"It's a shame about you being where you are though," Trapnell went on. "I mean, with the liquor business now, there's a lot more money than there ever was before. An unbelievable amount of money in fact. Only you probably won't wind up with one red cent of it because the Sangremanos have declared that they aren't going to run liquor."

"Yes, sir, that's what I heard."

"Of course, the scuttlebutt down in the Vaglichio territory is that the Vaglichios made an offer to handle whiskey for them, but Tony Sangremano even turned that down. What do you think of that?"

"I don't know. I guess I haven't given it that much thought," Pendarrow said.

"You should give it some thought. I figure the cops on the whiskey beats are makin' at least a hundred dollars a week extra."

"A hundred a week?" Pendarrow gasped. "That's more than I get paid."

"You're damn right it's more than you're making now. That's more than I make...or it would be more if I didn't have a little arrangement going for me." Trapnell stroked his chin for a moment as he studied Pendarrow, then he opened the middle drawer of his desk and took out an envelope. "I'll tell you what I'll do," he said. "I'm going to share some of my good fortune with you." He shoved the envelope across his desk toward Pendarrow. "There's two hundred and fifty dollars in there," he said.

Pendarrow looked at it in surprise.

"Go ahead, pick it up. It's yours."

Hesitantly, Pendarrow reached for it "What...what do I have to do for it?"

"Nothing," Trapnell said. "Absolutely nothing. That's the point, you see."

Pendarrow looked around the office for a moment as if unsure whether or not anyone was watching him. Then he picked the envelope up, peered in just long enough to see a stack of twenty-dollar bills, then stuck the envelope into the pocket of his uniform jacket.

"Thanks," Pendarrow said.

"That's all," Trapnell said, waving his hand. "You can go."

Pendarrow stood up and started toward the door. He didn't ask anything else, but it was obvious by the expression on his face that he was still confused as to why he had been given the money.

"Oh, there is one thing," Trapnell called, almost as if it were an afterthought. Pendarrow stopped at the door and looked around, waiting for the other shoe to fall. "In a couple of weeks, you are going to get another envelope. That envelope will contain another two hundred and fifty dollars. On the night of the day you get that envelope, say, oh, sometime between nine and ten, while Tony Sangremano is in his office tallying the daily receipts, you might see a couple of Vaglichio's men cruising around. If you do see them, don't worry about it. They'll just be looking for places to put in liquor joints if they can ever get Sangremano to change his mind. But, of course, if Sangremano knew that they were in his neighborhood looking around, he'd dig his heels in and never would deal with us."

"That's all they'll be doing? Looking for a place to put in their joints?"

"That's all. And all you have to do is leave them alone."

"Seems like I'm getting a lot of money for something like that," Pendarrow suggested.

Trapnell smiled. "Yes, doesn't it? But that's the beauty of this liquor operation, you see. Everyone makes money, no one gets hurt."

"All right," Pendarrow said. "If I see them, I won't say anything."

"Good man," Trapnell said. He stood up and smiled broadly. "Remember, your signal is the second envelope."

"How will I get the second envelope?"

"You'll get it," Trapnell said mysteriously. He laughed. "You know, all we policemen have to do is stick together and we'll not only take the streets back from those greaseballs, but we'll turn a dollar or two while we are doing it. You'd better go now," Trapnell said. "They'll be calling your watch soon."

Tim Kelly met Pendarrow and Trapnell just as they were coming out of Trapnell's office.

"Is there anything wrong, lad?" Kelly asked.

"No, Sergeant," Pendarrow answered.

Kelly looked at Pendarrow for a moment, then he nodded. "You'd better get ready."

"Yes, sir."

"Lieutenant Trapnell. Would you be sparin' me a moment now?"

"Sure thing, Sergeant Kelly."

Kelly followed Trapnell back into his office, then closed the door behind him.

"What can I do for you?" Trapnell asked.

"'Tis bad enough you're dirty, Trapnell," Kelly said. "I'll not be havin' you dirty up my men."

"Where do you come off being so holier-than- thou?" Trapnell asked. "Are your pockets that clean?"

"No, 'tis my great shame that I've taken money when I wasn't supposed to," Kelly answered. "But I don't anymore an' it's only because my own past isn't clean that I don't turn in the likes of you. Now I'm warnin' you, don't you be for dirtyin' up my men."

Trapnell held up his hands in surrender. "We were just talking a little, that's all," he said. "Don't get your bowels all in an uproar."

"Sergeant Kelly, the men are ready for inspection," someone called through the door.

"Aye, lad, thank you. I'll be right there," Kelly answered. He looked at Trapnell one last time. "I mean what I say about keepin' away from my men," he said. "If I find you spreadin' your dirt around, it's both your arms I'll be breakin'."

"May I remind you, Sergeant Kelly, that these are lieutenant's bars I'm wearing?" Trapnell said, pointing to the silver bars on his shoulder epaulets.

"Aye, I see your bars, Lieutenant," Kelly said. "And I'll be pinnin' them to your arse if you mess with me or any of my men."

Trapnell watched Kelly leave, then he leaned back in his chair and propped his feet up on his desk. When the whiskey started running, there was going to be a lot of money made, unless someone screwed things up. Sergeant Kelly just might be that someone. Trapnell decided he'd better keep an eye on him.

ILLINOIS

There had been only two paying customers today, a farmer who wanted to see his farm from the air, and a young man who wanted to impress his girlfriend, but who kept his eyes tightly closed for the entire flight.

"Ten dollars," Mike said. "That's all we made today." The sun had set an hour before and the two men were sitting on the piece of canvas they had thrown out alongside the plane. Overhead the sky was bright with a full moon and alive with thousands of twinkling stars.

"Actually, nine dollars and twenty cents," Johnny corrected. "Don't forget we gave that farmer a bargain. And we won't even get to keep all of that, because we promised Mr. Jensen five dollars for letting us use this field." Johnny reached down into an open sack of lemon drops and popped one of them into his mouth. He sucked on the confection the way other men smoked and when Mike teased him about it once, he said that it was easier than trying to light a cigarette in an open cockpit.

"Yeah, that's right," Mike said. "I almost forgot that." He laughed. "That will leave us with four dollars and twenty cents for the day's work. We aren't exactly getting rich with our little enterprise, are we?"

"Not like this, we aren't," Johnny agreed.

"How much do we have in our till?"

"Right now we have a total of forty-four dollars and twenty-three cents," Johnny answered.

"That's enough," Mike said. He got up and stretched, then walked back to the tail of the plane and began to relieve himself.

"Don't piss on the fabric," Johnny warned. "It'll eat right through the dope."

"You tell me that every night." Mike giggled. "Don't you think I know not to piss on the fabric?"

"You said forty-four dollars was enough. Enough for what?" Johnny asked.

"To get a few of the things we need," Mike called back over his shoulder. "One of us is going to have to go into town. We are just about out of everything. We need some bread, coffee, bacon, a few more cans of beans…"

"Oh, Lord, yes, don't forget the beans," Johnny interrupted sarcastically. "I just don't know what I'd do if I didn't get to eat another bean."

"Why, Johnny, you hurt my feelings. I thought you liked my beans."

"Oh, I love them," Johnny teased. "Anyway, you think you can find anything open? It's getting pretty late, isn't it?"

"Yes, but don't forget this is a farming town. That means the people have to work all day so the only time they can shop is at night. The grocery store is open until ten. I already checked."

"Do you want to go?"

"I don't mind going," Mike said, coming back to the front of the plane as he buttoned his fly. "Let me have a couple of bucks."

Johnny took two dollars from the little leather bag where they kept their money. "Get some…"

"Lemon drops, I know," Mike said, smiling. "Don't worry, I'll get you some."

"Hope you can find them. This little town doesn't look big enough to have such frills as lemon drops," Johnny said. "What's the name of it, anyway?"

"Sorento, Illinois."

"Sorento? How about that? An Italian name out here in the middle of nowhere. I wonder if any of my *paisanos* are here?"

"You want to go into town and find out and let me stay with the plane?" Mike asked.

"No thank you, you go ahead," Johnny answered. "These little burgs give me the willies." He lay back down on the canvas and folded his hands behind his head. "Besides, I don't have the energy to walk two miles into town and then two miles back. I'll be fine right here, thank you." An owl hooted. "With the owls and the frogs," he added.

Mike laughed. "All right, wilderness boy. I'll see you when I get back."

Johnny lay for a while longer after Mike left, just listening to the hooting of the owls and the serenade of the frogs from the pond. Then he decided that as long as he was going to stay with the plane he might as well do something useful, so he got up, walked over to the engine, opened the cowl, and pulled the fuel strainer.

"Just as I thought," he said as he looked at it. "We've been picking up a little trash in our gas. A little more and the fuel flow could be choked off. Wouldn't it be an unpleasant surprise if at about fifty feet off the end of the runway the engine would suddenly quit?" He shook his head and put the little wire mesh strainer up to his lips, then blew through it to clean it out.

From her bedroom on the second floor of the farm-house, Lucy Jensen saw one of the two young men walking down the road on his way into town. By the light of the full moon, she could make him out well enough to see that it was the shorter of the two men, the one with the reddish-blond hair. That meant that the tall, good-looking, dark-haired man was still in the field with the airplane.

Lucy looked back into the darkness of her home. From her position by the window of her bedroom, she could hear, floating down the hall to her, the steady sawing of her husband's snores. It wasn't even nine o'clock yet, but already he was sound asleep and had been since before eight. It was always like this with him...in bed before dark, out of bed before dawn. Melvin Jensen was a hard worker and a good provider, but that was about as far as it went. He seemed to have no interest in his wife beyond the cooking and housekeeping that he expected her to do for him. Lucy could barely remember the last time they had been together as man and wife. On those rare occasions when they did make love, it would always leave her totally frustrated and on edge.

They didn't sleep together anymore. They didn't even share the same bedroom. Mel was the one who suggested they have separate bedrooms because she liked to read at night and the kerosene lantern kept him awake. Lucy felt no loss at leaving his bed, nothing ever happened in it anyway.

When Lucy married Mel two years ago, she had no idea there would be so much missing from her life. At the time Mel was fifty-two and she was twenty-one and her older sister had warned her that she might have some problems marrying someone who was so much older than she was. Unfortunately, Lucy's sister had been too modest to be specific and Lucy never knew exactly what her sister was talking about. By the time she figured it out it was too late. She was married now and condemned to a life of frustration.

Lucy was a young, healthy woman, with hungers and desires that were going unfulfilled. How she wished her sister would have had the gumption to tell her exactly what she had meant by her warning. How she wished she had a man to make a woman of her.

Some of the younger men in the county, perhaps suspecting what Lucy was going through, had flirted with her a few times. Lucy always found their attention flattering, the more so since she now knew what they were thinking about when they looked at her with that hunger in their eyes. But she had never taken any of them up on their unspoken offer, nor did she intend to. She did have occasional erotic thoughts but they were never about anyone she knew. Her erotic dreams, whether waking or sleeping, were always filled with nameless, faceless men. However, from the moment that airplane had landed in her husband's pasture today, her fantasies had been very specific and the object of her fantasies had been very identifiable. Today, all of her fantasies were built around the dark-haired young pilot who dropped down from the sky, the one who was still out there by the airplane, all alone.

Lucy looked toward the field where the airplane was sitting. Despite the fact that night had fallen, the airplane was quite visible from her window, a dark wedge carved out of the silver splash of moonlight. She could see not only the airplane but beyond the plane to the pastureland and the distant grove of walnut trees as well. It was a landscape etched in shades of pearl and black.

On impulse, Lucy, barefooted but carrying her shoes with her, stepped cautiously out of her bedroom. The hall was thickly carpeted and she could feel the rich texture beneath her feet as she walked silently across the upstairs landing. As she passed her husband's bedroom door on the other side of the landing, she could hear him, still snoring loudly.

The house was dark but a pool of moonlight coming in through the glass door at the front of the stairs acted as a beacon to guide her. She moved slowly and silently down the stairs.

As she reached the middle landing of the stairs, she was startled by a sudden clicking noise followed by a whirring sound. Lucy froze as she felt her hair prickle and she grabbed at the banister in sudden numbing fear.

The clock chimed once.

It was nine-thirty.

Lucy relaxed with a small laugh.

At the front door, she slipped into her shoes, then went outside, down the porch steps, and out toward the pasture. There was a gentle breeze blowing and it moved through her hair and pressed the thin nightgown against her so that it became almost a second skin. It was sexually stimulating and she found herself being aroused by its gentle kiss, as surely as if the caressing breeze were a man's tongue, exploring her body. That imagery stimulated her to such a state of sexual excitation that she felt her knees grow weak and her loins surge as she walked toward the plane. She had to grab hold of the barnyard fence and hang on until the surge of feeling passed.

Johnny finished with the fuel screen and put it back in place. He had just finished tightening the restraining nut on the fuel line when someone called out to him.

"Hello?"

It was a woman's voice, quiet and hesitant. Surprised, Johnny looked around.

"Is there anyone here?" the voice asked.

"I'm up here, by the engine," Johnny answered, closing the cowl.

A young woman materialized out of the darkness. At first, Johnny gasped because he thought she was naked. Then he saw that she wasn't actually naked. She was wearing a light silk nightgown, but the breeze had molded it so close to her body that it could have been a second layer of skin. It was a startlingly erotic sight, the more so because she had appeared so unexpectedly in the middle of a farmer's field. It was the young woman he had seen with the farmer earlier in the afternoon. He smiled at her.

"You're the farmer's daughter, aren't you?" he asked. He thought of all the farmer's daughter jokes he had heard and he would have laughed, except that this was true and the situation was much more sensual than it was humorous.

"No," the girl said, smiling. "I'm Lucy Jensen. I'm the farmer's wife."

"His wife?" Johnny asked, clearly surprised by the revelation. The farmer had been old and stern-looking, while this girl was young and vibrant.

"He was a friend of my father's," Lucy said as if finding it necessary to explain. "His first wife died and he was so lonely. He had this nice farm and Pa thought..." She stopped in the middle of her explanation and let her arm and her voice drop. "But then, I don't reckon you'd be all that interested in that," she concluded.

"Oh, no, it's fascinating, really," Johnny said. He stared at her, absorbed by the sensuality of what he was seeing. The nightgown accented, rather than concealed, the hard, upthrust little breasts, topped by nipples that were sticking out like little fingers, a flat stomach, smoothly rounded thighs, and, through the thin material, the strong hint of a dark patch of pubic hair just at the junction of her legs. Johnny's erection was already straining at the front of his pants. "Is there something I can do for you, Mrs. Jensen?"

"No, I mean, I, uh, just wanted to get a closer look at this contraption, that's all," Lucy said. She moved up closer to Johnny and put her hand on the smooth fabric of the lower wing. Now Johnny could see the raw hunger in her eyes and he knew that she wanted him as badly as he wanted her. In fact, she almost frightened him with the intensity of her desire, but he knew he wasn't going to let this opportunity get away from him.

"Is that all you want?" Johnny asked quietly. He moved closer to her so that they were only a breath apart.

Lucy stripped out of her nightgown, while, quickly, Johnny took off he clothes.

"Mister, I don't know what it's like where you're from, but out here, we don't look too kindly on this sort of thing," a man's cold voice said.

"Oh, shit!" Johnny shouted, seeing the business end of a double-barreled twelve-gauge shotgun, aimed right at his privates.

"Mel! What are you doin' out here?" Lucy gasped, trying to shield her body with her hands, not from Johnny, but from her husband.

"Get on back up to the house," Mel said. "I'll talk to you after I take care of this fella."

"What…what are you going to do to him?"

"Me an' him's goin' to take us a little walk," Mel said. "We're goin' over to the walnut grove." He waved his shotgun. "Come on, you. Get movin'."

Lucy, who was still naked, met Mike in the road as he was coming back from town.

"Hurry!" she pleaded with Mike. "Oh, please, hurry! My husband is going to kill him!"

Mike didn't waste time asking what it was all about. By what he was seeing, he knew.

"Where are they?" he asked.

"Mel's takin' him across the pasture to the walnut grove. It's on the other side by the..."

"I know where the grove is," Mike shouted back, already breaking into a run. He had seen it when they flew in and he had gauged the height of the trees very carefully before they took off on the first flight that afternoon.

When Mike reached the airplane, he gathered up Johnny's clothes and dropped them down in the front cockpit, then he reached in to set the switch, magneto, and throttle. Then, quickly, he began pulling the propeller through. As soon as the engine caught, he grabbed the chocks from under the wheels, then, even as the airplane began rolling, climbed into the rear cockpit and opened the throttle.

Johnny heard the engine kick over from the middle of the field. He recognized it immediately but Mel, who wasn't as familiar with the sound, looked around to see what it was. When Mel looked around that gave Johnny a slight opening and he took advantage of it, and he gave his captor a mighty shove, then started running across the field toward the sound of the airplane.

The shove was strong enough to knock Mel down and by the time he regained his feet, Johnny had already put forty yards between them in the dark. Mel let loose a blast with both barrels but by then Johnny was far enough away that only one or two of the little pellets carried far enough to hit him and they didn't have enough energy to penetrate the skin. They did sting enough that Johnny let out a yell.

From the airplane, Mike saw the muzzle flash of the shotgun blast and he started toward it, taxiing fast enough now that he could lift the tail skid from the ground. Mike raised up from his seat slightly so he could peer over the spinning disk of the propeller. When he did, he saw Johnny running toward him. Mike corrected the direction of the plane, aiming the nose directly toward Johnny. He chopped the throttle just before he got to him. The airplane slowed and the tail skid dropped but it was still moving as fast as Johnny could run.

"Get in!" Mike yelled.

Johnny ran alongside the plane until he could grab the rim of the front cockpit. Then, with a mighty heave, he pulled himself off the ground and dived headfirst down into the well of the front cockpit. He was no sooner in the plane than Mike opened the throttle again, this time to full power. He hauled back on the stick just as soon as he had airspeed and the plane climbed out over the walnut grove, skimming by so close to the taller trees that the bottom wing of the DH-4 was slapped by a few leaves from the smaller branches.

Johnny was head down in the front cockpit with both his legs sticking straight up in the air. Mike saw him wriggling back and forth as he was trying to get right side up, and the sight was so funny that he began laughing and he laughed until he cried. When, a moment later, Johnny finally managed to get himself righted, he turned to look back at Mike, saw him laughing, and yelled something at him in anger, though Mike could not hear him over the engine noise. Mike throttled back so he could hear.

"What did you say?" Mike called.

"I said I want to know what you are laughing at?" Johnny replied angrily. "It's not funny, goddamnit! I nearly got myself killed!"

"I can't help it," Mike said. "You've got to admit that

looking at your bare ass shining in the moonlight is a funny sight. Tell me, Johnny. Was she worth it?"

Johnny thought about it for a minute, then he too began to laugh. "Well, she would have been, I think," he shouted back.

"I'm glad you think so. Now, are you going to put on some clothes, or do you want to just fly around naked, looking for the next good time?"

"What the hell?" Johnny giggled. "Why don't I just advertise to the ladies?" Johnny turned back to face the front of the airplane, reached up to grab the top wing, then, to Mike's astonishment, climbed up to the wing where he stood with his feet braced against the center wing strut and, totally naked, held his arms straight out to each side, laughing into the wind.

CHAPTER 3

NEW YORK CITY

Sammy Solinger was a little man with white, curly hair, dark brown eyes, and a nose somewhat like a hawk's beak. He was little in physical stature, but he certainly wasn't a small man in his field, for Sammy Solinger was one of the most successful movie producers in the business. In 1916, the movie magazine *Picture Play* said that he was the best. Solinger had actually paid the magazine to make that statement, but it became a self-fulfilling prophecy since he had produced several successful pictures in a row, almost living up to the press he had bought.

Like many others before him, Solinger actually started his movie business in New York City, fifteen years earlier. Just before the war, however, Solinger moved to Hollywood along with most of the other motion picture producers in order to escape several lawsuits brought against them by the Edison Company. The Edison Company held patents for motion picture cameras and film, and every time someone would attempt to produce a movie without first making arrangements to pay a royalty to the Edison Company, they would wind up in court. California was a continent away from New York and southern California was eager for growth. As a result, their courts were somewhat kinder to the independent producers than were the courts of New York, thus a new industry was born.

Solinger missed New York terribly and he wished he could come back. It wasn't just sentiment, either. As he saw it, there was a growing problem with producing movies in California, due to the competition for money for production. Any two-bit con man with a movie camera and a few rows of film could, and did, call himself a movie producer. Movie producers were always in need of money and those who provided money for such productions were so besieged by these would-be producers that they were getting more and more difficult to deal with. They had even reached the point of demanding control over the production. They wanted the last word as to what film would be produced, who would write it, who would star in it, and even who would direct it. As a result, the producer himself was losing all control.

Solinger wasn't willing to go along with that. He intended to be the final authority on all the films he produced and if the men who came up with the money didn't like that, then to hell with them.

Solinger had been able to get away with his independence so far because he could point to a string of money-makers he had produced. But his last two productions had lost money, and financing was getting more and more difficult to obtain. Now he was in the midst of a big, important war film, a film bigger than anything even G. W. Griffith had ever done. Unfortunately, the movie was running far over budget and the backer was getting nervous. He was getting so nervous, in fact, that he told

Solinger to bring the film in with the money he had already received, or buy out of it. He was not prepared to put up one more dollar.

That left Solinger with nowhere to go, for the other financiers had already let it be known that they were not interested in bailing out a failing project. Hollywood was already counting Solinger out and many were betting that the picture, which he was calling *Glory Dust*, would never be finished. What they didn't realize was that Sammy Solinger was not yet ready to roll over and play dead. He had another source of money, an offer that had come to him in a letter from Giuseppe Sangremano.

"Myself, I do not go to see the moving pictures," Sangremano had written. "The pictures dance and flash before my eyes and they give me a headache. My daughter goes many times however, and she can say the names of all the people who act in them. My daughter wants to be a person who appears in these moving pictures. Such people, I am told, are called stars. I am also told that it is very difficult to become a star, but I love my daughter very much and I want to make things easy for her. In my lifetime, I have made some good business, so I can be very generous to the man who will do this for her."

It had been almost six months since Solinger received the letter, along with a less personal and more detailed business letter written by one Al Provenzano. The last thing Solinger wanted to do was put some wop's daughter in his movie, but something told him not to dismiss the offer out of hand. Therefore he replied promptly, explaining that he was in the midst of a production now, but would get in contact with Mr. Sangremano again at a later date. Now he was in New York to do that very thing. If Sangremano had enough money to finance a picture for his daughter, then he had enough to bail

Solinger out on the picture that was currently in production. And as far as the girl was concerned, Solinger would take a look at her. If he could use her in something he would. If not, well, by then the money would already be in hand and there would not be anything Sangremano could do about it. With any luck, the picture would be successful, and he could return Sangremano's money.

The taxi ride from Grand Central Station to the Plaza Hotel felt good to him and he realized that he was actually happy to be back in New York. "You got no business in California," his brother had told him when he left, fifteen years ago. "This is where we belong, not California. There are no Jews in California."

His brother was wrong. There were Jews in California, but they were displaced Jews, like Solinger himself, so there were no long-established ethnic neighborhoods with the delis, and the bakeries, and the kosher butcher shops. Of course, Sammy Solinger was not kosher, but he liked the comfortable feeling of being in a place where he could be kosher if he wanted. Coming back to New York was like putting on a pair of old comfortable slippers.

When Solinger checked in to his suite at the Plaza, he made a telephone call to the number that Provenzano had given him.

Katherine was reading *Picture Play* magazine when the phone rang. Her mother was actually closer to the phone, but her mother had never quite learned to trust the instrument.

"I don't like to talk to someone unless I can see into their eyes," she explained. "Without you can see into their eyes, how do you know if what they are telling you is true?"

Though she didn't actually admit it, Sophia was also intimidated by the fact that her English was so poor that she had a difficult time making herself understood over the phone.

"Hello," Katherine said, picking up the receiver.

"May I speak with Giuseppe Sangremano, please?"

Katherine gasped and looked at the phone. "Who is this?" she asked sharply. "Are you making a joke?"

"A joke? No, of course not," Solinger said, surprised at the reaction he had gotten. "I'm sorry, have I gotten the wrong number? Is this not Giuseppe Sangremano's telephone number?"

"Yes it is," Katherine said. "Giuseppe Sangremano was my father."

"Did you say he *was* your father?"

"Yes. My father died a month ago."

"Oh," Solinger replied. He let out a soft sigh. "I'm very sorry to hear that. I didn't know."

Now Katherine softened somewhat. It seemed incredible to her that there could be someone who did not know about her father, but the man on the other end of the phone line sounded genuinely sorry.

"I'm sorry if I sounded rude," Katherine said. "I thought everyone knew. It was in all the papers."

"Again, I apologize," Solinger said. "But I don't live in New York anymore, so I missed the papers. My name is Solinger, Sammy Solinger. I live in..."

"You are the movie producer!" Katherine said sharply, her voice rising in excitement.

"Yes."

"And you are calling here? Why?"

"Your father made me a business proposal," Solinger said. "I was going to speak to him about it."

"A business proposal?" Katherine asked. "Was it about me? I am his daughter. Papa said he would arrange it for me to be in the movies."

Solinger chuckled. "Yes, it was about you as a matter of fact," he said.

"Well then, you can talk to me," Katherine said. "Where are you?"

"I am at the Plaza Hotel."

"Don't go away," Katherine insisted. "I'll be right down to see you."

"Now wait a minute, wait a minute. I don't know if that is such a good idea, Miss Sangremano," Solinger said.

"Why not?" Katherine asked. "It is about putting me in the movies, isn't it? Isn't that why you came?"

"Well, yes," Solinger said. "But there are other considerations to discuss as well. Business considerations that would be inappropriate to discuss with you alone."

"You mean because I'm a woman?" Katherine asked.

"Oh, no, my dear," Solinger answered easily. "I simply mean it would be inappropriate to discuss it with you because you are going to be one of my stars. Movie stars never discuss business themselves. They have someone else do it for them."

"I'm going to be a movie star? Oh, do you really think so?" Katherine asked, excited just to hear the word spoken.

"Trust me," Solinger said easily. "I am the man who makes such things happen. But, as I said, movie stars never discuss their own business arrangements. They have agents to do that for them. Perhaps someone like Al Provenzano could do that for you," he added.

"You know Al Provenzano?" Katherine asked, surprised to hear Solinger say his name.

"Not personally, but I did receive a letter from him," Solinger explained. "In that letter he represented himself as someone who handled your father's business. Is he still employed in that capacity?"

"Yes," Katherine said. "Only he works for my brother now."

"Well then, perhaps your brother is the one I should talk to?" Solinger suggested.

"No," Katherine said quickly. "That is, not yet," she amended. "He doesn't know about this. If you must talk to someone besides me, you should talk to Al."

"Very Well, Miss Sangremano. Suppose you and Al meet me in my hotel room at one o'clock this afternoon. Could you do that?"

"You want me to come too?"

"Certainly, if you wish. Provided, of course, that you bring Mr. Provenzano."

"Your hotel room, yes. I'll be there," Katherine promised excitedly. She started to hang up the phone, then picked it up again. "Don't go away!" she said.

Solinger laughed. "Don't worry, Miss Sangremano. I'm not going anywhere," he promised.

"Katherine, what is it you talk?" Sophia asked when Katherine hung up the phone. "Who do you meet in a hotel room?"

"Mama, that was Mr. Solinger," Katherine said excitedly.

"Mr. Solinger? You go to a hotel room to meet a mister? We do not even know someone named Mr. Solinger and you go to meet him like some *puttana?*"

"Mama, you don't understand. It isn't like that. I'm not going alone. Al is going with me. Besides, Papa knew Mr. Solinger. Papa wrote him a letter about me. Mr. Solinger is going to make me a star, Mama."

"A star? A star? What is this star?"

"In the movies, Mama," Katherine said. "I am going to be in the movies."

"Ahh, I don't know," Sophia said. "I think the girls who are in the movies, they are not very nice. I have seen the pictures of them, with their eyes like so." Sophia made circles around her eyes to indicate that they were overpainted. "Their dresses show too much and they kiss men who are not their husbands."

"It is all very respectable, Mama," Katherine said; "It is only make-believe, for the movies."

"This is what you want?"

"Yes, Mama. And Papa wanted it for me too. I told you, he is the one who wrote the letter to Mr. Solinger.

"I do not like."

"Mama, please!"

Sophia sighed. "Okay. If you go with Al Provenzano, I will not worry. He is a good man, your papa listened to him. If he says it is okay, then I will say it is okay."

"*Grazie*, Mama. *Grazie*," Katherine enthused, kissing her mother on both cheeks.

"In his hotel room? What sort of man is it who would meet a woman in his hotel room?" Al Provenzano responded when Katherine told him of the telephone call she had received from Solinger.

"You sound like Mama," Katherine exclaimed. "Besides, meeting in a hotel room means nothing to a man like Sammy Solinger. He is a movie producer and movie producers do things differently from everyone else. Haven't you ever read any movie magazines?"

"No, I haven't."

"Well, if you had, you would know that this is the way they are."

"Indecent? That's the way they are?"

"Al, it can't be indecent if you are with me too," Katherine said. "I can see where it might be wrong for me to go alone to see him. But you will be with me."

"I'll tell you what I'll do. I'll talk to your brother Tony. If he says it's all right to see him, we'll go see him."

"No!" Katherine said.

"No? What do you mean, no? Katherine, you know that without Tony's approval, nothing can be done."

"Yes, I know that," Katherine said. "But don't you think we ought to at least find out what Mr. Solinger wants, before we see Tony? I mean, if we go see Tony now, we have nothing to tell him. Besides, he's been so terribly busy getting all of Papa's business changed over so he can do it his way. Let's don't bother him until after we have had a chance to meet with Mr. Solinger."

"Katherine, I cannot do that," Al explained patiently. "I am your brother's consigliore. I can take no action without his approval. I will go to his office and see him now. If he says okay, I will take you to see Solinger."

"And if he says no?"

"If he says no, there is nothing I can do."

"But, Al, Papa said it was okay."

"Katherine, your papa does not run things now," Al explained. "Your brother Tony is the new Don."

"The big shot with his own office," Katherine pouted. "Papa never had an office, but what Papa did is not good enough for Tony. Okay, we will go see him. But if he says no, that will not stop me. Maybe I can do nothing with Mr. Solinger, but I will find a way to get into the movies, with or without Tony, the big shot with his own office."

Sitting in his new office, Tony looked up from a ledger book he was writing in and smiled at his brother. Vinnie was sitting at a desk also, playing with a rubber band.

"Is that all you can find to do at your desk?" Tony teased. "Play with a rubber band?"

Vinnie sighed and put the rubber band down. "It's this," he said, making a sweeping motion with his hand.

"It's what?"

"This, all this. The office," Vinnie said. "I don't belong in an office, Tony. I should be out on the street, checking on things. This...this doesn't seem right."

Tony laughed. "I know, I know, you think it is a foolish waste of time and money," he said. He held up his finger. "But it is important, Vinnie. Remember, we are businessmen, you and I. We are not hoods. And businessmen must have an office."

"Yeah, but it's your office," Vinnie pointed out. "Not mine."

"That isn't true, Vinnie," Tony replied. "This office belongs to both of us. Your name is on the door just like mine."

The office was on the third-floor front of a building just off Mulberry, with a window that looked out over Spring Street. The signs were in gold-foil letters, not only on the frosted glass of the door but on the window as well. The lettering read, "Sangremano Enterprises, Antonio J. Sangremano, President, Vincent G. Sangremano, Vice President."

Giuseppe Sangremano had not found it necessary to use an office. He did all the Family business from a table in the back of Scali's Restaurant and he kept notes on pieces of paper that he would stuff into his pockets, each pocket a separate file. Sometimes a multi-thousand-dollar deal would be secured by nothing more than a few lines scribbled on a table napkin. Whenever Tony would question his father about it, Giuseppe would explain that he didn't like to leave paper trails. "You never know who might be following them," he would say, waving his finger as he instructed his son and heir in this bit of precautionary behavior.

What Giuseppe didn't realize but what Tony understood perfectly was that creative obfuscation could be even more effective than leaving no trail at all. And one still had all the records necessary for conducting an efficient business operation.

On the other hand not just anyone could do what

Tony was doing. He had spent years preparing for the day he would be able to put his ideas into practice. No one understood quite what he was doing yet, but they would come around. The merchants who were handling the punch cards, the bookies, the pimps, the loan sharks, which he liked to call bankers, were all surprised by the detail of his records. Tony tried to explain to them, and to Vinnie and to Al, that though their operations weren't exactly legal they were still businesses, and as with any business, it was very important to maintain a profit-and-loss sheet for each of them. For example, by examining the records he had just constructed, he now knew where extra punch cards could be placed to increase the revenue on that particular enterprise.

Tony Sangremano closed the ledger book and leaned back in his chair to stretch. It was hard work, creating books from scratch on all the operations the Sangremano Family controlled, and Tony had to spend many long hours in his office in order to get everything brought up to date.

Al Provenzano came through the door then, and when Tony and Vinnie looked up at him, they were surprised to see that Katherine was with him.

"What is it?" Tony asked quickly, rising from his chair. "Mama," he said. "Katherine, is something wrong with Mama?"

"No," Katherine said. "What would make you think something is wrong with Mama?"

"Nothing," Tony said. He smiled sheepishly. "I mean you being here, that's all. I've never seen you in the office before."

"You haven't had it all that long," Katherine said. She smiled sweetly. "I just wanted to come down and take a look at it."

"Well, what do you think? Nice, huh?" Tony asked.

"Yes," Katherine said. "Very nice."

"See, Vinnie, even Katherine thinks the office is nice." He looked at her. "But I don't think you really came to see how nice the office is. There's something else on your mind."

"Yes, there is," Katherine admitted. "Tony, did Papa ever say anything to you about a man named Sammy Solinger?"

"Solinger? Solinger? No, I don't think so. You ever hear of him, Vinnie?"

"No," Vinnie said.

"Al, do you know who he is?"

"Yes," Al said.

"Well, who is he?"

"He's a movie producer," Katherine said excitedly. "And he wants to put me in the movies."

"Yeah?" Tony replied. "Why?"

"Why? Because I'm a good actress."

"You were in some school plays," Tony said. "I saw them, you were very good. Did this man, Solinger, see you?"

"No."

"Then how does he know you are a good actress? Why is he willing to put you in one of his plays?" When Katherine didn't answer, Tony looked at Al. "Do you know why he is here, Al?"

"Before he died, the Don wrote a letter to him, telling him that your sister was interested in being in the movies."

"I see," Tony said. "Have you spoken to this man, Solinger?"

"Not yet," Al said. "I wanted to see you first, to fill you in on your father's letter. He asked to speak with me today, because I enclosed one of my letters, with your father's, explaining my position with the Family. We got a reply telling us that he was in the middle of a production at the moment and would get back to us later. We heard nothing else from him until he arrived in the city. He called the number that he thought was your father's and he spoke to Katherine. Evidently, he wants to meet with Katherine and me, today."

"I see," Tony said. "Just exactly how much do you know about this guy, Al?"

"Probably much more than he realizes," Al replied. "Your father had me find out all I could, so I have been keeping up with him for the past several months. Right now Solinger is making a picture for Redwood Studios called *Glory Dust*. It's one of those pictures they call an epic. It's a war movie with lots of sets and expensive scenery and so forth. From what I've been able to learn, they've run out of money. I believe Solinger is here to see us to get the money he needs to finish that picture."

"Why would he think he could get the money from us?" Tony asked.

"Because the Don offered to invest in his business."

"I didn't know that," Tony said. "I thought I knew all of his business, but I didn't know that Papa was interested in movies. Why wasn't I told about it?"

"He didn't intend for it to be a Family business," Al explained. "It was something he was doing for Katherine."

"For Katherine?"

"Yes," Katherine put in quickly. "Don't you think Papa could do something for me if he wanted to?"

"Of course I do, Katherine," Tony said. "It's just that I never heard of it before, that's all." He looked back at Al. "So, Papa was going to give this man money, for what... putting Katherine in his picture?" Tony asked.

"Yes, that was the idea your father had in mind."

"And you think that's why Solinger is here, now? To put Katherine in this...this epic?"

"Uh, no," Al admitted. "I think Katherine is the carrot Solinger intends to hold out. I believe he is going to say that if we give him money for *Glory Dust*, he'll find a part for Katherine in his next picture."

"Doesn't sound like much of a deal to me," Tony said. "Tell him thanks, but no thanks. We aren't interested."

"Tony, no!" Katherine said sharply. "You aren't going to do this to me!"

Tony looked over at her, surprised by the sharpness of her response.

"What do you mean?" he asked.

"Look," Katherine said. "I've not asked for any of this, have I?"

"For any of what?"

"This!" Katherine said, taking in the office with a wave of her hand. "Papa's business. It's all yours now, yours and Vinnie's, and Johnny's too if he wants it and ever decides to come back. But what about me? What is there for me? I don't have anything to do with any of it."

"Of course you don't," Tony said. "You're a woman."

"Yes. But I'm Giuseppe Sangremano's daughter. And part of what he built for you and Vinnie and Johnny, he also built for me."

"Katherine, be reasonable. Have you ever wanted anything you couldn't have? A new dress? Jewelry? Anything? You know that what's ours is yours."

"I don't want a new dress, Tony. Or jewels, or a car. I want a life. Can't you understand that? I want a life."

"And that's what you figure being in the movies is? A life?"

"Yes. I know I can make it as an actress, Tony. All I need is the opportunity. Papa was about to give me that opportunity. Only you don't care, so you are about to just throw it away...throw it away without even giving me a chance."

Katherine was crying by the time she finished her tirade and all three men offered her their handkerchiefs. She took the one closest to her and dabbed at her eyes. Tony leaned back against the front of his desk and folded his arms across his chest.

"Katherine, if what Al says is true, the man isn't even here to offer you a part. He's here to get money for the movie he's doing now."

"Do it, Tony," Katherine pleaded. "Please do it. If you don't help him now, when he needs it, he won't even give me a second look later."

"Does it really mean that much to you?"

"It means everything to me," she replied.

Tony looked at Al. "And Papa really intended to invest in the business? Where were you in all of this? Did you advise him on it?"

"It was for Katherine," Al said.

"That doesn't count," Tony replied. "You were his consigliore. It was your job to point things out to him so that he wouldn't let his heart get in the way of good business."

Al smiled. "Yes. Well, it could be that movies are good business," he said.

"What do you mean?"

"Tony, do you know anything about the movie business?" Al asked. "Do you have any idea how much money they earn?"

"No. None at all," Tony admitted.

"Over forty million people a week go to the moving picture shows. At an average cost of fifteen cents a person that is…"

"Six million dollars a week," Tony said quickly. His eyes sparkled. "My God, that's over three hundred million dollars a year!"

"Yes," Al said.

"You know, Al, maybe this is a business worth looking into."

Vinnie laughed. "So, what are you sayin', Tony? That we're going to start making movies now?"

"No," Tony said, waving his hand. "But if there's that much money in the movies, there's bound to be some business in it for us." He looked at Al. "This man, Solinger. What's he like?"

"He's a producer," Katherine said quickly. "One of the best in Hollywood. He has made several wonderful pictures."

"He's a hardheaded businessman," Al said. "One of the reasons he's having a hard time coming up with the money to finish this film is because he insists on having artistic control over all his pictures."

"Artistic control? What does that mean?"

"That means he wants to pick the writer and the story, the director and all the actors."

"Yeah, well, I don't care about all that," Tony said. He stroked his chin for a moment. "But he's got to have a place to show the movies, right? He's got to have theaters."

"Yes," Al answered.

"How many theaters in New York?"

"I don't know," Al said. "There must be hundreds... maybe even a thousand or more."

"Nobody's got the theaters organized, do they? I mean, nobody's ever thought of it before."

Al smiled. "No," he said. "I don't think so."

"Yeah, well, we're going to do that. And we're going to decide what picture goes in what theater. That way, we'll have it from both sides...the theater owners will have to come to us if they want to show a certain picture, and the movie makers will have to come to us if they want to put their picture in our theaters. This guy, Solinger, he might be of some use to us."

"That's all very interesting, Tony," Katherine said. "But where do I fit in?"

"We'll take care of you," Tony promised. "Al, when you make the deal, we have to have an ironclad understanding that Katherine gets a job in the movies."

"Not a job...a part!" Katherine said.

"Okay, a part," Tony said. He smiled broadly. "You want to be in the movies, I'm going to see that you are in the movies."

"Oh, Tony!" Katherine squealed in delight, hurrying to put her arms around him. "Thank you, Tony. Thank you very much!"

Tony laughed, then gently disentangled himself and looked over at Vinnie. "Vinnie, I want you to go with them when they see Solinger."

"Me? Why you want me to go?"

"Yes, why?" Katherine asked.

Tony put his hand gently on his sister's shoulder. "Don't worry," he said. "I'm just going to send Vinnie along to make certain about the deal we are buying into."

"Vinnie, you won't frighten him, will you?" Katherine asked.

"No," Vinnie answered. "Why would I do that? I just want to make sure he listens to reason, that's all."

Solinger received his visitors in a silk dressing gown. He met them in the sitting room of his suite, where he had a table set up with coffee, pastries, and fruit. He greeted them effusively and offered them a seat.

"Would you like something a little stronger than coffee to drink?" he asked, pulling a bottle from the pocket of his dressing gown. "I had one of the bellboys get it for me. It's genuine Canadian."

"Thank you, no, Mr. Solinger," Vinnie said. "It's against the law."

Solinger looked up at them and smiled. "What? Against the law? Are you kidding me? Since I got here, I did a little research on you people. I know who Giuseppe Sangremano was and I know who you are."

"And who are we, Mr. Solinger?" Vinnie asked.

Solinger poured a generous amount of whiskey into his cup, then screwed the cap back on and put the bottle away.

"You're gangsters," he said, stretching his lips across his teeth in what might have been a smile.

Vinnie stood up and started for the door. "Come along, Katherine, Al," he said. "I think we made a mistake in coming here."

"Wait, wait!" Solinger called to them. "Listen, I didn't know you were going to be so sensitive. I want you to know it doesn't bother me."

"If you really think we are gangsters, why would you want to do business with us?" Al asked.

Solinger barked a laugh. "You think I haven't done business with gangsters before? You think we don't have gangsters out in Hollywood? We got 'em out there, all right. The only thing is, they're quiet men who wear silk suits..."

"And silk dressing gowns?" Vinnie added pointedly.

Solinger looked at his dressing gown, then laughed again. "Yeah," he said. "And silk dressing gowns." He took a drink and studied Vinnie, Al, and Katherine over the rim of his cup. Finally, he took an audible breath and put the cup down in his saucer with a clink. "Look, let's be frank with each other, okay?" he said. "You get your money from what? Gambling? Loansharking? Prostitution? Maybe a little protection? You get that money and you got no way to show where it comes from in case the wrong people start gettin' too curious about your business. So, you need a place to put your money...a legitimate place, right? You can hide a lot of money in a business like mine. You need me."

"Let's get something straight, Mr. Solinger. You came to New York to see us. We didn't come to California to see you," Vinnie said.

"That means nothing. I've got family here in the city. Besides, it was your old man who contacted me first. The truth is, I've got people lined up to put money in my projects."

"That's not the way I heard it," Vinnie said. "Tell him what we know, Al."

Al took a piece of paper from his pocket and held it up, though he didn't open it.

"I have here a list of the backers you have gone to see in the last two months," he said. "All of them have turned you down."

"You do your homework pretty damn good, don't you?" Solinger growled.

"In our line of work you have to," Vinnie said.

"All right, all right, I need you too," Solinger admitted. "The thing is, we can be good for each other. You invest a little money now in the movie I already have in progress. That will bail me out of the fix I'm in, and let you get your feet wet, so to speak, without getting in too deep. The good thing is, this movie is almost in the can, so you won't have to wait too long to see how it comes out. Then, if we're both happy with our business arrangement, we can get together and plan my next movie." He looked over at Katherine and smiled. "A movie with this beautiful young woman as the star."

"How much money do you need to complete the picture you are working on now?" Al asked.

"Another half mil ought to bring it in," Solinger said.

"A half a million dollars?" Vinnie asked, stunned by the amount.

Solinger blinked. "Well, yes. Listen, is that too steep for you? I mean, if it is, then we got no business. Movies make a lot of money, but they cost a lot to produce. This is no penny-ante operation here."

"You got a telephone in the other room there? I think maybe we ought to call my brother on this."

"Yeah, sure, make whatever telephone calls you have to make."

"Thanks."

Vinnie and Al went into the other room to call Tony, leaving Katherine and Solinger in the sitting room.

"Coffee, Miss Sangremano?" Solinger offered, raising the coffeepot in invitation.

"Yes, thank you."

"So, have you seen many of my movies?" Solinger asked as he poured the coffee.

"I've seen them all," Katherine said.

"Which one did you like best?"

"*Dreams of Youth.*"

Solinger looked up in surprise. *Dreams of Youth* was a very "arty" picture, full of allegory and symbolism. It had been praised by critics and ignored by the public. It was one of the films that lost money for Solinger, though it was his personal favorite. It was not the type of film he would expect a star-struck young woman to appreciate.

But then, Katherine Sangremano wasn't like the normal star-struck woman he was used to seeing. She wasn't sexy and beautiful... she wasn't even pretty, though the makeup artists could go a long way toward correcting that.

Hollywood was full of beautiful young women who were trying to become movie stars, long-legged, sultry sirens who changed beds between directors and producers as often as those same beds had their sheets changed. Most were vacuous women who were depending on their body to get them by.

"What did you like about *Dreams of Youth*?" Solinger asked.

"It's difficult to put into words," Katherine answered. She smiled and when she did, she was almost pretty. "I saw it several times and it was like…like looking through a piece of prism glass to see many different colors of the same light. Only instead of colors, I saw many different meanings. I know it sounds silly, but it made me cry."

Solinger was stunned by the young woman's observation. He had paid thousands of dollars to publicity directors to try to explain the picture to the public, but none of them had described it as well as she just did. And she did it in no more than two dozen words. Solinger was still staring at her in surprise when the two men returned from the bedroom.

"I talked to my brother," Vinnie said. "We are prepared to offer you a deal, provided you can listen to reason."

"Yeah? What kind of deal?"

"We'll put up the five hundred thousand dollars you need to finish this picture. When it's finished and it comes to New York, it comes to us. We'll make the deal with the theaters."

"No can do. I have a contract with a half dozen distributors who handle New York."

"Don't worry about that," Vinnie said. "We'll take care of getting you out of those contracts."

"How are you going to do that?" Solinger asked.

"We will talk to the distributors."

"You can talk until you are blue in the face. These contracts are worth a lot of money to those people. They aren't going to just turn their back on them."

Vinnie smiled. "You let us worry about that," he said. "We are going to make them listen to reason."

It was the second time Vinnie had made that statement. The first time, it had passed over Solinger's head. This time, he read something more ominous in it.

"That's all you want?" he said. "The right to distribute my film in New York?"

"All your films in New York," Vinnie said. "From here on out."

"You're asking a hell of a lot."

"What is your percentage of the gross?"

"Forty."

"You won't be losing anything with us. You'll be getting the same percentage as you are now. The only thing, we feel we can get the gross up. In the end, you'll be making more money."

Solinger stared at them for a long moment. He had no choice, if he didn't come up with the money soon, he was going to lose this picture and everything he had invested in it. To hell with it. Let them distribute this picture. If he could get out of the contracts he was in now...he could do it again with these people. He had to have the money, there was no way out.

"All right," he agreed. "You can distribute my pictures."

"And we don't wait for the next picture for you to use my sister," Vinnie said. "You use her in this one."

"In this picture? No way. This is a war picture, there's no place in it for women. Besides, it's almost finished."

"Find a place," Vinnie said. "Nurse, grieving wife, sister, find a place. You can go back and put it in."

"All right," Solinger agreed. "Normally, I don't like my backers telling me who I can use or what the picture is about. But, in this case, I'll make an exception."

Vinnie smiled. "I thought you would listen to reason," he said.

There was that expression again. It was so perfectly innocent, but it gave Solinger a cold chill.

"So, how do I get the money? You write me out a check or what?" Solinger asked.

"You'll need my sister in California, won't you?" Vinnie asked.

"Yeah, sure."

"When she comes, someone will come with her. They will bring the money with them."

"Six weeks," Solinger said. "I'll need the money within six weeks. If I don't get it, they'll close me down and there won't be anything I can do about it." He looked over at Katherine. "And there will be no part for her," he added.

"You'll have the money in six weeks," Vinnie promised.

CHAPTER 4

TWO WEEKS LATER

Pendarrow had been walking his beat for almost an hour. It was a little after nine o'clock and the heat that had built up during the day was still around, hanging just over the streets and the sidewalks like something palpable. It seemed unusual to be this hot, this early. What was it going to be like in July or August? As Pendarrow mopped his face with a handkerchief, he wished the police would design a uniform that would take the heat into consideration. Perhaps a short-sleeved shirt could be worn on nights like this. Instead, he was expected to wear not only a long-sleeved shirt, but a heavy uniform jacket, over the shirt. Well, he had made some accommodation. Tonight, as soon as he had completed the watch inspection, he went into the men's room and took off his shirt. He was wearing the uniform jacket all right, but he had absolutely nothing on beneath the jacket.

On hot nights like this, everyone seemed to move closer to the city. The doors and windows of all the apartments were thrown open and, in many cases, mattresses were brought out onto the fire escape and people slept outside to attempt to beat the heat. Some of the more affluent people had window fans and Pendarrow could hear their droning hum and smell the cooking odors they pumped out into the streets as the fans exchanged the air inside the apartments with that from outside. Somewhere, someone was playing a recording of Caruso and Pendarrow could hear the tenor's voice floating down an alley. The streets were full of kids playing stickball and kick-the-can. Here and there, young lovers would sit on a front stoop of an apartment building, trying to carve a few square feet of privacy out of the teeming neighborhood.

Pendarrow checked his watch, saw that it was time to report in, and walked to the call box at the corner of Mulberry and Spring streets. The call-box key was hanging from a cord around his neck and he raised it up to the lock and opened the door. There, just inside the call box, was a white envelope. It hadn't been there an hour ago. Hesitant, he reached in and took it out.

Pendarrow opened the envelope, then gasped. Inside he found twelve twenty-dollar bills and one ten. There was also a piece of paper with the words. "Green Oldsmobile, two men."

Two hundred and fifty dollars. The second half of the payment he had accepted from Trapnell. Someone, somehow, had put the money in his call box. This was the signal Trapnell told him about. Tonight, some of Vaglichio's men would be perusing the area. And all he had to do was...nothing.

Pendarrow looked around quickly to see if anyone was watching him, then slipped the envelope into his jacket pocket. After that, he called the station.

"Pendarrow," he said when his call was answered. "I'm just checking in."

"Everything all right?"

"Yeah," Pendarrow replied. "Everything is fine."

The car drove by again, a green Oldsmobile with two men inside. It was the third time Pendarrow had seen the car since he found the envelope. The note in the envelope had said "Green Oldsmobile, two men," so Pendarrow, as instructed, paid no attention to the car, even when it stopped and one of the men called over to a young boy who was leaning against the wall in front of a pool hall. The boy, about sixteen, flipped away the cigarette he had been smoking and sauntered over to the car.

Weasel saw the green Oldsmobile and the two men in it almost as quickly as Pendarrow did. And like Pendarrow, he knew that they weren't a normal part of the neighborhood. That didn't mean too much, though. There were always people down here trying to find a card game, or a whore. Sometimes they drove around looking for a speakeasy but those who came here for that were out of luck. Tony Sangremano was not in the whiskey business.

Though Tony wasn't in the whiskey business, that did not mean there was absolutely no place a person could buy liquor. There were a few enterprising and courageous men who were attempting to fill in the gap. They were enterprising because they were manufacturing liquor in their own house. It was generally pretty raw stuff and it had earned the name "bathtub gin." They were courageous because they were in business for themselves, without the Sangremanos' support, or permission.

For the most part, however, the Sangremano territory was dry. Weasel didn't understand why Tony was letting such an opportunity get away from him. He wished he would change his mind because there would be more opportunities for him if there were a few speakeasies about.

Weasel was always looking for opportunities. That was why he had shown up at Dunnigan's, ready to run numbers for him on the day of Don Giuseppe Sangremano's funeral. He had earned a few dollars that day, and as Weasel hoped he would, Dunnigan had used him a few more times. So far at least, the numbers running had not turned into anything steady and dependable. And the two boys in his "gang" were too young and inexperienced to do him any good. Of course, they were not any younger than Weasel himself, but Weasel had been on the streets, on his own, for nearly two years. Two years on the streets made a body grow up pretty fast and Weasel was far ahead of Guido and Dom.

The Oldsmobile stopped on the street right in front of the pool hall and one of the men signaled for Weasel to come over. Weasel flipped away the cigarette he was smoking and went out to see what the man wanted. Maybe there was a buck in it for him.

"Hey, kid, we want you to deliver a package for us," one of the two men said. This was the one on the passenger side.

"Who to?"

"Tony Sangremano. You know him?"

"Are you kidding me?" Weasel asked. "Everybody down here knows Mr. Sangremano."

The man laughed. "Yeah, I guess they would, wouldn't they? Tell me, he's a pretty good guy, is he?"

"Yeah, sure," Weasel said. Who were these clowns? Did they actually think he was going to say Tony wasn't a pretty good guy?

"That's what we heard."

"What we mean is, is he a man somebody can do business with?" the driver asked.

"It depends on the business you wantin' to do," Weasel replied.

"Anything we can. We just want to make a buck, you know what I mean?"

"You tryin' to get started down here, in Sangremano territory?" Weasel asked.

"Yeah, if we can work somethin' out with the man."

"No whiskey," Weasel said. "Tony won't have nothin' to do with any whiskey."

"That's what we hear. It don't matter none, it don't have to be whiskey. We can find somethin' else, maybe a little bankin' business," the passenger said. He picked up a package wrapped in brown paper and tied with a red ribbon and bow. He handed it through the window. "Listen, my mama, she baked this. You know mamas. They figure no Italian can turn down a favor on a full stomach. See that Mr. Sangremano gets it, will you?"

"What is it?"

"What is it? It's a nice rum cake. Smell it, okay, but don't squeeze it."

"Here, kid, just so you know what you're deliverin'," the driver interjected. He reached out across the passenger, handing Weasel a small piece of cake. The cake was wrapped in a napkin. "Take a taste, tell me how you like it."

Tony tasted it. "It's good," he said.

"Goddamn right it's good. Carmine's mama is a good cook. Look, you take it in, tell Mr. Sangremano a nice Italian mama baked it just for him."

"Shouldn't I tell him who it came from?"

"Naw, that ain't necessary. Me and Carmine, we'll come aroun' tomorrow and see him. We'll tell him then. Maybe he'll be in the mood to talk a little business with us."

"A dollar," Weasel said.

"What?"

"You want the cake inside, it'll cost you a dollar for me to deliver it."

"That's pretty steep, ain't it?"

"You see anybody else around here can do the job for you?"

"You're quite the little hustler, ain't you?"

"A dollar," Weasel said again.

"Give him the money, Carmine," the driver said. The driver smiled at Weasel. "Ever'body's got to have some action goin', right, kid?"

"Right," Weasel said, taking the package and the dollar.

Vinnie was having a difficult time understanding where Tony was going, but Vinnie would come around. Tony was sure of that. Vinnie had been very good, so far, in neither questioning Tony's authority nor challenging what he was trying to do, even though Tony knew that Vinnie disagreed with him. Vinnie, for example, wanted to get into the liquor business and not just in a small way. He wanted it all, including bottling his own hooch, then slapping a Canadian label on the bottles and passing them off as imported bond.

Quietly, Tony was studying the possibilities of going into the liquor business. It was just that he did not want to rush into it until he was adequately prepared. The liquor business did have a high potential for profit, though of course there was an even higher potential for problems. It was Tony's intention to study those problems, learn from the mistakes of others, then eliminate them. With all the preliminary study and the details taken care of, Tony figured that by the time the Sangremano Family entered the liquor business they would be able to run it as smoothly and efficiently and, what was most important, as profitably as if it were General Motors.

But of course, that didn't mean anything to Vinnie. Vinnie was the kind of man who thrived on problems. He especially loved physical confrontation. He was younger than Tony, but even when they were children Vinnie seemed to intuitively recognize that Tony was the kind of person who would rather depend upon his brain than his brawn. Vinnie was bigger and stronger than his older brother, but he never bullied Tony. Vinnie respected Tony's intelligence and he was very protective of him. Once when they were young, two larger kids, Tony's age, started harassing Tony. Vinnie tore into them. He was smaller and younger than they were but he already had something that neither of them had. He had an absolute lack of fear as well as a love of physical contact. Vinnie did not care how many times he got hit as long as he was able to get in his own punches. He would willingly trade three for one, if need be. Kids did not normally think that way, and it gave Vinnie an overwhelming advantage in any fight. As a result, Vinnie's ferocity set both of Tony's antagonists running.

———

Without the words being spoken, a bond greater even than the bond of brotherhood joined the two boys that day. Later, Tony described it as a symbiotic relationship, and he explained the term to Vinnie.

"Yeah, I understand," Vinnie said. "Your brains and my brawn. Together, no sonofabitch can take us."

And then, of course, there was Johnny. Johnny was totally different from either Tony or Vinnie. Tony liked to think of him as being someone who had some of his brain and some of Vinnie's brawn. Johnny had no interest in the family business at all. It wasn't that he was particularly negative about it; he seemed, literally, to have no opinion about it one way or the other. As far as Tony could tell Johnny wasn't even particularly interested in money. All he seemed to care about was flying that airplane he bought. The airplane and, of course, women. Johnny had always been a big one with the women.

"A big one," Tony said aloud, and he laughed at his own joke. Unlike Tony and Vinnie, Johnny had been an all-star athlete in high school where he played baseball, football, and basketball. And of course, even in high school, he had been very popular with the girls. Though no one else but Tony and his father knew of it, Giuseppe had once paid a great deal of money to the father of a girl Johnny had gotten pregnant. Not even Johnny knew the girl was pregnant; he was only fourteen at the time and the girl was nineteen. The irate father came to Giuseppe and suggested that Giuseppe might be inclined to find someone who could "take care" of his poor little girl, to save her reputation. He wanted Giuseppe to find an abortionist and to pay for it.

Giuseppe refused because he did not believe in abortion. He was willing, however, to pay handsomely to put the girl in a private boarding school for unwed mothers. The girl's father accepted Giuseppe's offer. Tony later discovered that the girl's father used the money to buy an abortion anyway, while he kept the rest. Tony did not tell his father what he found out because he was afraid his father would have the man killed. That was the way Giuseppe was. The thought of aborting an undeveloped fetus could bring him to tears, but if he believed it was justified he could order the murder of a husband and father without so much as a second thought.

A knock on the office door interrupted Tony's musing and he got up from the desk and walked over to open it.

A boy was standing just outside the door in the hallway holding a package. The package was wrapped in brown packing paper, although it did have a bright red bow taped to it.

"Hello, kid," Tony said. He had seen the boy a few times, although he could not think of his name.

"Godfather, this is for you," the boy said, handing the package to him.

"Well, thank you," Tony said. "And this is for you." Tony pulled out a dollar, but the boy waved it away.

"That's okay, Godfather, you don't need to pay me anything, the men who gave me the package to deliver paid me."

"You didn't have to tell me that," Tony said. "You could've been paid twice."

"I welcome the opportunity to do you the favor, Godfather."

"What's your name?"

"Most people just call me Weasel."

Tony smiled. "Okay, Weasel. I'll remember you," he said.

Weasel smiled broadly. "Thank you, Godfather."

Tony took the package into his office and placed it on the corner of his desk. Weasel had called him Godfather. That was another thing Tony wanted to change. Actually, Tony did not qualify as a Godfather, even under the old traditions. That was a title of respect that he would have to earn. But realistically, he never wanted to be thought of as a Godfather, for he didn't care for the image that it evoked. Godfathers were dictators, sometimes benevolent, but most of the time malevolent. Tony did not want to be regarded as a dictator, either for good or for evil. While Tony was growing up at his father's side he had made a study of those people who addressed his father as Godfather. Some did it out of love, others out of respect, but a significant number of them did it from fear.

Tony had no desire for his people to fear him. Nor did he need them to love him. But he did want their respect and felt he could eventually earn it.

In the meantime, if they wanted to continue to give him little gifts as they had his father, what was the harm? It would be an insult not to take them. He knew the kind of gifts they were for they had shown up at his father's house at significant occasions such as Christmas, Easter, his father's birthday, anniversaries, first communion days, and even at his and Vinnie's weddings. Most of the time the gifts were something simple like a gallon of homemade wine, several jars of homemade jelly, pies, cakes, or cookies. Giuseppe always made a big fuss over them and Tony remembered staying back in the shadows, watching the absolute rapture in the faces of the old Italian women who were having praise for their taralles heaped on them by the Godfather.

"Papa, you can get taralles anytime you want from the bakery store. Why do you carry on so when some old woman gives them to you?" Tony had asked.

"It pleases me to make them feel good about their gifts," Giuseppe had answered. "Never forget, Tony, when someone gives a gift, they are giving you a part of themselves. If you can make them feel good about that, they will not mind so much later when you ask for a gift of their soul."

At the time Tony had thought that was a very strange answer and it was many years before he understood it. Finally, he realized that this was the source of his father's power. Giuseppe Sangremano traded in favors large and small, and he had built a large checking account of souls receivable that was never overdrawn.

Tony considered that demeaning for both parties and

he had no intention of doing anything like that. And at some time in the future, he would begin to refuse gifts such as this one just brought to him. He would, however, wait until everyone understood exactly what he was trying to do with Sangremano Enterprises so that no one's feelings would be hurt.

In the meantime, he smiled, it wouldn't hurt to accept the gift of a few pastries now and then. What was in this box, he wondered. A pie? A cake? Cookies? He untied the string, then opened the lid.

The bomb in the box exploded with a flash of white flame and a thunderous roar that could be heard two blocks away. Tony was leaning over the box when it went off and his body took the full charge. His right arm was literally blown from his body and it went crashing through the window with the gold letters, to fall on a Dodge that was passing by on Spring Street. The driver of the Dodge, seeing the severed, bleeding, and still-twitching arm lying on the hood just in front of his windshield, stopped in panic, then staggered out of the car and began throwing up.

Jason Cardoba, a CPA who had an office just down the hall from Sangremano Enterprises, was also working late that night. He was the first one into the office after the explosion. The lights in the new office had been blown out by the explosion so it was illuminated only by the hall lights. It was dark and gloomy and filled with smoke as Cardoba picked his way over the broken glass and shattered furniture. He looked around for Tony but he could not find him. Then he realized that there was not enough of Tony left to be called a "him." The walls and ceilings were spattered with pieces of flesh and bone, blood and guts. Like the Dodge driver in the street three floors below, Jason staggered back out of the room and leaned against the wall of the hallway as he began puking on the floor.

Up in the Bronx, Joe Provenzano was attending Julio Pizaro's wedding. He had rearranged his schedule to be here just so he could see Maria Vaglichio again.

The wedding reception was held in a rented hall and decorated for the occasion with red, white, and green bunting, as well as large photographs of the bride and groom. There were over two hundred guests for the reception including Maria's grandfather, Sam, her uncle Luca, and her father, Mario.

Joe had not come to the reception in his police uniform but he may as well have. Even in mufti, he looked different from the others. He had dark hair, dark eyes, and a swarthy complexion, just as the other young men did. But his shoes were leather, not snakeskin, his shirt was cotton, not silk, and his haircut was not expensive. There was also something about his demeanor that had "cop" written all over him. As a result, he stood out as sharply as if he had been Chinese.

Johnny had not seen Maria since Giuseppe Sangremano's funeral, nor had he spoken to her tonight. He had looked at her though, and once, when someone came up to engage him in conversation, he happened to glance over and see that she was staring at him. She looked away in quick embarrassment when she realized he had caught her.

There were a few other times during the evening when they would steal glances and, finally, she lost her embarrassment and actually smiled at him. Now, with no one at the punch bowl, Maria walked over to it.

"Please, Miss Vaglichio. Allow me," Joe said, stepping quickly up to the punch bowl to pour her a cup.

"Thank you," Maria said. Her voice sounded like the song of angels.

"My name is Joe Provenzano."

"I know who you are," Maria said. "You are a police-man, aren't you?"

"Yes."

"The other day, you saved three little girls from a gunman. Everyone was talking about it, about how brave you were."

"There wasn't much to it," Joe demurred.

"You are also the nephew of Al Provenzano, consigliore for the Sangremanos, aren't you?"

"Yes," Joe said. He handed her the cup of punch. "Does that bother you?"

"It doesn't bother me," Maria said. She took a swallow and studied him over the rim of her cup. "But it bothers my father a great deal."

"Then I won't ask your father to dinner."

Maria chuckled.

"But I will ask you."

"No," Maria said sharply, and she looked around quickly, to make certain no one had overheard. "No, you mustn't. I can't."

"Dinner, in a public place?" Joe said. "What could be wrong with that?"

"No, I can't," Maria said again.

"You can't? Or you don't want to. Maria, if you aren't interested at all, then tell me now and I won't bother you anymore. But if the only reason you are turning me down is because you think you can't see me, then, I promise you, we could work something out."

"Wait," Maria said, holding up her hand to stop him. She looked around anxiously, then when she saw that no one was close enough to overhear them she said, "Stay right here." She turned and started to leave.

"Maria?"

"Wait right here," Maria said again, calling back over her shoulder.

Puzzled, Joe did as he was asked. He watched her move through the room talking and smiling with all the others until, finally, she was lost in the crowd. He was confused. Why had she told him to wait, if she was going to walk away like that?

A few minutes later another girl came up to the punch bowl and smiled at Joe. He recognized her as Ellen Pizaro, the bridegroom's sister. "Hello, Joe. Would you pour me a cup of punch, please?"

"Yes, of course," Joe said. Even as he poured the cup for Ellen, he was looking through the crowded room trying to find Maria.

"You know where I live, don't you, Joe?"

"Yes. You live just over the bakery."

"Be there at seven o'clock next Friday night."

"I beg your pardon?" Joe asked, surprised by the girl's comment.

Ellen smiled broadly. "You do want to see Maria, don't you?"

"What? Yes. Yes, of course I do."

"Then be at my place, seven o'clock next Friday night," she said. She drifted back into the crowd.

"I'll be there!" Joe said. He walked over to stand against the wall, scarcely able to keep the broad grin off his face. He wanted to sing out loud. Maria did want to see him. She had made arrangements herself!

Right then, two men came in through the door of the reception hall and stood beside Joe for a moment or two, holding their hats in their hands as their eyes searched the room. Joe recognized them as Carmine Petacci and Freddie Sarfatti, a couple of goons who worked for the Vaglichios, generally doing strong-arm jobs. They were not dressed for the party, so Joe knew that they were here for some other reason. Spotting Luca, the two men walked over to him. One of them whispered something in his ear. Luca smiled, then went over to say something, quietly, to Don Vaglichio, who was sitting at the head table with the bride and bridegroom's parents. Don Vaglichio nodded, but the expression on his face did not change. Joe glanced up at the clock and saw that it was just a couple of minutes past ten. He did not know why Carmine and Freddie were here but he would be willing to bet that something had just happened within the last half hour and they had something to do with it. Whatever it was, it had been at the Vaglichios' direction. Joe was certain of that.

ST. LOUIS, THREE DAYS LATER

After crossing the Mississippi River just north of the Eads Bridge, the DH-4 began descending. It circled once around the city, then landed at Lambert Field, an airport named after the president of Lambert Pharmaceuticals, maker of Listerine, and one of St. Louis's earliest aviation enthusiasts and financial supporters. They taxied to a stop in a spot pointed out to them by a line boy, then, after they killed the engine, Mike and Johnny climbed down from their airplane.

"Do you want fuel?" the line boy asked.

"No," Johnny answered. "Just leave it there."

"Leave it? Don't worry about that, mister. There's no way I'm going to try to move this thing. It looks like it's about to fall apart," the boy said derisively.

The airplane was beginning to show quite a few signs of fatigue and wear. It had already accumulated many hours of flying time with very little maintenance except that done by Mike and Johnny. With no money for actual replacement parts, the two men managed to keep their airplane flying by using pieces of baling wire for control cable, garden hose for engine fuel and oil lines, and ash, pine, or elm instead of the hard-to-get spruce to replace or repair damaged spars and ribs. Wherever a corn stalk or a stick had poked a hole in the fabric they patched it with pieces of cloth cut from flour and feed sacks. The rocker arm oil leak that had never been adequately repaired continued to pump away and by now had smeared a large brown stain from the nose halfway back to the empennage. The DH-4 was no more than a vagabond collection of stained, bent, and patched bits and pieces of wood, cloth, and wire that was somehow able to hold together. It was a refugee from the junkyard, and as they walked away from it, Mike looked back to see it sitting right in the middle of a long line of shiny new Curtis Robbins. The contrast between the new airplanes and the one they had been flying was so vivid that Mike groaned.

"What is it?" Johnny asked.

"Look," Mike said, pointing back toward the airplane. "The boy is right."

"Yeah, I guess it is kind of ugly, isn't it?"

"Ugly? It would have to improve a lot to be ugly," Mike suggested.

"Never mind. If Robertson Aviation will take us on as airmail pilots, we can afford to get our plane fixed up real nice."

"Fixed up? The only thing we could do to fix up that thing is take the old airplane off the propeller and put a new one on."

"And then replace the propeller," Johnny added, laughing.

"Don't let it hear us talking like this, though," Mike teased. "I wouldn't want to hurt its feelings."

"No, I wouldn't think of hurting its feelings," Johnny

said. "Say, Mike, do you think the airmail pilots are flying those nice new jobs there?" he asked, pointing to one of the shiny new Curtis Robbin biplanes.

"I don't know. Maybe. Listen, have we really thought about this? I mean, are we sure we want to be airmail pilots?" Mike asked.

"Well, yeah, we're sure," Johnny answered. "At least I am. Aren't you? We did talk about it."

"I know we did," Mike answered. "And I guess I am ready to give it a try. For a few months anyway."

Johnny laughed. "They tell me a few months is all an airmail pilot lasts."

"Before quitting?"

"Yeah. Or getting killed."

"Really? Well, I don't think I was born just to be killed flying somebody else's bills around," Mike said.

"Me neither," Johnny agreed. "That's why the thought of being an airmail pilot doesn't bother me any."

By now they were at the little office building that served as the Robertson Aviation Company office. Johnny pushed the door open and they went inside.

The interview lasted no more than fifteen minutes. When the interviewer was convinced that both Mike and Johnny had enough flying experience to handle the job, he agreed to hire them, telling them to wait for a few minutes while he walked over to the hangar to get the chief pilot. The chief pilot, he said, would assign them a route and give them a schedule of when they would be flying. As they settled down into the overstuffed chairs of the waiting room, Mike saw a copy of the St. Louis Post-Dispatch sitting on a small end table and he reached for it. It had been several weeks since either of them had looked at a newspaper and he had no idea what was going on in the world now.

The front page of the paper contained news of the

Supreme Court upholding the Volstead Act. The 1920 census report was in and New York was the largest city in the country with a population of 5.6 million people. It was not until he turned the page and saw the article on page three, however, that Mike saw a story that really grabbed his attention.

Mob Chief Killed In Gangland Bombing Associated Press

NEW YORK, NY June 15th—Antonio J. Sangremano, said to be a mob chief in New York's Lower Manhattan and the borough of Queens, was killed today by a bomb blast. Police say the bomb, concealed in a package that was delivered to Sangremano, was probably the work of someone in a rival gang.

Tony Sangremano had only recently assumed power in the gang that was headed for many years by his father, Giuseppe Sangremano. Insiders say that Tony Sangremano's brother Vinnie will be the new chief. Police and others fear that the bombing will now precipitate a response from Vinnie Sangremano, resulting in an all-out gang war.

"We will not sit idly by and watch a gang war develop in the streets of our city," the mayor of New York said. "Nor will we allow gangs, such as that headed by Tony Sungremano, to terrorize our citizens. Today I am informing all policemen to be on a special alert for any signs that Vinnie Sangremano may be trying to avenge the death of his brother."

Funeral arrangements have been tentatively scheduled for June 18th, pending notification of the deceased's brother. Johnny Sangremano, the youngest brother of the Sangremano family, is believed to be flying about the country as a gypsy aviator and is unaware of his brother's death.

Mike lowered the paper and looked over at Johnny, who had picked up a Collier's magazine. Johnny was smiling at one of the jokes he was reading. Today was the twentieth of June. Since the family had been unable to contact Johnny, Mike was certain that Tony was already buried. Nevertheless, Johnny had to be told.

"Johnny," he said, handing the paper toward him, folded in such a way as to bring the story about Tony to the front. "I think you'd better read this."

"What is it?" Johnny asked, still smiling. Then, when he saw the expression on Mike's face, he took the paper from him and began reading.

"Oh," Johnny said a moment later. "Oh, Jesus." He pinched the bridge of his nose.

"I'm sorry, Johnny," Mike said.

"This…this kind of stuff wasn't supposed to happen anymore," Johnny said, waving at the newspaper. "Tony was going to turn everything into a business, no more *luparas*, no more vendettas."

"You want to go back to New York?" Mike asked.

"Yeah," Johnny said. "Yeah, I guess I'd better. It's too late for the funeral but I think I ought to be there. You keep the plane, I'll take the train back."

"Wouldn't you rather fly back to New York?"

"No," Johnny said. He looked out the window toward their airplane, then laughed softly. "To tell the truth, I don't know if that old crate would hold together long enough to get us back."

"Maybe we can sell it."

"Yeah, maybe."

"I'll come back to New York with you."

"No, that's all right, you don't need…"

Mike put his hand out to touch his friend on the shoulder. "I won't interfere with your family, Johnny. I won't even see them. But if you're leaving now, I am too. I don't think I'd enjoy it much without you along."

"I'm sorry this has messed up all our plans, Mike. It's not fair to you to…"

"Ah, don't worry about it," Mike interrupted. "It's about time I went back home and got a job and settled down anyway." He smiled. "Let someone else fly the mail."

"What kind of job are you going to get?"

"I don't know," Mike admitted. "The only thing anyone in our family has ever done is police work. But I'm not all that anxious to become one of New York's finest."

"Good," Johnny said, smiling. "I'd have a hard time explaining to Vinnie that my best friend is a cop. Vinnie isn't real crazy about cops."

NEW YORK

A line of perspiration beads popped out on Officer Pendarrow's upper lip. The police officer's hands shook noticeably and his eyes were wide with fright as they followed Vinnie. Vinnie was pacing back and forth in the back room of a little tobacco shop on Baxter. Also in the room were one of the Sangremano capo-regimes, Luigi Sarducci, and Sarducci's second in command, Angelo Cardi. Sarducci and Cardi had brought Pendarrow in off the street a few minutes earlier and were standing on each side of him. Vinnie had just asked him a question, but didn't seem pleased by Pendarrow's answer.

"Now, let me see if I understand what you are telling me, Officer Pendarrow," Vinnie said. He turned back toward the policeman and folded his arms across his chest. "You are telling me that you didn't see anything suspicious on the day my brother was killed. Yet you were on duty that day, and were, in fact, walking the beat right in front of my brother's office. I know this is true because many people who heard the explosion have told me that they saw you there but a moment earlier. Do you deny that you were there?"

"No," Pendarrow said in a halting voice that was choked with terror. "I don't deny it. I was there that night."

"But you didn't see anyone come inside?"

"People went in and out all the time, for chrissake," Pendarrow whined. "Mr. Sangremano, that is a business building."

"But it was after hours."

"It was a hot night, everyone was up and moving around. People went into the building."

"Did you see any of them carrying a package?"

"No."

"The bomb had to get in there some way. Don't you agree?"

"I suppose so."

"You suppose so?"

"Yes! Yes! I agree," Pendarrow said.

"Who brought the package?"

"I don't know."

"Pendarrow, I am a bereaved man. My poor father died of natural causes a short while ago, then my brother was murdered. Surely you can understand why I would want to know who did this? You can understand that, can't you, Pendarrow?"

Pendarrow nodded. A whimper escaped his lips.

"I didn't hear you."

"Y-yes," Pendarrow said.

"Officer Pendarrow, I think it is time for you to listen to reason."

"I didn't see anything," Pendarrow said.

Vinnie nodded at Cardi and Sarducci. Cardi reached down and grabbed Pendarrow's right arm and forced the policeman's hand, palm down on the arm of the chair. Without any further preliminary, Sarducci then slammed a ballpeen hammer down on the knuckle of one of Pendarrow's fingers. Sarducci was very precise with the blow, hitting the index finger exactly on the knuckle, while avoiding all the other fingers.

Pendarrow let out an agonizing yell, but it was stifled when Cardi crammed a rag in his mouth. The yell died in Pendarrow's throat but tears sprang to his eyes.

Vinnie nodded again and Cardi pulled the rag out of Pendarrow's mouth.

"Oh, Christ, oh, oh, Christ," Pendarrow moaned.

"Now, you see, Officer Pendarrow, I told you it was time for you to listen to reason and you didn't do so. When people don't listen to reason, I sometimes find it necessary to make an adjustment."

It was not until that moment that Pendarrow was able to attach the real significance to what had seemed, at the time, an innocuous statement.

Vinnie pointed to Pendarrow's smashed finger. "Pendarrow, you should be more careful around the call boxes," he said. "When you slam the door on your finger like that, you can cause a serious injury. Don't you agree?"

"No," Pendarrow said. "Yes," he corrected. He nearly sobbed the word. "I don't know," he said, breaking down into a series of barking sobs.

"Please, get control of yourself," Vinnie said. "Now, I'm going to ask you again to listen to reason."

There was that statement again. Pendarrow's blood ran cold and he looked up, choking back the sobs.

"I...what do you want? What do you want to know?" Pendarrow whimpered.

"Tell me about the night my brother was killed."

"I...don't know for sure," Pendarrow said. "But I saw a car, a-a green Oldsmobile with two men, drive by two or three times...like they were casing the place." He didn't dare say that he had been told, in advance, to look out for the two men. "I don't know if they had anything to do with it...maybe it was just a coincidence."

"Who were they? Were they Vaglichio's men?"

"I don't know," Pendarrow lied.

"Mr. Cardi, Mr. Sarducci, a further adjustment is needed," Vinnie said calmly.

"Wait!" Pendarrow screamed. "I can tell you about the kid!"

Vinnie nodded and Cardi released Pendarrow's arm. Pendarrow pulled his hand back and held it protectively, even though he knew there was no way he could really protect it if they wanted to hit it again.

"What kid?"

"I don't know his name, but I can describe him. He's a pimply faced kid about fourteen or fifteen and he was wearing a sailor hat. He wears it a lot, I've seen him before. I think he hangs out around the Pool Emporium."

"I know the kid he's talkin' about, boss," Sarducci said. "They call him Weasel. Dunnigan uses him as a runner sometimes."

"What about the kid?" Vinnie asked. "What does he have to do with my brother getting killed?"

"Maybe nothing," Pendarrow said. "All I know is one of the men called him over to the car."

"What happened next?"

"I don't know what happened next," Pendarrow said. When he sensed a movement beside him he cringed in terror. "I swear to God, Vinnie, I don't know!" he cried out. "I had to leave the street for a few minutes and when I got back, the car was gone, and so was the kid. That was about ten minutes before the bomb went off."

"Why didn't you tell me this before?" Vinnie asked.

"I was afraid," Pendarrow said. "I was afraid if you knew I saw two men I didn't know cruising around in your territory and I didn't check up on them, you'd be mad. But I swear to you, Vinnie. I didn't have any idea they were going after your brother. I thought maybe they were a couple of guys just looking for a little action."

"What kind of action?"

"You know. Women, gambling, that sort of thing. I didn't think there was anything wrong with them, honest."

"Let him go," Vinnie said.

Cardi and Sarducci stepped away from the chair and Pendarrow looked up anxiously at each of them.

"That's it?" he said. "I can go?"

"Yeah, you can go."

Pendarrow hesitated for another moment, then he got up quickly and started toward the door.

"Pendarrow?" Vinnie called. His voice was as cold as ice. "Turn around."

When Pendarrow turned around he saw that Vinnie was pointing a pistol right at him. Pendarrow's lower lip began quivering and his face went white. "Oh, Jesus," he said quietly. "Oh, sweet Jesus." The air grew rank as Pendarrow soiled his pants.

"You won't say anything about our little conversation here, will you?" Vinnie said. "I wouldn't want the kid to know we were looking for him."

"I won't say a word," Pendarrow said. "I swear, I won't."

"Get out of here."

"Yes, sir. Yes, sir," Pendarrow said. He had been turned into a quivering mass of jelly.

"You goin' to go after the kid, boss?" Sarducci asked after Pendarrow was gone.

"Yeah," Vinnie said. "But first, I want to make a telephone call."

Vinnie walked over to the wall phone and called home. His wife answered it on the fourth ring.

"Yeah, it's me," Vinnie said. "Any word from Johnny?"

"He's in St. Louis," Gina said. "We just got word. He called long distance about an hour ago."

"St. Louis? What the hell is he doing there?" Vinnie growled.

"Vinnie, you know he was flying that airplane of his all around the country. He said he didn't find out about it until he saw it in the paper in St. Louis."

"Is he comin' home?"

"He's taking a train out tonight," Gina said. "He'll be here in two days."

"Not soon enough," Vinnie said.

"That's the quickest he can get here," Gina said.

"If he was to get here now, it wouldn't be soon enough," Vinnie said. "Tony's already in the ground."

"Vinnie, I hope you aren't going to hold that against Johnny. It wasn't his fault he wasn't here. He didn't know anything about it."

"Johnny owes me," Vinnie said. "He owes the family."

"Vinnie, go easy on him. Tony was his brother too," Gina reminded him.

Vinnie hung up the phone and looked at Sarducci. "Okay, now tell me about this kid Weasel. What do you know about him?"

"I don't think he has any folks," Sarducci said. "Do you, Cardi?"

"No, I know the kid too, and I can tell you he don't

have none. His mama was a whore, I don't think she ever knew who Weasel's old man was. You remember her, Vinnie. She was the one called herself Alma, a pretty girl. She used to work the Liberty Hotel. She died a couple of years ago during the big flu epidemic."

"Yeah, I remember her. Where does the kid live?"

"I don't think he lives anywhere in particular," Sarducci explained. "Mannie lets him stay in the back of the Pool Emporium, but he don't stay there all the time. I heard that lately he's been runnin' the numbers for Dunnigan."

"Yeah, he's a hustler, all right. He's always trying to make a dollar," Cardi said.

"Just what will he do for a dollar?" Vinnie wanted to know.

"I'll tell you what he wouldn't do," Sarducci said. "He wouldn't set up your brother. At least, not if he knew that was what he was doing. He's too smart to do anything like that."

"Yeah, but the thing is, if he did do it, I mean even if he didn't know what he was doing at the time, it's a sure thing that he's figured out by now that he was responsible for it. And if so, we aren't going to be able to get near him 'cause the moment he sees any of us, he's going to take off running," Cardi said.

"We'll find a way to get to him," Vinnie said. "And when we do, you can bet that he'll be more than anxious to help us find the men who did this."

"Hell, Vinnie, the Vaglichios did this, you know that."

"Yeah, I know," Vinnie answered. "But before I go after them, I want the button men, you know what I mean? I mean, I want the men who actually did the job. I want everyone who works for the Vaglichios to know that the Vaglichios can't protect them. When Vaglichio's soldiers see two of their own go down, they're going to think twice before doing something like this again."

"Yeah," Sarducci agreed. He grinned. "That's pretty good thinkin', boss. They figure they can't be protected, they ain't goin' to be that anxious to work."

27TH PRECINCT, THE NEXT DAY

"You sonofabitch! Nothin' to it, you said," Pendarrow yelled across the desk to Lieutenant Trapnell. He held up his bandaged hand. "Look what they did to me! I could have been killed!"

"You could have been, but you weren't," Trapnell said. He pointed to the wounded hand. "And, what the hell, you got paid five hundred dollars for that finger. You don't have anything to bitch about. Five hundred dollars is a pretty good price for one lousy finger. What did you tell them?"

"What did I tell them? I told them nothing," Pendarrow said. "I told them I saw some kid talking to two men in a car, that's it."

"Good. Keep your nose clean, you'll come out of this all right. Maybe I'll be able to use you again sometime."

"Use me again? To hell with that. All I have to say about this is don't do me any more favors," Pendarrow said angrily. He turned and stormed out of Trapnell's office, slamming the door so hard behind him that the echo reverberated all through the building.

It was almost an hour after that encounter before Sergeant Kelly stopped by Trapnell's office.

"So, you set it up to have Tony Sangremano killed, did you now?" Kelly said.

"What? Who told you that?" Trapnell asked. "Did Pendarrow tell you that?"

"Sure and he didn't have to," Kelly said. "A blind

man could see how it went down. You've gone across the line, Trapnell. What you did makes you a party to murder. Have you thought of that?"

"No, and you shouldn't think about it either," Trapnell growled. "You've been around long enough, Kelly, to know that it's not healthy to think too much about things that don't concern you."

"Aye. But what concerns my men concerns me. Didn't I tell you to stay away from them?" Kelly asked. "If I find any way to prove you were part of the killin', I'll be for takin' out a warrant on you myself."

When Kelly left Trapnell's office, he walked quickly down to the water fountain and leaned over to take a drink. He wasn't really thirsty but he needed to do something to get control of himself. He knew that confronting Trapnell as he had just done was a dangerous, perhaps even a foolish stunt. But if he could frighten Trapnell into making a wrong move, he might actually be able to get enough on him to get him indicted. Trapnell was one of the leaders of the ring of police who were on the take. If Trapnell were to be caught, it would have a serious effect on all the other "dirty" cops. And it would go a long way toward helping Tim Kelly regain the self-respect he had lost in front of his son, so many years ago.

Fifty feet away from the water cooler where Tim Kelly was standing, Trapnell was behind the closed door of his office talking on the telephone.

"Kelly," he was saying quietly. "Sergeant Tim Kelly. Yeah, that's the one. He's beginning to cause us a few problems."

GRAND CENTRAL STATION, NEW YORK

Grand Central Station shook with the power of three dozen rumbling trains and smelled of steam and smoke.

Mike and Johnny were able to hurry past the redcaps and the baggage claim. They had no luggage other than the little canvas bag each had carried with them on the airplane and were carrying now. They moved through the crowded waiting terminal, then out onto Park Avenue where several taxis were queuing up for the arriving passengers. Like Grand Central Station, the avenue was alive with swirling color and movement. It was a symphony of honking horns, rattling engines, police whistles, the cry of vendors, street musicians, and clicking shoes on concrete.

"Well, I guess this is where we say goodbye," Johnny said, sticking his hand out.

Mike shook it. "I guess so. It feels strange getting back to the city, doesn't it? But we've been playing around long enough. It's time we both settled down."

Johnny took out a sack of lemon drops, offered one to Mike who declined, then stuck one in his mouth. "Yeah, you're right." Johnny chuckled. "But we had fun, didn't we?"

"The most fun I ever had in my life," Mike agreed.

Johnny shoved an envelope toward Mike. "Listen, Mike, we have two hundred eighty dollars left from the sale of the airplane," he said. "I want you to have it."

"No, not all of it," Mike replied. "I'll take a hundred and forty, that's my share."

"Take it all," Johnny insisted.

"No," Mike said, shoving it away. "Why would you try and give all of it to me?"

"The money doesn't mean anything to me. I don't need it. You might."

Mike laughed. "The money doesn't mean anything to you? Do you know who you're talking to, Johnny? Don't forget, I've watched you squabble with a farmer for half an hour over a difference of half a dollar in what he was charging us to spend the night in his field."

Johnny laughed with him. "Yeah, I did put up some pretty good fights, didn't I? But that was then, this is now," he finally said. "I guess I'm about ready for a few changes to be made in my life."

"A few changes? What do you mean?" Mike asked, still smiling.

"The truth is, I've been giving it a lot of thought on the way back." Johnny sighed. "Mike, I've decided what I'm going to do. I'm going into the business."

"The business? What business?"

"You know what business I'm talking about."

"No, I..." Mike stopped in midsentence and looked at Johnny. The smile fell away from his face, replaced by a look of disbelief and disappointment. "Johnny, no. You don't mean you're joining the Mafia?"

"Mike!" Johnny said sharply, his eyes flashing a warning. He raised a warning finger. "I told you, never say that word. Goddamnit, that can get you killed!"

"Listen to yourself," Mike said, stung by the severity of the reprimand. "It sounds like you are threatening me. Is that what you intended, Johnny? Are you threatening me?"

"No, of course not," Johnny replied. "But I did warn you. Take the warning seriously, Mike. Be careful, that's all I'm saying."

"Why are you doing this, Johnny? You know what kind of business your family is involved with."

"Yes, I do know. But with Papa and Tony both dead, I have no choice. Anyway, it doesn't seem right for me to leave Vinnie all alone."

"Right? It doesn't seem right? How can you use that word with what your family does? I would think the word 'right' would stick in your throat."

"Wait a minute, here. Listen to the righteous one. Just who the hell are you to judge me?" Johnny asked sharply. "And who are you to tell me about my family? Are there no skeletons in your closet? Correct me if I'm wrong, Mike, old friend, but aren't you the same person who confessed to me that your father was the very kind of policeman that my father so easily corrupted?"

"We aren't talking about my father or yours. We are talking about right and wrong," Mike said.

"Listen, there is right and there is honor, and sometimes right is one thing and honor is another," Johnny answered.

Mike looked confused. "What the hell is that supposed to mean? That statement doesn't make any sense. But then, that's understandable because you aren't making any sense," he accused.

"Maybe not. But I know what I'm going to do. My mind is made up."

"You don't really want to do this, do you?"

"I told you, I have no choice. I am destined for this. It's in my blood."

"Johnny, didn't you once tell me that I'm not my father and you aren't yours?"

"Maybe I did say that," Johnny admitted. "But if I did, I was just kidding myself. It wasn't real when I said that," he went on. "Where were we? In a farmer's field somewhere on some other planet?" A nearby car honked angrily at a pedestrian, who shouted back at the driver of the car. "That wasn't real. This is," he added, taking in the busy street with a wave of his hand. He tried again to pass the envelope over to Mike. "Now take the money, Mike. It will help you get started in whatever it is you are going to do."

Just walk a little slower on your beat, Mike remembered. Suddenly he felt a chill pass over his body and he reached out to push the envelope back firmly.

"You may be like your father, Johnny, but I'm not like mine. I won't take one cent more than is due me, don't you see? Not from you, not from anyone."

A screen dropped over Johnny's eyes. It was the kind of screen a person would put up when he wanted to separate himself from whoever he was talking to. Mike had seen the same protective screen in others but he had never seen it in Johnny. At that moment a gulf opened up between them and Mike didn't know if either of them would ever be able to reach the other again.

"Okay," Johnny finally said. "I understand."

"I don't want to make you mad," Mike said.

"That's all right," Johnny replied coolly. "I guess there are some lines that even friendship can't cross." He counted out the exact amount due Mike, then handed the bills to him.

"Thanks," Mike said. He put the money in his billfold, then reached out to shake Johnny's hand again. "I'll see you around," he said.

"Goodbye, Mike," Johnny replied pointedly:

The two men held their handshake, and for a moment, the screen in Johnny's eyes almost came down. It was as if this conversation had never taken place. They weren't in New York, they were in Ohio, or Indiana, or Illinois, bound together on their quest for adventure. But almost as quickly as the screen came down, it went up again and Johnny turned and walked over to get into a waiting taxi. Johnny looked back as the taxi drove away but didn't wave. His eyes were sad and distant, and Mike wasn't at all sure that Johnny even saw him.

Mike had a feeling that he would never forget that moment, for it was the exact moment that he realized that, like his father, he was going to be a policeman.

"No, lad, not a policeman," Mike's father told him that night as the two talked. Mike had entertained his parents with stories of all the adventures, both humorous and frightening, he had experienced during the barnstorming. Later, he and his father had sat in the kitchen drinking coffee and spoke, really spoke, for the first time in many years.

"You don't want me to be a policeman? Why not, Pop? I thought you would be pleased."

"Pleased? Pleased to see Trapnell and his bunch get your hands dirty? Now why would you be thinkin' that would please me?"

Mike frowned at his father. "I'm not sure I know what you're talkin' about," he said.

"Mikey, don't you be for tellin' me that you're forgettin' how a ten-year-old boy once shamed his old man, shamed him for makin' him see the brigand that he was."

Mike stared into his coffee for a long moment. "I'm sorry about that, Pop. I was just a kid then. I had no right..."

"No, don't you apologize. Don't you dare apologize to me for that. You had every right," Tim said forcefully. "I had done wrong and you knew it. But what you don't know, lad, is that from that day to this, not so much as a nickel have I taken that wasn't rightly mine. Aye, and I've paid for it too, and I don't mean just in the mean livin' I've made for your poor old mother. I mean in tryin' to live up to what's right in the midst of so many who are wrong." Suddenly Tim smiled broadly. "But I wouldn't trade a minute of it, lad. No, not one minute, for I've carried in my heart the picture of that ten-year-old callin' me to task for what I had done. And I've felt a pride in comin' up to the high standards that boy set for his old man."

Mike went to his father and embraced him. They had

not embraced since Mike was a child and he felt a lump in his throat and tears in his eyes.

"I love you, Pop."

Awkwardly, Tim patted his son on the back, then the two men separated and Tim found that it was necessary to blow his nose.

"The Bureau of Investigation," Tim finally said after a long pause.

"What?"

"The Bureau of Investigation," Tim said again. "'Tis a federal police force with power to tell the local and state police where to get off. 'Tis for sure such a job would keep you out of Trapnell's clutches."

"How would I go about getting such a position?"

"Well, there's a federal judge doin' all the recruitin' now. He can give you the badge and put you on the payroll. Then, I'm told there's goin' to be a young lad with the Bureau who'll soon be comin' up here from the headquarters in Washington. His name is Hoover. John Edgar Hoover. After the judge swears you in, you should talk to Hoover in order to find out just what you're lettin' yourself in for."

"Okay, Pop," Mike said. "Let's go see the federal judge. I'm ready to sign up."

THE BRONX

"Salve, mister? Salve?" Weasel asked, holding out a small jar of blue salve. For three days now, Weasel had been working all the restaurants, streets, and stores of the Village, selling his salve. He had only sold four jars, but he kept coming back. Those who saw him working admired his spunk and determination to keep trying in the face of what appeared to be a total lack of success in selling his product. What they didn't realize was that

Weasel didn't care if he sold any salve or not. He was getting paid twenty dollars a day to search all of the Vaglichio territory until he could find the two men who gave him the package to deliver to Tony Sangremano.

Weasel liked to tell everyone he was eighteen, though he was four months short of his seventeenth birthday. His real name was Jimmy Pallota. Actually, Pallota was just a name Weasel's mother had taken, having once seen it on the side of a delivery wagon. Weasel, who had never been called anything but Weasel, wasn't even sure that his first name was Jimmy. He had never seen a birth certificate and when he asked his mother one day what his real name was, she hesitated for a long moment before telling him, as if she were coming up with it for the first time. His mother admitted to him that she didn't know who his father was. She had never told him anything about her own family, who her parents were, where she was from, or whether she had any sisters or brothers. Weasel was a person without a past and since his mother died, without a present. But he was a bright and ambitious young man who did not intend to be without a future. That was very nearly the case, however, when he got involved in the killing of Tony Sangremano.

When the bomb went off that night, Weasel had been the most surprised person around. Surprised and frightened, for he realized at once that he had been the instrument, albeit unwillingly and unknowingly, of Tony Sangremano's death.

Weasel figured it would be just a matter of time before the Sangremanos found out about his part in it. When they did find out, they would come for him.

Weasel planned to run from them, but he was tricked. The Sangremano who came for him was Johnny Sangremano. Weasel had never even seen Johnny Sangremano.

As a result, his guard was down and he was shining Johnny's shoes when he found out who he was.

To Weasel's relief, the Sangremanos didn't want to kill him, they only wanted him to help them find the men who had driven the car that night. And what's more, they were even willing to pay him for his help. It was turning out better than he thought.

Weasel saw the two men he was looking for in Leto's Restaurant on the third day of his search. For a moment he considered doing nothing. He had found them once, he could find them again, and in the meantime he would be earning twenty dollars per day. He didn't actually consider that option very long though. On the one hand, he was afraid that the Sangremanos might find out he was playing games with them. He had come out lucky with them once, he didn't want to take the chance with them again. Another reason Weasel decided not to wait was because he felt that fingering these men now would be an investment in his future. He went into a telephone booth at the corner and called the number Johnny had given him.

"This is Weasel. I found them," he said when the phone was answered.

"Where are they, kid?"

"Leto's Restaurant. It's on 222nd Street."

"Yeah, I know where it is. Go back to the restaurant and stay until we get there."

"Okay," Weasel agreed.

Weasel hung up the phone, then went down the street and into the restaurant. He began moving from table to table, trying to sell his salve.

"Hey, you, kid," the restaurant owner called. "Get outta here tryin' to sell that shit. My customers don't want to be bothered with it."

"Leave the kid alone, Nick," one of the two men

Weasel had spotted said. "He's just tryin' to earn a dollar for chrissake."

"I don't need him 'round here botherin' my customers none."

"I'm a customer," the man said. "He ain't botherin' me. What about you, Carmine? He botherin' you?"

"No," Carmine answered. "The kid ain't botherin' me none."

"Come on over here to the table, kid, let's see what you got," the man invited.

Weasel walked down to the table where the two men were sitting and showed them his bottle of salve.

"What's this s'posed to cure?" the man asked.

Carmine laughed. "Hell, Freddie, you've seen that shit in the magazines, ain't you? It'll cure warts, ingrown toenails, put hair on your chest, and make you a better lover."

"A better lover? Hey, you can't be no better lover than I am," Freddie teased, laughing and poking Carmine playfully. "You could prob'ly use a jar though. Tell you what, kid. Maybe you better sell me a jar for Carmine. All the women tell me he ain't so hot."

Freddie took out a dollar bill and handed it to Weasel.

"Bullshit," Carmine said.

"You hungry, kid? Sit down an' eat with us," Freddie invited.

"No, that's all right," Weasel answered, taking the dollar and handing the jar to Carmine.

"Say, do I know you? Seems like I seen you somewhere before."

"I shined your shoes a couple times," Weasel lied. He didn't want the man to make the connection.

"Really? Most the time I just let the nigger over in the Crown Barbershop shine my shoes. Don't remember you doin' it any. But it sure seems like I seen you somewhere."

"It's been a year, maybe, since I done it," Weasel said. "You was real busy that day, you prob'ly didn't pay no attention to me."

"Yeah, I guess. Well, come on, sit down with us and have somethin' to eat."

Reluctantly, because he couldn't think of any way to get out of it, Weasel sat at the table with Freddie and Carmine. The waiter brought a plate of spaghetti. As Weasel began to eat, he looked at the two men at the table with him. They were laughing and joking as if everything were normal. They had no way of knowing that in just a few minutes they would both be dead. It made Weasel feel strange, sitting there with two men who were about to die. It didn't frighten him. He thought about it and was proud of the fact that he wasn't frightened. If anything, he was almost excited by the prospect. His knowledge gave him power over them. It was a power unlike anything he had ever experienced before and he had to admit that he liked it.

As Weasel contemplated the situation, he ate heartily, laughing at the jokes Freddie and Carmine were cracking with each other and with him. He even managed to get in a few of his own. He was relishing the situation so much that it seemed like no time at all before Sangremano's men got there.

"Everybody stay where you are!" a voice suddenly shouted. "Where are they, Weasel?" There were two men standing at the front door, holding submachine guns.

Weasel got up and started running toward the men with the guns. "That's them!" he shouted, pointing to the table where he had been sitting. "They're the ones who did it!"

"Mother of God!" Freddie yelled, suddenly recognizing Weasel. "We've been set up! This is the kid we gave the bomb to!"

Carmine had just twisted a large bit of spaghetti onto his fork. Now he dropped it and started trying to get his gun out from under his jacket. Weasel dived for the floor and slid on his stomach under a table near the wall just as the two men in the door started shooting, moving their submachine guns back and forth as if they were spraying a garden with water hoses.

The bullets whined and whistled all over the room, smashing into tables, breaking glass, and shattering the crockery. Carmine and Freddie were hit with perhaps a dozen bullets each, and Weasel watched in morbid fascination as the blood started squirting from their bodies like jets from a fountain. Freddie pitched forward across the table, Carmine fell back onto the floor. The two gunmen moved over to the two bodies and, at point-blank range, emptied their guns into them. Slowly and methodically, they put new magazines into their guns, then looked around the restaurant. There were ten or fifteen others in the restaurant but they were all crouched behind the counter or under the tables.

One of the assassins looked over at Weasel and for a moment Weasel's stomach flip-flopped in fear. They were about to kill him.

"Get in the car, kid," he said. "We'd better get you outta here."

"Yes, sir," Weasel answered. He hurried out of the restaurant and slipped into the back seat of the car. The engine was running and the driver was sitting calmly behind the wheel, humming an aria from a Puccini opera. When the two men got in behind Weasel a second later, the driver put the car in gear and drove off. Weasel twisted around in his seat to look through the back window at the front of Leto's Restaurant. A crowd of people had gathered around, but all of them were looking at the grizzly scene inside. Nobody was chasing after them, and nobody was even looking at them closely enough to identify the car.

"You done good, kid," one of the men said. He took an envelope from his pocket and handed it to Weasel. "This is for you."

"What is it?"

"Open it and see," he said, grinning at Weasel.

Weasel opened the envelope and saw that it contained a wad of twenty-dollar bills. He counted out five hundred dollars, then gasped. This was more money than he had ever seen in his life!

"Gee, thanks, Mister..."

"Sarducci. You been doin' some work for Dunnigan?"

"A little, yes, sir."

"He's a goddamn mick. What's a nice Italian boy like you doin' workin' for an Irishman?"

"I need the work," Weasel replied.

"Yeah? Well, you're workin' for me, from now on," Sarducci said. He stared pointedly at Weasel. "Do I have your loyalty?"

"I'd never do anything to cross you," Weasel said.

"Good. Startin' today, you're on my payroll. Fifty a week."

"What do I do?"

"You'll do anything you're told to do," Sarducci said. "Just like we do." Then, as if the job he had just done was no more than a simple errand, he turned his attention to something else. "Hey, Cardi, you want to catch the baseball game tomorrow?" he asked.

Weasel shared neither his money nor the news of his good fortune with his two friends, Guido and Dom. Instead, he invested some of his money in a double-breasted navy pin-striped suit and a real barbershop haircut. Shortly thereafter, he presented himself at a whorehouse. He figured it was about time he lost his virginity.

The whorehouse was on the second floor of a building at Lexington and Forty-seventh Street. He chose one far from where he usually hung out so that he wouldn't encounter any of the women who used to work with his mother. Weasel climbed the stairs, then pushed the door open and went inside. A woman of about twenty-eight wearing a cloche hat and a worn chemise dress was sitting on a stained sofa. She was filing her nails and a cigarette dangled precariously from her lips, but she looked up when Weasel came in.

"What do you need, honey?"

"What do you mean, what do I need? Why do men come into a whore house?"

"Ain't you a little young?"

"I got the money and a hardon," Weasel said. "What else do I need?"

"How much money do you have?"

"It takes five dollars, don't it? That's what I have."

"Let me see the money."

Weasel pulled out a five-dollar bill and showed it to the woman. She reached for it, but he pulled it back.

"Do I get a woman or not?"

"Yeah. You get a woman."

"Who?"

"How about me?"

Weasel looked her over for a brief moment. "I guess you'll do."

"Well, look, don't do me no favors, kid," the woman replied. She took a deep drag of her cigarette and stared at him through the smoke. "Okay," she finally said. "Come along with me."

Weasel followed the woman down a long, narrow hallway and into a small room. The room had a bed, a small table, and a chair. The bed had no linens, and the mattress smelled of urine. On the chair, a fruit-jar lid doubled as an ashtray. The woman ground her cigarette out in it. There were half a dozen others, branded with her color lipstick. Weasel wondered if she had been in here half a dozen times already today, or if the full lid was merely the sign of poor housekeeping.

"Okay, honey, get undressed," the woman said.

Quickly, Weasel slipped out of his new suit, then turned to watch the woman as she began to get undressed. By now he was so hard that he hurt.

She smiled at him. "You've got a pretty good pole there for a kid," she said. "Has it ever been used before?"

"Sure," Weasel lied. "Lots of times."

The woman pulled the dress over her head, then took off her bra and slipped down her panties. Her breasts sagged somewhat, and there was a slight roll around her middle, but she was a woman and she was naked and that was all Weasel needed.

"You've done it lots of times, huh?" the woman said, smiling as she lay on the bed. She held her arms out toward him. "Okay, why don't you just come show Wanda what you can do?"

"I can do plenty," Weasel boasted.

The woman laughed, a patronizing little chuckle, deep in her throat. "Really?"

"Don't you believe me?"

"Honey, I can take care of you in two minutes," she said. "Come here, let me show you."

Weasel moved over to the bed and she reached up and grabbed him.

"Hey!" Weasel said, surprised by her action. "Hey, what are you…uhn…"

Weasel wasn't able to finish his question. The action of her hand brought on an immediate orgasm, and he felt his knees grow weak. He would have fallen had it not been for the bed. He leaned forward and caught himself with his hands.

The woman took her hand away, grinning mischievously at Weasel.

"Do you see what I mean?" she asked.

"Yeah," Weasel answered sheepishly. "I guess I do."

"This was your first time, wasn't it?"

"Yeah, it was."

The woman looked at Weasel, and at the shame and dejection in his face. She smiled softly and put her hand to the side of his face.

"I'll tell you what," she said. "I guess I was a little unfair. Next time you come in, ask for Wanda. I'll give you one for free."

CHAPTER 5

"'m going to call the meeting off," Vinnie said disgustedly.

"Why?" Johnny asked.

"Why? What do you mean, why? Because there's no way we can get to the sonofabitch now, that's why. If you were meeting downtown someplace you could blast him, then get the hell out of there. But their beach house has a private road a quarter of a mile long, with guards every hundred yards or so. Even if you were able to sneak a gun in, it won't do you any good. You can't kill him because if you do, you won't get away."

"What's this place like where they want the meet?" Johnny asked. "The beach house."

"I don't know," Vinnie sneered. "Bein' as we don't exactly socialize together, I've never been on their invite list when they gave a party."

"I've been inside it," Angelo Cardi said.

"You have?" Vinnie asked in surprise. "How come you've been in there?"

"It was my uncle Paulie. He used to be one of Don Vaglichio's soldiers."

"What's it like?" Johnny asked.

"It's like a fort or somethin'. Did you know that house has iron shutters and reinforced walls? And doors? Them doors are really somethin'. They're made out of steel and you couldn't drive a tank through 'em if you tried."

"You want me to call it off, Vinnie?" Al asked.

"Yeah, we may as well call it off," Vinnie said. "We'll just have to wait a while and get him when he's not suspecting it."

"We can't do that," Johnny insisted.

"Why not?"

"Because if we don't act, it's going to mean trouble," Johnny explained. "Everyone will think we've lost all our strength. Then they'll start moving in on our territory and we'll be right in the middle of a war with no allies. We have no choice, Vinnie. If we are going to survive as a Family, we have to get Don Vaglichio now."

"Yeah? Well, you heard what Angelo said," Vinnie replied. "The house is a goddamn fort. You got any ideas on how to get through?"

"Maybe I do."

"You do, huh? I'd sure as hell like to hear 'em," Vinnie said.

Johnny turned to Angelo. "You say you've seen the place. Is it a two-story house, or one story?"

"One story," Angelo replied.

"Good."

"Good? What do you mean, good?" Vinnie asked.

"What the hell difference does it make whether it's two stories or one?"

"Believe me, it makes a difference," Johnny said. "Could you draw a picture of it?" he asked Angelo.

"A picture? Jeez, I don't know, Johnny. I'm not what you would call an artist."

"It doesn't have to be much," Johnny explained. "All I really want is a floor plan."

"A what?"

"A floor plan. It's like a map of the house, showing the location of all the rooms. You know, like where the living room is, the parlor, the dining room, the kitchen, that sort of thing."

"Yeah, well, I didn't see the dinin' room or the kitchen," Angelo said. "I just seen the hall where you come in and the parlor, that's all. But I know Don Vaglichio, he stays in the parlor all the time he's there. He likes to listen to the Victrola."

"Okay, show me where in the house the parlor is located, and where the Victrola is," Johnny said. He gave Angelo a piece of paper and a pencil. After thinking for a moment, Angelo drew a square, then put the rooms that he knew about in the places he knew them to be.

Johnny smiled as he watched Angelo draw the picture. "Good," he said. "You're doing a good job, Angelo."

"Johnny, you mind telling me what the hell this is all about?" Vinnie asked.

"Don't cancel the meeting, Vinnie. I know a way to get to him," Johnny said.

ON LONG ISLAND

Don Vaglichio stood for a moment at the parlor window of his beach house and looked out across the beautifully sculptured front lawn. A dark blue Cadillac was parked in the circle of the front drive, its nose pulled right up next to the splashing fountain. The chauffeur was using the water from the fountain to wash the car. The silver work of the grille and bumper gleamed brightly in the midday sun, while a blue star flashed brilliantly from deep within the highly polished hood. There were also a couple of black, nondescript, four-door Dodge sedans parked in the drive. These were escort cars and the Dodges, filled with bodyguards, would accompany the Cadillac everywhere it went. One car preceded the Cadillac and the other followed. In that way, it would be virtually impossible for anyone to get to him. Some might think that such close scrutiny would be a pain in the ass but Don Vaglichio had learned to deal with it. In fact, except for reflective moments such as this, he was able to put them so completely out of mind that he seldom even noticed their presence.

He was thinking of them now, though, as he stood at the window. He looked out to see if they were doing their job. One guard was standing on the front porch, a lupara held loosely in his arms. Another was at the entrance to the driveway and another, Don Vaglichio knew, was all the way down by the entrance of the private road. In addition, there were two or three men in position on the private road and a couple more out back. There were also two men who roamed all around the estate. Telephones had been placed strategically throughout the estate so that one of the outlying guards could phone in a report the moment he saw something, thus alerting those closer to the house.

The estate itself was on a little spit of land that stuck out into Long Island Sound, thus it was impossible to approach it by any means other than the private and well-guarded road. Even the water approaches were secure. Large underwater obstructions had been placed in such a way that they would tear the bottom out of any boat that attempted to approach the house by any way other than the narrow, controlled access.

In the unlikely event someone would make it onto the estate grounds, they would still have to get into the house. The house, with reinforced walls, doors, and windows, was quite literally a fort. Living in a fort was nothing new to the Don. He had lived in one all his life, even when he was a young man in the old country.

He had been born and grew to manhood in Sicily, in the little village of Misilmeri. There, tiny stone houses perched precariously on the edge of the steeply sloping hills. The peasants labored in the fields and paid their tributes to the Godfather who watched over them, administering justice, settling disputes, and dispensing favors. That man was Don Stefan Vaglichio, Sam's father. He was the Capo di Capi of the Mafia, recognized and honored by all. Don Vaglichio and his family lived well behind the thick stone walls and heavily guarded grounds of Villa Vaglichio.

Sam had an older brother, Vito. Vito was the heir apparent to his father's position and he wore that mantle of authority as surely as if he were a crown prince. He enjoyed the position of power and the influence his name brought him. But those who knew the family well were already saying that Vito was not the man his father was.

"It is too bad that Cesare is not the oldest," they whispered, talking about Sam for Cesare was the name he had been born with and by which he had been known in the old country.

"Yes," another would say. "Cesare is a strong man with many of the qualities of his father. He respects his elders, honors his friends, pays his debts, and tends to business. Vito wishes only to chase the women."

The villagers were right when they accused Vito of being a woman chaser. Handsome enough to attract women in his own right, Vito also had the advantage of being the Don's son, and the wealth and power that implied. He went through the women of the village the way fire goes through dry timber, and like a consuming fire, he left ashes in his wake. Young women threw themselves at him, not realizing that they had absolutely no chance at all to ever live in Villa Vaglichio as Vito's wife, for Vito had a simple, inflexible, and impossible rule. He would never consider marrying a woman he hadn't tried...and he would never marry a woman who had given herself to him.

However, not all the women of the village threw themselves his way. One young woman who had turned away from his flashing black eyes and silver tongue was Justina Sangremano. Justina was eighteen. Her father, Carlo, had been killed by bandits a few years earlier, and Justina lived with her mother and sixteen-year-old brother Giuseppe.

Justina did not realize that spurning Vito's advances was like waving a red flag in front of a bull. He became driven in his quest to win her favors and when money and charm did not work, he resorted to the only sure thing. He raped her.

When Don Vaglichio found out what his oldest son had done, he became very angry. He felt badly for the young woman and he sent the girl's mother a letter of apology, along with a leather sack full of money, a large goatskin of wine and another of olive oil. In this way, he hoped to atone for his son's misdeed.

On the day after he sent the gifts, a powerfully built young man came riding up the road to the villa, asking to see the Don. He was leading a donkey, and strapped to the pack saddle of the donkey were two goatskins, one hanging on each side. The young man was Giuseppe Sangremano, Justina's brother. Cesare went to the door to greet the visitor. Cesare, who was two years older than Giuseppe, had seen Giuseppe at work in the fields, but this was the first time he had ever seen him up-close.

"I have come to speak with Don Vaglichio," Giuseppe said when Cesare opened the door.

"I'll tell my father you have requested to see him," Cesare said. He turned away from the door.

"No!" Giuseppe shouted. The sharpness of his answer stopped Cesare in midstride and he looked back in curiosity. "I am not requesting to see him. I am demanding to see him."

"That isn't the way you ask," Cesare replied, irritated by the young man's audacity.

Giuseppe loosened the drawstring at the top of the leather bag he was carrying, then swung it around to send gold coins flying all over the room. The coins jingled and rang as they skittered across the floor. From their scattered positions on the stones, they caught the morning sun and flashed brilliantly, two dozen golden stars winking in the morning light.

"Tell him I have brought something for him."

"I don't know what you are trying to prove, but I'll tell him no such thing," Cesare said.

Cesare's father interrupted him then. "I'll talk to the boy, Cesare," he said. "What is it, son? What do you want with me?"

"I want you to see what I do with the wine and the oil," Giuseppe said. He walked out to a donkey, took out his knife, and cut a gash in one of the bags. A crimson flow of wine began gurgling out. He then walked around to the other side and slashed that sack as well. It began dribbling a golden stream of olive oil to join with the wine that was already staining the flagstone walk.

"I see the money on the floor and the wine and oil on the ground," Don Vaglichio said. "But I do not understand why you do these things."

"Do you think my sister is a whore?" Giuseppe asked.

"No, of course I do not. And you should know better

than to speak of your sister in the same sentence in which you use that word."

"I asked you the question, because you have dishonored her by sending my family money, wine, and oil," Giuseppe said angrily.

"I sought only to make appeasement," Don Vaglichio explained.

"There is only one way you can make appeasement," Giuseppe replied. "Turn Vito over to me."

"No, I cannot do that," the Don answered. "In the first place, you are only sixteen. Vito is twenty-three. It wouldn't be a fair fight."

"I'll take my chances," Giuseppe said.

"No. Even if I thought the fight would be fair, I wouldn't do it. He is my son. You must realize that I could never turn over my own son."

"He dishonored my sister," Giuseppe said. "Under the code, you have no obligation to defend him."

Now, Don Vaglichio grew angry and he bristled at the contempt of the boy. "Don't you quote the code to me, young man. I am the code," the Don said, pointing to his own chest.

"I will kill him," Giuseppe said easily.

Don Vaglichio looked at the boy, then looked at the many guards who were standing around the grounds. He shook his head sadly.

"You have much courage," he said, "but little sense. There is no way you can kill Vito. You are fortunate that I do not have you killed. Leave now. Leave while I still have some compassion for you."

Giuseppe glared at him for a long moment, then he climbed into the saddle and reached down to pick up the reins of his donkey. Without another word, he rode off.

"Wouldn't you like to see the balls on that boy though?" Vito said, laughing. He had come down to the living room and had remained back in the shadows and out of sight. "He has no sense, that one. Can you imagine, him asking you to turn me over to him?"

Don Vaglichio looked at his son, but didn't say anything. He turned away as if he were going to walk off, then suddenly and unexpectedly, he whirled back around and whipped his hand across in a wicked backhand slap that hit Vito so hard it brought blood to his lips.

"You whore-chasing pig," the Don snarled. "Would that I could choose my sons, I would have chosen that one over you!"

"Papa, it isn't like you think. She wanted me, Papa. She wanted me," Vito insisted.

Don Vaglichio looked at Vito, then rolled his lip back in disgust. "How could anyone want you?" he asked. "Get out of my sight," he added.

The next morning Don Vaglichio woke early, as was his custom, and went down the stairs to the dining room. He looked out through the window at the meadow out behind the house. The meadow was alive with wildflowers, and a heavy dew was on the grass and in the petals of the flowers. In the early morning sun, these droplets of water formed a million tiny prisms, and they flashed golds/blues, reds, and greens in shimmering beauty. Don Vaglichio liked this time better than any other, for it was quiet and peaceful and he could sit in his chair and drink his tea and eat a pastry and plan his day. The rest of the household was still asleep, for they had not yet learned the joys of early morning solitude.

The last thing the cook did the night before was to bake a pastry for the Don's breakfast, then lay the wood for a small fire so he could prepare his own tea. Don Vaglichio put a few twigs of kindling into the little stove, then started the fire. Preparing his tea every morning was, like the solitude, a part of the ritual he enjoyed.

When the little pot began to whistle, Don Vaglichio poured the hot water onto the tea leaves. He held the steaming cup under his nose, sniffing the bouquet, then he lifted the silver cover over the pastry tray to see what delicacy the cook had prepared for him.

What he saw in the next instant hit him with the force of a hammer blow to the stomach. He felt his heart accelerate, then he turned and began to throw up, spraying his vomit on the one-hundred-fifty-year-old Tabriz rug.

There on the silver tray, stuck in a coagulated pool of dark red blood, was Vito's severed head. Vito's eyes were open and opaque and his mouth was twisted into a sardonic, mocking smile.

Sam was told later that his father's scream that morning could be heard in the most distant house in the village.

It was no secret who did it. Giuseppe Sangremano had made good on his promise to kill Vito. The question was, how did he do it? That house, like this one, was a veritable fortress.

Giuseppe had gotten in, did his terrible deed, then got out. He left Sicily on the same day.

Sam thought his father would offer a big reward for Giuseppe but he didn't. After the funeral and the initial shock and grief were over, the Don told Sam that Vito had been the cause of his own death. He extracted a promise from Sam not to seek revenge and Sam agreed.

When Sam and Giuseppe met in America several years later, Sam told Giuseppe of the promise he had made to his father. He took an additional vow, in front of Giuseppe, that he would never go back on that promise. That did not mean that the two men were ever friends. In fact, in the early days of establishing territory, they had fought a bitter war with much killing on both sides. Most recently, Sam had agreed with Luca that Tony needed to be eliminated. But the killing of the earlier wars and the killing of Tony, even the reprisal killings of Freddie and Carmine, had nothing to do with the emotions and vendetta of those events that happened half a century ago. What was going on now was strictly business. It was something Don Giuseppe Sangremano would have clearly understood.

"Don Vaglichio?" The call summoned Sam from his reverie and he looked over toward the front door. The chauffeur had just stuck his head in. "You goin' to need the car? The reason I asked, I'm goin' to change the oil right now and that'll take a few minutes."

"No, go ahead," Sam replied. "You change the oil. We got to keep the car runnin' good all the time. You never know when we might need it."

"Okay. I'll get right on it," the chauffeur said. "It shouldn't take too long," he promised.

After the chauffeur left, Sam turned to look back into the parlor. This was a comfortable house and the parlor where he spent most of his time was particularly to his liking. Sam liked to surround himself with nice things and the parlor was a perfect example of that. A two-century-old Tabriz carpet was on the floor, the same one that had been in his father's villa. In addition to the rug, there were hand-carved tables and a sofa and four matching chairs from England. Each chair was covered in a single, unbroken piece of soft leather, taken from cows that were raised without barbed wire so that there would be no chance of damage to the skin. The sofa was too large for a single skin but the seam was so skillfully hidden that no one could tell. The room was decorated with marble statuary from Italy as well as several original oil paintings. None of the paintings were by any artists of note but they were the kind that Sam particularly liked: fleshy nudes, naked nymphets, and pastoral scenes. A few colorful vases rounded out the decor.

The most treasured piece in the room, however, was the Victrola. Sam walked over to it and ran his hand over its rich burl wood, enjoying the golden glow of its polished surface and the texture and workmanship of the instrument itself. "A Victrola," Sam liked to say, "is a musical instrument, no less than a violin or a cello. And like a violin or a cello, a Victrola must be constructed by the best artisans of the finest wood, and crafted in such a way as to allow the full musical tones to resonate."

Sam opened the cabinet to take out a record. When he pulled out the record case he noticed that one of the felt-lined slots was empty. He looked up to see that the record that was supposed to be in the slot was lying, unprotected, on the shelf.

"Goddamnit!" he shouted, though as he was alone in the house no one heard him. "Doesn't anyone know the value of good things?"

Angrily, Sam took the record down, then lovingly wiped it clean with a soft cloth. It was a recording of Caruso singing "Ave Maria." He put the record on the turntable, wound the crank, then set the turntable in motion. He put the arm and needle very carefully into place, then smiled with satisfaction as the famous tenor's full rich tones began pouring out of the speaker. Don Vaglichio sat down in a chair right next to the Victrola, leaned his head back, and closed his eyes. The music touched some chord deep within him and as he was listening, he was able to shut out everything else; his anger at finding the record out of its slot, the chauffeur and the oil change, the disposition of the bodyguards, the purpose of the meeting he was about to have with Johnny Sangremano, even the annoying drone of an airplane, high overhead. There was only the music. Some may not understand, he thought, but this was as close to heaven as he would ever get.

Johnny sucked on a lemon drop as he banked the plane around and peered down between the two tips of the left wings. He could see the little spit of land sticking out into the Sound, the private road, and the house just as it had been described to him. The big blue Cadillac was there, with the hood up and someone working on the engine. That meant that Don Vaglichio was there, waiting for him. The smug bastard probably thought he had put one over by setting the meet here.

Johnny came out of the banking turn, then started climbing out over the water. When he reached thirty-five-hundred feet, he turned back toward land and about three miles ahead could see the Vaglichio estate quite clearly. He steered toward it. When he was almost directly overhead, he throttled back his engine, heard it pop and snap as the exhaust heat cooked off the fuel that was not ignited in the cylinders, then nosed it over. Silently, the plane began falling through the air.

Johnny pointed the nose straight down. Through his windscreen and the blur of the slowly turning propeller, he could see the Vaglichio estate. Using the rudder, he adjusted his descent until he was lined up directly over the left-front portion of the house. It was here, he was told, that the parlor would be located, and if his information was correct, Sam Vaglichio would be in the parlor.

As the airplane fell out of the sky the noise increased. The engine was still throttled back but the wind was passing through the struts and braces with the velocity of a hurricane so that it began emitting a high-pitched whine. The house grew larger and larger in the windscreen and Johnny moved his hand over to the toggle switch that controlled the current to the electromagnet on the bottom of the plane. Hanging from that electromagnet was a single 250-pound bomb.

The airspeed indicator showed 120 miles per hour, terminal velocity for an unpowered descent. The altimeter was winding down so quickly that Johnny couldn't keep track of it. He saw the needle pass through five hundred feet and he knew he only had a couple of seconds left in which to release the bomb and climb away. He flipped the toggle switch and felt the bomb fall away, adding power for his climb-out at the same time.

The Vaglichio chauffeur heard the power being applied to the engine and he looked up. His eyes grew wide with shock as he saw a large black object falling from the plane, heading right for the roof of the house.

"Sam!" the chauffeur shouted, not bothering in the excitement of the moment to call him Don. He started toward the house.

The bomb punched down through the roof of the house almost dead center over the parlor. The roof itself didn't activate the fuse, but the floor of the attic and the ceiling, made of stouter material than the roof, did. With the fuse activated, the bomb continued downward, exploding at a level of approximately four feet above the floor. The bomb consisted of 250 pounds of high explosive, enclosed in a steel casing. The reinforced walls of the house contained the explosion for no longer than a half-second, then they blew out. During that half-second, however, the force of the explosion within the contained area was greatly intensified. That was enough to totally obliterate everything within the room...the leather sofa and four matching chairs, the paintings and statuary, the crafted Victrola and all the records...and Don Vaglichio.

Headlines from various New York papers

MOBSTER SLAIN FROM AIR

SAM VAGLICHIO MURDERED BY BOMB BLAST

MOB WARFARE BECOMES MODERN WARFARE

The stories were all pretty much the same, describing how Sam Vaglichio was killed by a bomb dropped from an airplane. One story, which was typical of all the others, read:

> There has always been a degree of violence between the mobs, but the recent murder of Sam Vaglichio took that violence to a new and very dangerous level. Not content to murder their enemies with pistols and knives, the mobsters had already begun to terrorize the city and innocent citizens with submachine guns. Now, borrowing a page from the recent World War, they have taken their mob warfare to the air and one wonders if tanks and artillery will soon be added to their growing arsenal.
>
> The Mayor's Office and the New York Police Department have all but admitted that they are unable to handle the situation.
>
> "We have done all we can do," the police commissioner said, "so we have turned to the only avenue left open to us. We have asked the federal government to provide us with assistance in combating this scourge of lawlessness and violence. In response, the federal government has provided us with an agent from the Bureau of Investigation.

A prominent member of the Mayor's Council on Crime Control, Councilman George Chambers, has made no secret of his feelings about calling in federal help.

"You cannot convince me," Councilman Chambers said in a recent interview, "that the City of New York is incapable of handling its own problems. And if it were necessary to go to the federal government for help, then what help could we possibly expect from a mere two law officers. Perhaps if they were competent I would have some faith in them. But these are the same people, remember, whose first attempt to 'clean up' the city was made in the back room of a laundry."

Councilman Chambers is referring, of course, to a raid conducted by Agent Mike Kelly and his Flying Squad a few weeks ago. Though reporters were tipped off that the raid would result in the closing of a notorious bookie operation, it turned out to be a false alarm.

Since that time there have been no other attempted raids and Agent Kelly has even released the policemen who were detailed to him, back to their original assignment. What plans Agent Kelly may have for the near future are not known.

"Not very flattering articles, are they?" Bill asked, tossing one of the newspapers onto the corner of Mike's desk where a pile of them sat. It was almost ten o'clock in the evening but Mike and Bill, who had no particular place to go, were still in their office in the back of the municipal headquarters building. A headline on the wall behind Mike's desk read, "FEDERAL CLEANUP BEGINS IN LAUNDRY."

"No, they aren't," Mike agreed. He had his pistol apart, cleaning it. "I know who did it, Bill."

"Beg your pardon?"

"I know who killed Sam Vaglichio."

"Well yeah, I guess it was the Sangremanos, wasn't it?" Bill asked.

"Yes, it was the Sangremanos. Specifically, it was Johnny Sangremano." Mike held the cylinder up and stared through it before he picked up a cleaning rod and began poking a patch through the six empty chambers. "He was the only one who could have done that. That was quite a job of flying, you know, to deliver a single bomb to a single house like that. It took some skill."

"Is your friend that good?"

"No," Mike said coldly. "That is to say, yes, Johnny Sangremano is that good of a flyer. But he is no friend of mine."

"I thought he was the one you went flying with."

"He is. But skillful flying or not, what he did by bombing Sam Vaglichio's house was commit coldblooded murder. And anyone who would commit cold-blooded murder is no friend of mine." Mike finished with the cleaning, then snapped the cylinder back into place.

Though everyone in the city braced for a retaliation from the Vaglichios over the killing of their father, that didn't happen. The reason that didn't happen was because Don Pietro Nicolo sent emissaries to the Vaglichio and Sangremano Families asking that a truce be called and summoning them to a meeting. The meeting was not only of the Vaglichios and the Sangremanos, but of the Five Families of New York, and other Families from all over the country.

The meeting included the DiCarlo Family out of Detroit. The DiCarlo Family was into "labor management." This was a particularly sweet racket for them, for they were able to work both sides of every dispute. They had infiltrated the unions while at the same time selling their services to the auto manufacturers to "take care of any rough spots," such as worker strikes or demonstrations, to make sure production ran smoothly.

The Coppola Family from Steubenville, Ohio, would

also attend. The Coppola Family was headed by Ignatzio "The Hammer" Coppola. In Steubenville, the Coppola Family was into prostitution and gambling, but on a national scale they had established a lucrative business in exporting murder. If someone in Cleveland, Cincinnati, Kansas City, or even Chicago and New York wanted a murder performed and they wanted the killing to be unassociated with their own Family, they could order the job from Ignatzio Coppola.

In Kansas City, the Masseria Family, headed by Mike Masseria, had the city under its thumb. The Masseria Family controlled whiskey, gambling, prostitution, and politics.

In New Orleans, it was the Macheca Family, now headed by Charles Matranga. Of all the other Families in the country, the Macheca Family was closest to the Sangremanos, for Giuseppe had started with the Macheca Family when he first came to America.

Though Alphonso Caponni, who now called himself Al Capone, controlled Chicago, he was not Sicilian and therefore not a true member of the United Families. His existence could not be overlooked, however, and there was little business done on a national scale that did not include him. He was considered a "loose cannon on deck" and as such was watched closely by the other Families. Capone was also invited to the meeting and though he did not attend, he sent one of his lieutenants.

The meeting was held in a small vacation resort in the mountains of Pennsylvania. Security was handled by Don Pietro Nicolo. His men were spread out over the grounds and around the building, checking everyone who came in or out. Those people who were not associated with any of the Families, and who showed up for the purpose of actually taking a vacation, were told that there were some problems with the sewer system and the resort was temporarily closed. The sight of several armed men enforcing this temporary closure was enough to send the would-be vacationers on their way without argument.

The resort was set up in a way to make the stay as pleasant and comfortable as possible. The bar was supplied with bonded whiskey and the kitchen turned out great quantities of food. There were no prostitutes available, however, for this was to be a working meeting and everyone agreed that prostitutes would just get in the way. Besides, prostitutes were generally considered to be a low-grade type of person without honor and incapable of keeping secrets.

The opening session of the meeting was held in the private dining room of the resort. A long, polished mahogany table, surrounded by massive red leather, cushioned chairs, served as the meeting table. Don Pietro Nicolo, who had called the meeting, sat in the middle of the table. Vinnie Sangremano sat at one end and Luca Vaglichio sat at the other. Johnny was by Vinnie's side, Mario was by Luca's side. Both men had their consigliore in the meeting room with them, though none of the other consigliores were present. None of the chief lieutenants were in the room either. This meeting was reserved strictly for Family. The Family heads sat around the table in no particular order, with the exception of Don Charles Matranga, from New Orleans. Because he had a special kinship with the Sangremanos, he sat very close to Vinnie.

As each man arrived in the room, they went to Don Nicolo and embraced him, then nodded perfunctorily at Vinnie, then at Luca, and finally at the others. There was a quiet buzz of conversation between the men as they waited for Don Nicolo to start the meeting and finally, when the last guest had arrived and was in place, Don

Nicolo nodded to one of the armed men at the door. The guard stepped out of the room then and closed the door behind him. The most powerful figures in the American underworld were left alone. They were all together for perhaps the first time in history.

Johnny looked around the table at these men. Some he had seen before, Matranga, Don Nicolo, and, of course, the Vaglichios. Some he had never seen, though he had heard of them. All in all, he had to admit to himself that he was much impressed with this gathering. These men could very well be considered as captains of industry, as surely as if they were the head of major American enterprises, and in fact they were. These were men who were bigger than life and they lost none of their mystique by being seen in person. They were generally corpulent men, with large noses, generous mouths, and heavy cheeks. They were men who were listened to. They were also men who had grown accustomed to power. For the moment they each found themselves in the unusual position of being present at a meeting, but not being in charge. They were, however, more curious about how this was going to work than they were jealous of their positions of authority. They were willing to defer to the man who had called the meeting and they waited patiently for Don Nicolo to speak.

"Gentlemen, I want to thank all of you for coming," Don Nicolo said, speaking Italian in a Sicilian dialect. "I want to say at the beginning that I did not ask you here in order to build my own power or reputation. I have no ideas to put before you. I have only a request, a request that will take the combined efforts of all our Families to fulfill. May I now make that request?"

Don Nicolo looked around the table at each man in turn and each of them answered him in the affirmative, with a silent nod of their heads.

"Thank you," Don Nicolo said. He took a deep breath and stroked his chin for a moment before he began.

"At each end of this table today, we are honored by the presence of the Sangremanos and the Vaglichios." Don Nicolo turned to Luca. "Luca, I remember your grandfather from the old country. He was a powerful Don and a gracious man who did many favors for many people, myself included. I remember your father too, for we were young men together in Misilmeri. There he was known as Cesare and though he changed his name to Sam when he came to America there were some among his old friends who could still call him Cesare. I am pleased to say that I was one of those old friends and I was greatly grieved when he was killed."

Don Nicolo then turned to Vinnie. "Vincent, I knew your father too. He proved his bravery in Sicily and many times again after he came to America. He was a man of honor. I knew, also, your brother Tony." Don Nicolo put the tip of his finger to his temple. "Tony was a man with many ideas, a very smart man. It is too bad he was killed, for I think the future of our Families may depend upon men of vision and honor, men like your brother. When he was killed, all of us lost."

Don Nicolo then turned to the table at large. "These two men of whom I speak, Don Cesare Vaglichio and Tony Sangremano, are both dead now. They died, not of natural causes, but by the hand of another Italian. Another Siciliano," he added. "In addition, the Vaglichio Family lost two decent and honorable soldiers, Carmine..." Don Nicolo had to put on his pair of glasses so he could read the names from a piece of paper. "Carmine Petacci and Freddie Sarfatti."

Don Nicolo took his glasses off and looked out over the table again. "I do not know why the Sangremanos and the Vaglichios began killing each other off. I do know that we are losing some of our finest men in the war that they have started. And, more importantly, I know that this war will not be contained to the two Families. And so now, my friends, I ask of you, the heads of all the other Families in the country, some suggestions as to how we may put an end to this killing, before it spreads across all the territory lines, and brings the police and the state and the federal governments down on our heads. Before it ruins us all."

"Don Nicolo," Don DiCarlo suggested. "Suppose we let each of them tell their side of the story. We can listen and judge as to who has the greatest grievance."

"And what would you do," Vinnie asked, "if you judge Luca's grievance to be greater than mine?"

"Nothing," Don Nicolo answered. "We are all men of honor here. Just knowing whose wrong is the greater is all that will be required."

Vinnie drummed his fingers on the table for a minute, then he nodded his head.

"All right," he said. "All right, I'll go along with that."

"Then, perhaps you will tell us your side of the story first?" Don Nicolo asked.

"You wish to hear my side?" Vinnie asked. "Here it is. As you all know, my father died a few months ago. My brother Tony took over the business. The Vaglichios..." Vinnie stopped and stared down the length of the table at his enemies while a blood vessel throbbed in his neck. Finally, he took a deep breath and went on. "The Vaglichios," he continued, "came to my brother with a business proposition. They had heard that my brother was not yet ready to go into the liquor business, so they asked if they could set up their liquor joints in Sangremano territory. My brother said no. The Vaglichios did not like his answer so they killed him. I believe the man who gave the order to have my brother killed was Don Sam

Vaglichio. Therefore, to avenge my brother's death, I had Don Sam Vaglichio killed."

"You also killed Carmine Petacci and Freddie Sarfatti, did you not?" one of the other New York Dons asked.

"Yes, I did," Vinnie agreed.

"Do you think that was a fair price to ask the Vaglichios to pay? Three for one?"

"Petacci and Sarfatti are not family," Vinnie explained. "I killed them to make a point, to show the other soldiers in the Vaglichio Family that they aren't safe. Killing them did nothing toward avenging my brother. As you know, that requires the killing of someone related by blood."

"And so you killed their father, a helpless old man," one of the other Dons said.

"Don Nicolo, may I speak for my employer?" Al Provenzano asked.

"Yes, if he wishes you to."

Al looked at Vinnie and Vinnie nodded his head.

"Thank you," Al said. "In the first place, Don Nicolo, you do a great disservice to Don Vaglichio to call him a helpless old man. He was cunning and very well protected. But you have brought up a point we wish to have considered. Don Vaglichio was an old man with not too many years of life remaining. Tony Sangremano, on the other hand, had many years remaining. He also had a wife and little children who were dependent upon him. Tony was a businessman who wanted only to run the enterprises his father had built. We had consulted many times on the establishment of a liquor business and it was his intention to start the operation as soon as he was prepared for it. You see, Tony was a very careful man who wished to do things properly and without making great difficulty for others. He wanted to set up the business so that all who depended upon him would profit from it, with each man getting his fair share. Tony

Sangremano had the right to develop the business in his own territory as he saw fit. The Vaglichios did not see it this way. They were greedy and cruel men and they sent two of their button men into Sangremano territory to kill him in his own office."

"Thank you, Counselor," Don Nicolo said. He turned to Luca. "And now, Luca, would you present your side?"

Luca told the Vaglichio side of the story, insisting that the decision to kill Tony was not an easy one, but one that was necessitated by business.

"We offered in all good faith to negotiate with Tony Sangremano for the rights to sell whiskey in his territory because he had already said that he did not intend to do so. We also offered points on the business so that the Sangremanos could enjoy some of the fruits of our labor. He turned these offers down."

"But did he not have the right to decide what business would take place in his own territory?" Don Nicolo asked.

"Don Nicolo, you know and I know that whiskey was going to be sold there. If the Sangremanos did not sell it, and we did not sell it, then who would have? The Irish perhaps? The Jews? The coloreds? Is that what we want? I am sorry Tony had to be killed, but in so doing, Vinnie became the new head of the Family and he has already started in the whiskey business. By doing that he has kept the Irish, Jews, and coloreds out and that is better for us all."

After the opening statement by both sides, there were several more questions asked by the various Dons around the table. Finally, Don Nicolo asked the Sangremanos and the Vaglichios if they would please leave the room so that the others could debate the issue and give the final decision. There was a scraping of chairs as the men of the two Families stood, then left the room. The

Vaglichios exited by one door and the Sangremanos by the other.

The Sangremanos had a suite of rooms on the top floor. While they waited to be summoned back to the meeting room for the decision of the other Families, Vinnie began going over some figures with Luigi Sarducci. Al was on the telephone and Johnny was sitting on the windowsill, looking out over the mountains. It was a beautifully clear day and Johnny saw an airplane, high and far in the distance. He was pretty sure that it was the mail plane between New York and Pittsburgh and for just a moment he wondered how things might have turned out if circumstances had been just a little different. He felt a tremendous tug at his emotions and he had to fight hard to keep from getting up and walking out of there, never to come back.

"Mike," he said under his breath. "Why did you have to pick up that goddamn paper out there in St. Louis? If we hadn't seen the story about Tony getting killed, that could be one of us up there."

"Did you say somethin', Johnny?" Vinnie asked from across the room.

"What? Uh, no," Johnny said. "I was just thinking out loud, that's all." He stood up and turned his back to the window and the mail plane and looked out over the room at his brother and the others. He was sure that none of them was aware of the plane flying so high and distant and free of this place. And even if they had been aware of it, they couldn't know what it meant to him.

"You okay?" Vinnie asked.

"Yeah, I'm fine. Say, Vinnie, you've been at this game longer than I have. Tell me what's going to happen."

"Nothin' is going to happen," Vinnie replied. He smiled broadly. "The Families don't want a war, so they're going to tell us to make peace. Whoever breaks the peace is going to hear from them. Since we were the last ones to strike, that's goin' to leave us ahead of the game."

"What about the Vaglichios? Will they go along with it?"

"It's going to eat at their guts, but they got no choice," Vinnie said. "Yeah, they'll go along with it." Vinnie laughed, then walked over and rubbed Johnny's hair. "Besides, if they don't, we'll turn our own private air service loose on them, huh, kid?"

There was a knock at the door then and a muffled voice called out from the hall. Vinnie nodded at Al, and Al opened the door. Don Nicolo's son Enrico was standing there just on the other side. Johnny knew that Don Nicolo's other son, Roberto, had probably gone to summon the Vaglichios.

"My father has asked if you would please come back down to the meetin' room," Enrico said.

"Yeah, sure," Vinnie replied. He smiled at Enrico. He and Enrico were the same age. Though they had not grown up together, they had seen each other many times at the various Italian social functions, such as Columbus Day celebrations, and the many weddings and funerals that had drawn the two Families together in the past. Their roles were quite different now, however, for Vinnie was the head of his Family, while Enrico was still the dutiful son.

"So, how'd it go in there, Enrico?" Vinnie asked.

"I think everything will be okay," Enrico said. "I'll let Pop explain the details."

"Good, good," Vinnie said. "I'm glad the Don was able to work things out."

"Vincent, Luca, Johnny, Mario," Don Nicolo said when everyone returned to the meeting room. "Come here, all of you. Come to the center of the room."

The four men came as beckoned.

"Now, put out your left hand, all of you," Don Nicolo ordered. "I want the four of you to grab hands in the middle."

When the men did as he asked, Don Nicolo smiled. "Do you see what you have done? You have formed a cross that goes right to your heart. I want this cross to be the symbol that ends the war between your two Families. Luca, Mario, you have lost your father. That is a great loss for anyone to bear and my heart aches for you. Vincent, Johnny, you have lost a brother, a young man with many years left to give. Now you must be responsible to bring up his family and that is asking much of you. My heart grieves for you as well. But from this day forward, there will be no more killing. Wars are too expensive and too public. It is best that we settle all our differences now. Luca, I do not want to come to your funeral and grieve for you. Vincent, I do not want to come to your funeral and grieve for you. This war must end. The other Families have decided...if there is another killing, we will join with the victim's Family and, together, we will punish the transgressor. Is this understood?"

"Yes, Padrone," Vinnie said.

"Luca?"

"I understand, Padrone," Luca replied.

Don Nicolo smiled and put his own hand on top of the other four. "Good, good," he said. "We have done good work here today, for we have preserved the peace. Now, let us all return to our homes and get on with business. We cannot earn money by enjoying a vacation in the mountains."

HOLLYWOOD, CALIFORNIA

Tony's murder did not stop the business arrangement the Sangremanos had made with Sammy Solinger. He got the five hundred thousand dollars in time to complete his picture. Now, all he had to do was create a small part for Katherine. With very little enthusiasm for what he was being forced to do, he arranged for Katherine and her mother to come to the studio for a screen test. At the last minute, he scheduled it for two o'clock in the afternoon. The phone rang at one-thirty.

"Sammy, this is Charlie Gibbons." Gibbons was in charge of production.

"Yeah, Charlie, what can I do for you?"

"Eddie just told me that he is supposed to shoot a screen test at two."

"Yeah."

"May I ask why the hell I didn't know about it? I've already got everyone else scheduled for other things this afternoon. I can't put together full crew on such short notice."

"I don't need a full crew," Solinger explained. "All I need is Eddie."

"One camera? You're going to shoot a screen test with one camera? What kind of test is that?"

"It's no test at all," Solinger admitted. "Look, don't worry about it, okay? It's something I've got to do. A promise I made."

Charlie laughed. "Don't tell me you're still using that old gimmick to get a girl in bed?"

"I don't have to do that anymore," Solinger said. "I have found that money is quicker and less trouble."

"All right," Charlie said. "Well, look, I don't know what this screen test is all about, but if we're going to shoot one at all, I can't let it just slip by without making some effort to do it right. My professional integrity is at stake here. I'm going to do what I can to scrape up a few more people."

"Suit yourself," Solinger said, hanging up the phone.

When Solinger went to the shooting stage at two o'clock, he saw that Charlie had managed to get another cameraman, plus a couple of men to handle the lights. In fact, he had put together a pretty good crew for a screen test that, in Solinger's mind, didn't amount to anything.

Katherine and her mother were on the set. The mother looked confused and suspicious, Katherine looked shy and frightened. A mouse, Solinger thought. She looks like a little gray mouse.

Katherine took her directions meekly, moving where he told her, going through the various poses with an almost painful shyness. Finally, Solinger told her that he had enough and he thanked her for coming down.

"Don't you want me to act?" she asked.

"What?"

"You haven't given me a scene to do. All you have done is take pictures."

"All right, you want to do a scene? I'll give you a scene. You wait right there for a moment."

Solinger walked over to a stand where there was some material left over from a previous shoot. He recalled that there had been a scene in the movie where the star, whose sister had been scandalized by lies, was determined to get even with the man who had caused all the trouble. In order to do that she first had to make him mad with desire for her. The scene was eventually cut from the script, however, because it had been impossible to capture just the right mood. Every time they tried to shoot it the actress playing the part would come across looking like either a prostitute or a silly young girl. It wasn't fair, of course, to expect Katherine Sangremano to be able to do the scene that an experienced actress couldn't do, but perhaps it would teach her a lesson and send her back to New York where she belonged.

"All right," Solinger said, returning with the script in his hand. "Here's the scene. Your sister was a young servant girl who discovered that the nephew of the man she worked for was stealing from him. When she threatened to expose him if he didn't give the money back, he went to his uncle and told lies about the girl, causing her to leave in disgrace. Now, you want to avenge your sister, but in order to do that, you will first have to make the nephew fall madly in love with you. So what you got to do, see, is pretend that the camera is that man. I want you to make the camera, and every man in the audience, go nuts over for you. Now, that sounds like a simple thing, doesn't it? You think you can do that for me?"

"Yes, I can do that," Katherine said.

Solinger smiled and tossed the script to one side, then looked over at Charlie and Eddie. "Did you hear her, boys? She can do that. Roll the cameras."

Charlie and Eddie had been on the crew of the movie this scene was taken from and they knew that after more than fifty takes that included crying, shouting and threats to walk out on the production, the scene was finally abandoned. They were curious as to why Solinger had given this shy young woman such an impossible task and they felt an instant pity for her.

Katherine knew nothing of the history of the scene. She knew only that she was asked to do it, so she walked back over to the set and sat on the sofa for a moment with her eyes closed, pinching the bridge of her nose as if she were in deep thought. Then she kicked off her shoes and stretched out on the couch with her head held erect by her right hand, while her left arm rested on the top of her leg. She threw her left shoulder forward slightly, and twisted her body to accent the curve of her hip. Then she fixed a smoldering glare at the camera while her lips pushed out in a pout.

It was two days later when the phone rang in Solinger's office and he heard Charlie say, "Sammy, come on down to the projection room. I've got something you ought to see."

"What is it? I don't have time for this," Solinger said.

"Find the time," Charlie said. "Trust me on this, it is well worth your while."

What Charlie wanted Sammy to see was the developed film from Katherine's screen test. When he told him what it was, Sammy started to leave but something in Charlie's voice made him stay and watch. What he saw was the most amazing transformation he had ever witnessed in his life. Katherine Sangremano, the plain, gray mouse of a woman with bee-stung lips, flat chest, and big, liquid-brown eyes, was, as seen through the camera, the sexiest woman Sammy Solinger had ever seen. And in fifteen years of making movies, he had seen a lot of them. There was something amazing and indefinable in the young woman's appearance. Solinger couldn't put his finger on exactly why there was such a charge of eroticism from the screen, though he thought it might have something to do with the combination of innocence and sexuality. He found that he was taking short breaths, and the palms of his hands were sweaty.

"My God," Sammy said when the screen flashed white and the film flapped in the take-up reel.

"What did I tell you?" Charlie asked.

"Keep this to yourself, Charlie," Sammy said.

"You are going to put her in your film, aren't you, Sammy?"

"You're goddamned right I am," Sammy said. He smiled at Charlie. "I've just happened onto a gold mine but I don't intend to go around like a fool shouting 'Gold!' Do you understand my meaning?"

"Yeah," Charlie said as he began rewinding the film. "I understand. You are going to stiff her."

"Listen, all she wants is to be in the movies," Sammy said. "She'll never know the difference."

CHAPTER 6

NEW YORK

A small bit of bread, wet and sodden, lay in a gutter of black rushing water. A rat, its beady eyes alert for danger, darted out to the prize, grabbed it, then bounded back to the comparative safety of one of the big warehouse buildings. The street in front of the warehouse was brick, and running down the middle of the brick street was a spur from the New York Central Railroad. The track ran to the far end of the buildings, glistened wetly in the dim light, then curved off toward the main line. At the place where the tracks curved, a streetlamp surrounded by swirls of cloudlike mist, barely managed to push away the darkness. In the darker shadows of the corner of one of the buildings, a uniformed police officer kept a close watch on the entrance to Warehouse 101B.

The police officer keeping watch was Mike's father, Sergeant Tim Kelly. This was not Tim's normal beat, nor was he officially on duty. He was here on his own because he hoped to find something that would put Trapnell away for a long time.

Tim had been working on this case for nearly two months now, talking with policemen in his and other precincts as well as with hoods on the street. Then, earlier today, he ran across a bit of information that he thought he might be able to use. He heard through a couple of his street sources that a truckload of whiskey was being moved tonight. The movement of illegal alcohol was a violation of the Volstead Act and normally, Tim wouldn't even get involved with it. Such a violation was a job for the Treasury agents, the special Prohibition task force of the police department, and the Bureau of Investigation. What made this particular tip interesting to Tim, however, was the fact that the whiskey that was being moved was said to be coming from Warehouse 101B. Warehouse 10IB belonged to the New York City Police Department. If the whiskey actually did come from there, it could only do so with the aid and assistance of members of the police department. Inventory responsibility for Warehouse 10IB was normally passed around from police officer to police officer. This week the officer in charge of inventory was none other than Lieutenant Herbert Trapnell. This was the break Tim had been looking for.

Tim had been there about an hour when the grinding of gears and the straining of a truck engine announced the approach of a vehicle. Tim looked down the street to see two fuzzy glows, headlights, yellowed by the night fog. The truck moved slowly down the brick street, then stopped with a squeal of brakes just in front of the warehouse. The driver tapped his horn twice, then a spreading bar of light began to appear in the darkness as the warehouse door was pulled open. The gears rattled and clanked as the truck was put into reverse, then the engine strained as the truck was backed into the warehouse. The door pulled shut again and the bar of light winked out. Once more the street was dark and empty.

Tim waited for a moment, then he crossed the street, slipping quietly through the fog. He knew he could not go in through the front, so he walked around the warehouse, trying every door and window until he found a window off the alley that was not locked. Pushing it up as quietly as he could, Tim hoisted himself up from the ground, then lay his stomach onto the windowsill and tumbled over inside.

The warehouse was cold, dark, and damp. He found himself way in the back, but he could see lights up in the front, and he could hear the subdued conversation of the men who were loading whiskey into the truck. He started toward the light and the sound.

Warehouse 101B was being used by the police to store not only liquor, but other confiscated items as well, from hijacked coffee to stolen automobiles. Tim picked his way carefully through the dark piles of booty until he got close enough to the little bubble of yellow light to see and hear what was going on.

"Only the bonded stuff," someone was saying. "None of that rotgut shit."

"What difference does it make?" someone else asked. "Hell, the suckers comin' to these places will drink anything, you know that."

"Not to this place. This liquor is going to the Babylon Gardens. They don't let nothin' but class people come to that joint. Anyway, from what I hear, we're payin' Trapnell enough for it."

"Yeah, well, don't worry. You're gettin' the good stuff. I ought to know, I already tried some of it out."

"Let's work faster. I want to get it loaded so I can get out of here," the driver said. "Bein' around all this shit is like bein' in a graveyard or somethin'. It gives me the willies."

A bright flash of light suddenly shined in Tim's face and he gasped and looked around in surprise.

"Well, well, well," a disembodied voice said from behind the glare of light. "Lookie who we have here."

It was late at night and Mike had already dismissed all the police who were assigned to him except for Bill Carmack. The two of them were sitting in the office alone, each lost in his own thoughts. There had been three more attempted raids since the formation of the "Flying Squad," and each of them had wound up just as the laundry raid, empty-handed. The press was having a field day with them and even the police were beginning to make jokes, though the jokes generally stopped when Mike came around.

"You know, Mikey," Bill said. "Everything we're going to try is going to wind up the same way unless we find out who's tipping off the hoods."

"I know," Mike said. He wadded up a piece of paper, then tossed it, like a basketball, toward the trash can in the far corner. The paper wad hit the rim, then fell in.

"How are we going to find out who it is?" Bill asked.

"We aren't going to find out," Mike said. "We aren't even going to try."

"What do you mean we aren't even going to try?"

"I mean I'm giving up," Mike said. "I'm going to the commissioner in the morning and I'm going to tell him, 'Thanks, but no thanks, I won't be using any New York policemen anymore."

"You're resigning?" Bill asked in surprise.

"No," Mike said. "I mean I'm just giving up trying to depend on the police. From now on, there will be no policemen in any of my operations."

"You're getting rid of everybody?"

"Yes. That's the only way I can be sure I'm getting rid of the stoolie."

"Mike, you know, that means me too. If you go to the commissioner with this, he'll insist that I return to my own precinct."

"I know. I wanted to talk to you about that," Mike said. "It doesn't have to mean you." Mike reached into his center desk drawer and pulled out a little leather case. He shoved it across the desk toward Bill. "All you have to do is take off that uniform, put this in your pocket, and you're a federal officer."

Bill chuckled. "What are you trying to do? Recruit me into the Bureau?"

"That's exactly what I'm trying to do. How about it?" Mike asked.

"You're serious, aren't you?"

"Very serious."

Bill looked at Mike for a moment, then he sighed. "I don't know, Mike," he said. "I really don't know. Don't forget, I've already got six years on the force."

"I know, I've already thought of that. If you come with me, that means you'll have to give that up," Mike said. "Also, you'll be starting at less pay and you'll be six years further away from retirement."

Bill laughed. "My God, you need lessons on how to recruit, you know that?" he asked. "You're telling me all the reasons why I should not join the Bureau. That's not how you are supposed to do it. Now tell me one reason why I should join the Bureau."

"You wouldn't be working with anyone who is dirty," Mike said simply.

Bill sighed. "Yeah, there is that, isn't there? I don't know, Mike, I'm going to have to think about it. You know, I've never pictured myself as anything but a New York cop."

There was a knock on the door of the office and Mike yelled for them to come in. It was the desk sergeant from the squad room out front and he had a strange, disquieting look on his face as he stood in the door.

"Agent Kelly?" he said.

"Yes?"

"I'm sorry to be the one to tell you this." The police sergeant paused for a moment before he went on. "It's about Sergeant Kelly."

"My father? What about my father?" Mike asked. Something in the expression on the sergeant's face and in the tone of his voice made Mike fearful of the worst. When the desk sergeant spoke again those worst fears were confirmed.

"Your old man was caught trying to boost a load of hooch out of Warehouse 101B. There was a shoot-out and your pa was killed. I'm sorry."

Four days later Mike Kelly was standing at his father's graveside. Sergeant Timothy Patrick Kelly had actually been buried the day before. Because he was under suspicion of having committed a felony, he was denied a burial with the honors normally due a policeman. Instead, he was buried very quietly with only his family and a few of his closest friends in attendance. Mike had been there for the burial, but he came back to the cemetery today, this time to be alone with his father.

The dirt mound over the grave was covered with flowers, many of them still fresh and fragrant.

"I know you didn't do what they said you did, Pop," Mike said aloud. "And since you didn't do it, that means you were set up. So I'm making you this vow right now. I intend to find the sonofabitch who did it, and when I do, I'm going to…"

"Mikey?"

Mike had not heard anyone approach so he was

surprised to hear someone call his name. When he looked around he saw Bill standing there. Bill was holding his hat in his hands, and he was dressed in mufti.

"Bill," Mike said. "What are you doing out here?"

"When I didn't find you in the office, I thought you might be out here," Bill said. "I decided to join you. I hope you don't mind the intrusion."

"No, I don't mind," Mike said.

"Mikey, I want you to know that I don't believe for a minute that Uncle Tim was involved in that whiskey heist. He may have been trying to stop it, but he sure as hell wasn't trying to steal it."

Mike put his hand on Bill's shoulder. "Thanks, Bill," he said.

"I want to help you find out who set him up, if you'll let me."

"Of course, I will let you. I can use all the help I can get. By the way, why aren't you in uniform?"

"I am in uniform," Bill said.

"What do you mean?"

"Isn't this what I would wear as a Bureau agent?"

"You mean you're going to join the Bureau?" Mike asked, smiling broadly and taking Bill's hand in his.

"I am if they will have me. And, of course, if you still want me."

"They'll have you and I still want you," Mike said happily.

"How soon can I be sworn in?"

"Right away. It's a little like getting married, you know," Mike explained. "All we have to do is find a federal judge who will perform the ceremony and you're in."

"As long as they don't throw rice," Bill teased.

"And why would they be throwin' rice at a foine Irishman like yourself, would you be for tellin' me that now, lad?" Mike teased, affecting a very thick Irish brogue. "Sure 'n 'tis spuds they'll be throwin' at the likes of you."

"Spuds is it now?" Bill replied in just as thick a brogue. "And would you listen to the lad who knows everything?"

Two days later, with Bill duly sworn in as the nation's newest agent of the Bureau of Investigation, the two men came back to the office after a late supper and saw an envelope lying on Mike's desk.

"What's this?" Mike asked, picking it up. He looked at it for a moment, swore, then set it back down unopened.

"What is it?" Bill asked, surprised by Mike's reaction.

"It's from that bastard, Johnny Sangremano."

"What's it say?"

"How the hell do I know? I didn't open the sonofabitch," Mike answered. "Besides, I'm not in the least interested."

"Sure you are," Bill said. "You were friends once."

"Don't remind me."

"Mike, what if it has some information we can use?"

"You read it," Mike invited.

"It's not to me, Mikey. It's to you," Bill said. "Read it," Mike said again. "Read it aloud. There's nothing that sonofabitch can say to me that I wouldn't want you to hear."

"All right," Bill replied. "If that's what you want." He picked up the letter, then walked over to lean against the windowsill and read aloud.

Dear Mike,
I was very sorry to hear about your father.
I won't even tell you that the Sangremano

Family had nothing to do with having him killed because I'm sure you know that we didn't. I will tell you this. As far as that job was concerned, your father was clean. However, I'm sure that because of the way things have turned out between us that you neither care nor need to have such corroboration from me.

Mike, I do hope you understand that I am risking quite a lot even to tell you this much. The whiskey robbery was a deal set up by Luca Vaglichio. There were some dirty cops involved, but your father was not one of them. As to why he was at the warehouse that night, I have no idea. I've been told the warehouse was off his beat. Maybe he was set up by someone who wanted him out of the way.

As you know by now, Luca Vaglichio is no ally of mine and I would like nothing better than to see him go down. Therefore, I have no reason to tell you this except that it is the truth. Your father was not set up by the Vaglichios.

Killing policemen is not a profitable enterprise to those of us on this side of the law. That leaves only one possibility; your father was killed by one of his own. It would seem that we aren't the only ones fighting among ourselves. Watch your ass, Mike. You never know where your enemies will be.

Mike, I wish you would go back to St. Louis and take that job flying the airmail. This new

*business you've gotten yourself into is no good.
Being a federal cop is no different from being a
local cop. We are bound to wind up on opposite
sides. Can't you see what you are doing? You are
making us enemies in a war that I cannot avoid
and that you have no business being in. Don't
get involved and don't come after us. If you do,
it's going to be bad. I'm part of the Family now
and I have no choice. As they say, blood is
thicker than water and Italian blood seems to
be the thickest of all.*

  Sincerely,

  Johnny

Bill finished the letter, then folded it and put it back in the envelope. He handed it over to Mike. "That's some letter," he said.

"Yeah," Mike agreed.

"You think he knows who the dirty cop is?"

"I don't know. But if he's telling the truth, if Vaglichio was the one behind the theft of the whiskey, then you'd better believe Vaglichio knows."

"Are we going after Vaglichio?"

"Yes," Mike said. "But not on the strength of this letter. We're going to have to have something more concrete before we can do that."

The phone rang and Bill picked it up.

"I would like to speak with Agent Mike Kelly," the voice on the phone said.

"Yeah, just a minute," Bill answered. He handed the phone to Mike.

"Kelly here," Mike said, taking the telephone stand in his left hand and putting the receiver to his ear with his right.

The voice on the other end was just a little more than a whisper. "At three o'clock this morning a load of whiskey is going to be brought across the Sound. It will be put ashore at a place called Eaton's Neck Point."

"Who is this?" Mike asked.

"A friend."

"How do I know you're not just telling me this to draw me away from somewhere else?"

"You have a tip on liquor being brought in some-where else?" the voice asked.

"No," Mike admitted.

"Then why are you worried?"

"Anonymous tips are generally not very reliable," Mike said.

"Then I guess maybe you'd better stay home." The phone went dead.

"Hello? Hello, are you still there?" Mike asked. He clicked the hook several times. Then, when he realized that his party was irretrievably gone, he hung up the receiver.

"What was that?" Bill asked.

Mike looked at the clock. "Three o'clock," he said. "That's just a little over five hours from now."

"What's a little over five hours from now?"

Mike studied Bill for a moment, then smiled. "Bill, do you like boats?" he asked.

"Boats? They're all right, I guess. Why?"

"Because we're going for a boat ride. Just the two of us."

"What, no girls?"

"No girls," Mike said. He opened the cabinet and took out two submachine guns, then tossed one of them over to Bill. "I'm afraid this will have to keep you company tonight."

———

When Joe Provenzano let himself back into the room, Maria Vaglichio was standing by the window, looking down onto the dark street.

"Hi," Joe said softly. "You look awfully pretty standing over there like that, with the light shining in your hair."

"Did you get the…uh…the things?" Maria asked nervously. She didn't turn around.

"Yes, I got them," Joe replied.

Maria turned toward him. Her eyes were big, brown, and trusting.

"It's a sin, you know."

"What?"

"It's a sin to use them." She waved her hand in front of her as if pushing something away. "Catholics cannot use them."

Joe crossed the room in a few quick steps and put his arms around her, drawing her to him. He could feel her quivering, nervously, in his arms, and as he pulled her to him the flutter of her heart thumped against his breast. She was frightened and vulnerable, and he suddenly felt very guilty.

"Do you want me to leave?" he asked quietly.

"No," she answered, just as quietly. "No, please, don't go. I couldn't stand it if you were to leave."

Joe put his hand on Maria's forehead and tipped her head back slightly, so that he could look into her eyes.

"Do you think what we are doing is a sin? Our love," he added. "Is it a sin?"

"No," Maria said. "No, it could never be a sin. It is too beautiful for that. Besides"—she laughed softly—"we've already done it several times. If it is a sin, it's done. Now it would only be a matter of degree."

"And do you want to get pregnant?"

"No! No," Maria said. "Joe, don't even say such a thing! My father would kill us both."

Joe squeezed her tightly. He knew that some girls might very well say that as a figure of speech. In this case, Maria wasn't exaggerating. If she got pregnant and Mario found out about it, he could very well kill them both.

"Then tonight, I'll wear one of these," Joe said. "And there will be no chance of your getting pregnant."

"What does it feel like? Will I be able to tell?"

"They say that you can't tell," Joe said.

"But if it breaks..."

"Don't talk anymore," Joe said.

Afterward, Maria lay hushed on the bed, gazing idly through the window at the lights of the city. She was still naked though Joe had put on his clothes.

"I'm glad we used the...the thing," Maria said.

"It's called a rubber."

Maria laughed. "That is what you put on your feet when it rains."

"It's the same thing," Joe said.

"You mean, making love with me is no different to you than putting rubbers on your feet and walking in the rain?" Maria asked.

"One is about like the other," Joe teased.

"Then perhaps the next time you want something, I

will tell you to go take a walk," Maria squealed, hitting him with the pillow.

"No, no, I take it back. I take it all back," Joe said, laughing.

Maria laughed and threw aside the pillow, then raised up to kiss him. As she leaned into him Joe felt her breasts brush against his chest. He could smell her perfume, blended with her musk, which had so aroused his senses a few moments earlier. He reached out and put his hand on her cheek to hold her kiss a bit longer.

"For the first time, I am not afraid that I am pregnant," Maria said. "It is a good thing, not to be afraid."

"I hope the time comes when you are my wife and we want you to be pregnant," Joe said.

"Oh, Joe, Papa will never let us get married."

"Maybe we won't ask him," Joe said resolutely.

An early morning freight chugged its way into the city, its cars loaded with a small portion of the daily supply of fruits, vegetables, poultry, and meat it took to feed the voracious appetite of New York's five and a half million people. The train could be heard, but not seen, for a heavy fog had risen from the surface of the Sound to wrap everything in its warm, wet, gray, impenetrable blanket.

A bell clanged from a nearby marker buoy while in the distance a foghorn bleated its mournful call. Water lapped quietly against the side of the powerboat Mike had borrowed from the Treasury Department. Of course, the Treasury Department had no idea Mike had borrowed the boat, for if they had known they would have had agents on board. Mike hadn't asked permission to take it. Instead, he just left them a note and now only he and Bill were aboard. That was by design, for if the tip he received panned out, he had no intention of sharing the operation with any other agency or department. Not only had his office become a laughingstock among the New York police, Mike was genuinely afraid that the government might close it down. He and Bill could well find themselves out of work, and though the prospect of being out of work didn't frighten Mike, he knew that Bill had given up a lot to join the Bureau.

Mike was glad Bill had taken the risk of leaving the force to join him, not only because he was Mike's cousin and someone he could trust, but also because he was someone who would be particularly useful on a night like this. Bill had been known, throughout the force, as someone who was an expert with firearms, any kind of firearm. He was the best shot in the entire police depart-ment with a pistol, a rifle, and the newest weapon in the arsenal, the forty-five-caliber Thompson submachine gun, sometimes called a "chopper." Mike looked over at Bill and saw him rubbing the barrel of the chopper, keeping it dry from the condensation that was building up with the fog.

"What time is it?" Bill asked when he saw Mike looking at him. It was the first either of them had spoken for a long time.

"I don't know for sure, but it must be nearly three," Mike answered. "I can't see my watch and I don't want to make a light for fear of being seen."

"I wonder if anyone is going to show up?"

"They'll show," Mike said. "I feel it."

"You feel it?"

"Yeah." Mike stared out into the night, though the fog was so thick he could see no more than a few feet. "It was mornings like this," he said quietly.

"What was mornings like this?"

"This was when you could expect the Germans to hit. They'd come running from the fog bank, popping up all of a sudden from out of nowhere. It got to where I could feel it beforehand, do you know what I mean? I can't explain it, but down inside, way down in my gut, I'd get this little...queasy...feeling. I knew when they were coming and I was never wrong."

"And you have that feeling now?"

"Yeah," Mike answered. "I have that feeling now. You think it's dumb?"

"No, I don't think it's dumb," Bill replied. "You can't be on the force for six years without getting a few feelings like that yourself, sometimes. If you say they're going to be here, then I believe you, and I'm ready for it."

"If it comes to shooting, Bill, how good are you with that thing?" Mike pointed to the submachine gun.

Bill smiled. "Firing a string of fifty rounds, I put forty-two inside the bull," he said.

Mike chuckled. "I'd say that was good enough."

They heard a sharp clanking sound.

"Hold it!" Mike hissed. "What's that?"

"The buoy bell?"

It clanked again, not the resonant clang of the bell, but a muffled clank.

"That's no bell," Mike said.

"It sure as hell isn't," Bill agreed.

"Get ready."

Both men stared out into the fog-shrouded darkness. After a moment they heard the steady throb of an engine. A boat was moving slowly through the water.

"How much farther?" they heard someone say.

"Not too far now. We'd better slow down, we don't want to run aground."

"This damn fog. I can't see shit."

The outline of the boat gradually began to materialize in the fog bank before them. Mike waited until the boat was fully materialized, then he turned on a big spotlight and captured the boat in its beam.

"Hold it right there!" he shouted through a megaphone. "Federal Agents!"

"Treasury men!" one of the men on the boat shouted and he opened up with a machine gun. Mike heard the bullets slapping into the boat around him and whipping by overhead.

"Return their fire!" Mike shouted.

Bill started blasting away with the Thompson, using the winking muzzle flashes of the bootlegger's gun as his target. One of the bootleggers let out a shout of pain, then the winking stopped.

There were three others on board the bootleggers' boat and they began firing as well. The spotlight Mike was using was hit. It exploded in a flash of sparks and a shower of broken bits of glass. The muzzle flashes from all the guns bounced back from the fog bank, creating the strange effect of brightening the night, while not improving the visibility.

Mike heard the engine of the bootleggers' boat rev up and he saw a white wake roll back from the bow. He knew then that one of them had gotten to the wheel and was trying to get away.

"They're making a run for it!" Bill shouted.

"Keep firing!" Mike replied. "We're going after them!"

Mike reached the wheel, started the engine, then gave chase. Because the bootleggers were still firing back at them, Mike had the advantage of being able to follow the winks of light for even though the boat had disappeared into the fog again, the muzzle flashes were bright enough that they could be seen. He bore down hard on them until he managed to catch up enough to have the boat in sight.

"Bill! Bill!" he shouted. Bill, who was now standing in the bow, firing at the boat, looked around. "Get down and hold on!" Mike called to him. "I'm not letting those bastards get away, even if it means I have to ram them!"

Bill dropped down onto the deck and grabbed hold of a stanchion. Mike opened the throttle to full power and the nose of the boat came up from the water. White spray flew past the deck as they skimmed across the water.

Suddenly Mike heard a loud crashing sound from the boat in front and he instantly chopped his throttle and threw the boat into a hard turn. The little powerboat dipped and bobbed crazily, but he avoided the channel marker that the bootleggers had hit. He came back around, then approached the damaged boat more slowly. As he drew alongside he could see that one of the bootleggers was lying on the deck while the other three were standing with their hands in the air.

Mike stopped his boat. "Keep them covered, Bill," he ordered.

"I've got them," Bill replied.

"Don't shoot! Don't shoot, Treasury men! We give up!" one of the bootleggers said.

"We aren't Treasury men, you ignorant bastards," Bill called back to them. "We're federal agents from the Bureau of Investigation! You got that?"

"It don't matter to me who you are."

Bill cocked his machine gun and raised it to his shoulder. "It matters to me, do you have that?"

"What?"

"I said do you have that?"

"Yes...yes, sir," one of the bootleggers replied. "You're with the Bureau of Investigation."

"See that you remember it."

"Get a rope on that boat," Mike called. "We're going to winch the front end up high enough to stop it from taking water. I'll be damned if I'm going to lose the evidence after this!"

Bill tossed a rope over to the bootleggers and told them to make it fast.

"Why the hell should we?"

"Because if you don't, you sonofabitch, your boat is going to sink. And you're going down with it," Bill told the man who asked.

"You'd better hurry," Mike advised them. "If it gets ahead of us, we won't be able to save it."

The three bootleggers worked feverishly until the rope was made fast. Mike started the winch and the front of the bootleggers' boat was raised, just enough to lift the hull out of the water. With it no longer taking water, Mike started towing it back to shore. Bill climbed over the rail to ride on the boat in tow, keeping an eye on the now-handcuffed prisoners.

There were three of them. The fourth man lying on the deck was dead.

"Who is that?" Bill asked.

"He's nobody. His name is Carboni. I'm the one you got to worry about."

"Is that so?"

"Yeah. You know who I am?"

"Can't say as I do."

"I'm Arnie Fusco. You ever heard of me?"

"Arnie Fusco," Bill said. He smiled. "Yeah, I've heard of you. You're small-time. You're one of Vaglichio's stooges."

"Small-time?" Fusco sputtered. "That's bullshit, copper. I'm one of his top men."

"Are you now? Well, aren't we the lucky ones, to catch a big fish like you?"

"You ain't caught nobody. Didn't you hear what I said? I'm one of his top men," Fusco repeated. He smiled. "Luca ain't goin' to let you get away with this. Especially not with the fix on."

"The fix is on?"

"Yeah, for this liquor shipment. Didn't anyone tell you?"

"No, I guess not," Bill said.

"You mean you weren't in on it?"

"No," Bill replied.

"Well, goddamnit, that's not my problem," Fusco said. "I mean we can't pay every goddamn cop on the entire force. Why the hell don't you guys talk to each other?"

"What's in the cases?" Bill asked.

Fusco smiled broadly. "Bonded hooch," he said. "From Canada. Good stuff too, the best. And let me tell you, some very powerful people are going to be pretty upset if this doesn't get through. You and your friend up there are going to be in a lot of trouble."

"You think so?" Bill asked. "Looks to me like you guys are the ones in a lot of trouble."

"All right, all right, I get it. You're pissed off because you weren't in on the deal. Okay, so how much do you want?"

"Are you offering me a bribe?" Bill asked.

"Am I offering you a bribe," Fusco mocked. "No, you dumb shit. I'm giving you a birthday present. Now, what will it take to put us ashore and let us make the delivery like we're supposed to?"

Bill suddenly, and without warning, hit Fusco in the nose. Fusco's nose swelled and a trickle of blood began running down across his mouth.

"You sonofabitch!"

Fusco yelled so loud that Mike heard it on the other

boat. He turned back to see what was going on. "What happened?" he yelled.

"Mr. Fusco tripped and fell on his nose," Bill replied.

"Who the hell do you think you are?" Fusco growled. "You can't get away with this!"

"Shh," Bill said. "You had better be quiet. If my friend knew you had offered us a bribe, he would shoot you and drop you overboard."

"You think you're going to keep us?" Fusco said. He laughed. "We got cops, judges, prosecutors, aldermen, everybody you can think of, on our take. And while you are explainin' why you made such a dumb ass mistake, me and my friends here will be eatin' lasagna in our favorite restaurant tonight."

"Yeah, well, all but Carboni there," Bill said, pointing to the dead man. "I don't think he's going to have much of an appetite, do you?"

"How the hell did they find out about it?" Luca wanted to know.

"What difference does it make?" Mario answered. "They found out. You know what that means, don't you? That means we are going to have to pay twice for the same shipment. Once to the suppliers and again to the cops to get it turned loose."

"These weren't cops," Luca explained. "They were federal agents."

"It doesn't make any difference; we'll get it back. We have to. Now that Tony is gone, Vinnie Sangremano is moving fast. He's opening up a new joint just about every other day, and he's got a good supply of liquor. If our clubs don't have the booze, you know where our customers will go, don't you?"

"Yeah, I know," Luca said. He took out a cigarette and tapped it on the gold cigarette case for a moment before he lit it. "Maybe he's moving a little too fast. We'd better keep an eye on him, little brother. Vinnie might turn out to be more of a problem than Tony was."

"What are you saying, Luca? Are you saying we ought to break the peace?"

"I'm saying that if we can't live with the peace that's been put on us, we may not have any choice," Luca said.

"If we're the ones break it though, we're going to have all the Families down on us," Mario warned.

"Maybe not," Luca said. "Maybe we aren't the ones who broke it. It could be, they've already broken the peace."

"How?"

"By moving into our territory. Even with a bond of peace, if your territory is invaded, you've got the right to fight back."

"Have they put some of their joints over here?"

"No. Something else," Luca said. "I just found out they've come into our territory to organize all the moving picture theaters."

Mario laughed. "Organize them into what?" he asked. "What business could they do with moving picture theaters?"

"The theater owners don't get any movies unless they come through the Sangremanos," Luca explained. "And the people that distribute the movies...they don't play them in the theaters unless they come through the Sangremanos too. The Sangremanos got it goin' for them both ways. And they're organizin' theaters all over the city, not just in their territory and our territory, but all over the city. They figure they can get away with it, 'cause nobody else is interested."

"Do you think there's any money in that?" Mario asked.

"Tony is the one that got it set up," Luca said. "And you know how he was about squeezing a dollar. You ask if there is any money in it? I figure there's got to be or he wouldn't have gotten into it in the first place. So, if we start something now, it isn't just our territory we're protectin', it's the territory of all Five Families." Luca smiled. "We won't be breakin' the peace, little brother. We'll be protectin' it."

CHAPTER 7

THE NEXT DAY, FIVE THOUSAND FEET OVER LONG ISLAND

"Okay, Mr. Vandervort," the pilot shouted, throttling back and pounding on the fuselage to get the attention of the young man who was riding in the front seat. "We're ready."

Jason Vandervort looked out of the airplane. "Where is the golf course?" he called back.

"Down there to the right. Do you see it?"

"Yes," Jason said.

"Look at the smoke over there," the pilot called. "It tells you which way the wind is blowing and which way you will drift."

"I see," Jason shouted. "So if I start here, then the wind will cause me to drift over that way so I can come down directly on the golf course, right?"

"Right."

"Okay, thank you very much. You have been most kind," Jason said. Loosening the seat belt that held him in, he stood up, then stepped out of the cockpit well and climbed down onto the bottom wing of the biplane. Squatting there and holding on tightly to brace himself against the ninety-mile-per-hour wind, he looked at the pilot and smiled. "Just pull on this thing, huh?" He put his hand on the retaining strap.

"No! No!" the pilot shouted excitedly, and waved his hand back and forth. "For God's sake, Mr. Vandervort, you pull that thing and everything is going to come off! That is the release for your parachute! The thing you pull is the D-ring, right there in front. The D-ring! It's that silver thing. Do you see it?"

"This?" Jason put his hand on the appropriate device.

"Yes, that."

"Right. Okay, I understand."

The pilot shook his head disapprovingly. "Listen, are you sure you want to go through with this?" he asked. "Why don't you just climb back into the seat there and let me take you back to the airport? Jumping out of a plane in a parachute isn't exactly like stepping off a chair, you know."

"Oh, but I've got to do it, don't you see?" Jason replied. "I made a five-dollar bet. I couldn't back out now."

"A five-dollar bet? You're doing this for five dollars? It doesn't seem worth killing yourself for that," the pilot said.

"I don't plan on killing myself," Jason replied.

"That's good," the pilot said. "'Cause I sure wouldn't want to think I helped you."

The young man laughed, then shouted a little poem.

"Here lies Jason Vandervort,

Squashed flat over a bet for sport."

"Very funny," the pilot said.

"See you on the ground, old man," Jason replied. Then, without another word, he leaped from the wing exactly as if he were diving off a diving board. The difference was this diving board was five thousand feet in the air.

When Jason first jumped, he felt his stomach come up to his throat. The sensation of falling only lasted for a moment or two, however, then it settled down and he had no sensation of falling at all. In fact, he felt as if he were flying and he spread out his hands and feet and looked down at the ground, far below, like a bird soaring gracefully above it all. A great calmness came over him and he had a curious sense of detachment as he looked down at the checkerboard formation of the ground, the clumps of trees, the golf courses, the houses and their estates, and the fields of the truck farmers. The houses, trees, cars, and roads didn't appear to grow any larger and he was ready to believe that he could stay up here for as long as he wanted.

Jason turned his head to look back toward the airplane he had just jumped from and when he did, the change in aerodynamics flipped him over onto his back. He could hardly believe his eyes, for the plane was now very small and very high, far above him. He had just left it! How had he come so far so quickly?

He managed to roll back over so that he was, once again, looking down at the ground. Now the features below him were noticeably larger than they had been when he first jumped, and he was sure he had come at least halfway down. It was almost as an afterthought that he moved his hand to a strap and started to yank on it, only to remember that this was one of the straps holding him attached to the parachute. Laughing at the near mistake, he corrected himself, found the D-ring, and pulled it. The chute streamed out behind him, then opened with a loud pop. He felt the opening shock all through his body, but especially in his legs where the main support straps were. He looked up to see the big white canopy billowing above him. By the time he looked down again, he was no more than a hundred feet or so above the ninth green of the golf course. True to the pilot's promise, he had drifted across the woods and the road and was right where he wanted to be.

Jason saw a foursome of players approaching the green. As yet, they were unaware that someone was coming down on top of them. Jason decided they could be forgiven for that. They would hardly expect to have somebody, quite literally, "drop in" on them.

"Fore!" he shouted. The golfers looked up in shock and one of them was so startled that he tossed his club to one side and ran off the putting green.

The others just stood there with their mouths open in surprise. Jason laughed at them.

Jason landed in one of the sand bunkers guarding the green. He fell to the ground, then rolled, just as the pilot had instructed him to, happy to see that the landing fall wasn't that bad. When the roll of the landing was complete, he slipped out of the parachute harness, then stood up and began recovering the parachute by wading up the cords and silk canopy. It had been an exhilarating experience.

"My word!" one of the golfers gasped, coming toward him and staring at him as if he were some mythological creature. "You are young Vandervort, aren't you?"

"Yes, sir. Hello, Mr. Montgomery."

"Are you all right?"

"Yes, thank you," Jason answered easily.

"Where on earth did you come from?"

"Not on earth," Jason replied. "From up there." He pointed. "I just made a parachute jump from an airplane."

"Good heavens! Did the motor quit? Where did it fall?" Mr. Montgomery began looking around anxiously.

"Well, I don't think it fell anywhere. It was functioning perfectly when I left it. Excuse me, sir, you are standing on part of the canopy."

Montgomery moved to one side to allow Jason to finish picking up the chute. It was obvious that he was still shocked by the incident and he continued asking questions.

"I don't understand," Montgomery said. "Why would you leap out of a perfectly good airplane?"

"Oh, I don't know," Jason replied. He laughed. "It seemed like a good idea at the time. Now, Mr. Montgomery, if you and your friends will forgive me for interrupting your golf game, I'll just get out of your way. I've made arrangements for someone to meet me over on the road."

"See here," Montgomery sputtered as Jason walked away. "Does your father know about this?"

"No," Jason called back. "But I'm sure he will find out soon."

With the parachute gathered under his arm, Jason started toward the road. There were several other players out on the course as well, and they, like the Montgomery party, had seen Jason come down. Now they waved and laughed, yelling at him as he passed them by. By the time Jason reached the road, he was beginning to experience somewhat of a letdown from the excitement and he almost wished he hadn't done it or that he had done it in the middle of the night so that no one would have seen him. The exhilaration he felt when he did such things was best experienced when experienced alone. Of course, a nighttime jump would have certainly been more dangerous, but danger wasn't exactly a deterrent. In fact, the more dangerous something was, the more appeal it held for him.

As Jason approached the road he saw a red Packard convertible waiting for him. He tossed the bundled-up parachute in the back of the car, then slipped into the white leather passenger seat as the driver pulled away. The driver of the car was Leah Sherman, a young woman with dark brown, bobbed hair, a red hairband, and a yellow feather.

An artist looking for a subject that would best illustrate the "flaming youth" that modern young men and women had become would have been hard-pressed to find a more attractive couple than the two in the car. Both were tanned and healthy-looking in the way that was typical of those who didn't have to earn their wages by swearing long hours in an ill-lighted, poorly ventilated factory. In fact, neither Leah nor Jason had to earn wages at all. Both of them came from very wealthy families, Leah's father was in real estate, Jason's was in finance.

Jason was only eleven years old at the time, but he could still remember the night his father and a handful of other wealthy men gathered in J. P. Morgan's library. They met to join their fortunes together to shore up the banking and investment institutions of New York and thus save the country from financial collapse during the great Knickerbocker Trust Crisis of 1907.

Jason was tall, blond-haired, and blue-eyed. He was not only wealthy, he was exceptionally handsome, so it was little wonder that women seemed to gravitate toward him. But it was more than looks and wealth that drew women to Jason Vandervort. Jason was a thrill-seeker. He drove cars and motorcycles at breakneck speed, he played polo, climbed mountains, and hunted big game. And always, at such events, there would be women around the periphery, drawn to him like moths to a flame. These were women who derived a degree of sexual excitement from the vicarious sharing of danger.

Leah Sherman was such a woman.

"What did it feel like, Jason?" Leah asked. "Was it exciting?"

"Yes, it was very exciting," Jason admitted.

"Was it frightening?"

"A little."

Leah's lips were a bright crimson smear. She stuck out the tip of her tongue and let it slide across them. When she looked over at Jason again her eyes were large, liquid, and inviting.

"Will you come over tonight?" she asked. Her voice was throaty with sexual excitement. Jason knew that she was very aroused right now, and if he had suggested it, he had no doubt but that she would pull the car up under the trees and let him have his way with her.

Jason chuckled. "I don't know if I should come over or not," he answered. "Your father doesn't care much for me, I'm afraid."

"You wouldn't let a little thing like my father's disapproval keep you away, would you?" Leah asked. "Besides, if we play our cards right, Daddy won't even know you are there," she added, smiling seductively at him.

"Oh? And just how are we to play these cards?" Jason asked.

"Don't come until after ten. Daddy is such a fuddy-duddy that he and Mama will already be in bed by then. Don't come up the front drive, park somewhere else and come in through the garden. I'll leave the French doors unlocked. All you have to do is step right through them."

"I think I should tell you, Leah, if I come, I won't be coming for a cup of tea," Jason warned.

"Ooohh," Leah said, shivering with unsuppressed

excitement. "I would certainly hope that you wouldn't be coming for tea."

Jason laughed. "In that case, I'll be there," he promised.

When they got back to the country club, at which place the idea of jumping from an airplane had been conceived, the others in the young couple's circle of friends were there to greet them. Leah began honking the horn as soon as she drove into the driveway and Jason reached into the back seat to grab a handful of silk. He held the deployed parachute up for all to see. They laughed and applauded. When they got out of the car, the young man who had made the wager with Jason was there to meet him. He was holding a five-dollar bill in his hand.

"I say, old man," the young man said to Jason. "It's no wonder your father is so wealthy. It must be in the Vandervort blood to do anything for a buck. To jump from an airplane for a mere five dollars...why, that is simply unbelievable."

Jason smiled as he took the proffered bill. "I suppose it depends on how you look at it, Roger," he replied. "It was such a kick I would have jumped for a nickel. Looking at it that way, I made a clear profit of four dollars ninety-five cents."

Everyone laughed, then one of the other young men turned toward Roger.

"Okay, Roger, now it's your turn," he said.

Roger's face went ashen. "No, no!" he replied, holding out his hands as if he were afraid they were going to force him into an airplane. "I can't. I won't."

Jason laughed. "Don't worry, Roger, nobody's going to make you do it. But I have to tell you, it is the berries. You're missing a great thrill."

"Not everyone's like you," Roger said. "Not everyone

has to find something exciting to do every single minute of every single day."

Jason laughed with the others, but there was more truth in Roger's words than he really wanted to admit. He had read about Freud and his method of psychoanalysis and he sometimes wondered if he should see a psychiatrist. Jason was convinced, in his own mind, that he suffered from a malady that was as compulsive as kleptomania, nymphomania, or any other mania. Jason had a compulsion to test the limits of danger as often and in as many different ways as he could.

Later that evening when Jason parked his yellow Stutz in the front drive of his father's house, he was met by the family chauffeur.

"Shall I wash your car and put it away, sir?" the chauffeur asked.

"You can wash it, but don't put it away," Jason replied. "I'll be going out again tonight." He was thinking of Leah's invitation. She was a beautiful girl and any man would, no doubt, find her charms irresistible. To Jason, there was the added fillip that he would be seeing her secretly, and under the very nose of her disapproving father.

"Very good, sir," the chauffeur replied.

The butler greeted him from just inside the foyer. "Ah, Phil, good afternoon," Jason said. "Are my folks here?"

"Yes, sir, Mr. Jason. They are having coffee in the library," Phil answered, taking Jason's hat. "Shall I tell them you are here?"

"No, thank you, Phil," Jason replied. "I'll just join them in there."

"Very good, sir," Phil replied.

Jason went into the library and kissed his mother on the cheek, then went over to draw himself a cup of coffee from the great silver samovar that sat on the credenza.

"How was the market today, Pop?" he asked.

Mr. Vandervort put down the Wall Street Journal he was reading. "Actually, it did quite well today. I wish I could believe that you really cared," he said.

"But of course I care," Jason quipped. "Don't you think I realize that it is your success in the market that allows us to live like this?" Jason took in the richly furnished room with a sweep of his hand.

Jason's father chuckled. "Oh, yes, I'm sure you appreciate what the market can supply for you," he said. "But what I mean is, I wish you cared enough to get involved in the business."

Jason took a drink of his coffee and studied his father over the rim of the cup for a long moment before he spoke.

"Pop, please don't misunderstand," he said. "I'm not being flippant about this. The truth is, I have nothing but the utmost respect for you and for what you do. Too much, in fact, to try and follow in your footsteps. It takes a special talent to be able to analyze the stock market as you do, and I know I don't have that talent. If I handled investments I'd run the company into bankruptcy in no time at all."

"You wouldn't have to handle investments to work with us, Jason. You have a law degree. You could work as a legal counsel for the company."

"I don't want to be a lawyer."

"Now is a fine time for you to decide that," Mr. Vandervort said. "After four years of college and three years of law school."

"I know. But, Pop, I just went to law school because I didn't know what I wanted to do when I finished college. Maybe someday, I'll be ready to settle down. Right now I'm just too...too restless."

"Is that why you keep trying to kill yourself?" the

senior Vandervort asked. "Because you are too restless to settle down?"

"Pop, I'm not trying to kill myself," he said. "Though I admit, I do like to find exciting things to do."

"Like jumping from an airplane?"

Jason's mother looked at his father. "Jumping from an airplane? What would make you say something like that?"

"It's all over the island that Jason made a parachute leap from an airplane today," Jason's father explained. He looked at Jason. "They say you did it to win a one-dollar bet. Is it true?"

"It was for five dollars, not one."

"Five dollars? Well, then of course, that makes all the difference in the world," his father said sarcastically.

"Oh, my heavens!" Jason's mother gasped. She set her coffee cup down so hard that it rattled the saucer. "Jason, you didn't really jump out of an airplane?"

"Yes, ma'am. I did," Jason said.

"And would you mind telling me just why you would do such a thing?" his father asked.

"I don't know," Jason answered. He was quiet for a moment, then because he felt that perhaps he should try to explain it even though it couldn't be explained, he continued: "I really don't know why I did it, Pop. Someone dared me, that's all. And at the time, it seemed like the thing to do."

"Jason, you'll be the death of me if you keep this up," his mother said nervously.

"You can't play games forever, son," Mr. Vandervort added. "You are going to have to find some profession to get into."

"If I could find some exciting profession to pursue I would do it," Jason said.

"Try rum-running," Mr. Vandervort said dryly.

"That's about the only thing with enough excitement to suit you. I saw in the paper where there was a big shoot-out on the Sound last night. Some gangsters were trying to bring in a shipment of booze and the police intercepted them."

"That's an idea," Jason replied, laughing.

"Please," Jason's mother said. "Don't give him any ideas."

———

That night Jason parked almost a block away from where Leah Sherman lived, then slipped down the alley to the rear of her place. He climbed over the back fence, then crossed the carefully manicured lawn to the sculptured hedgerows of the formal garden. When he reached the back of the house itself, he glanced toward the French doors and saw Leah waiting for him. She smiled as she held the door open and beckoned him inside.

"I didn't know if you would come," she said.

"I said I would."

"In here," she whispered, opening the door to her bedroom for him. Jason slipped in, then Leah came in right behind him. Once inside, she put her arms around his neck, then kissed him deeply, pushing her pelvis against him and thrusting her tongue into his mouth. Her lips and mouth were as sweet as nectar.

"Well, hello," Jason said when after a deep, probing kiss of several seconds duration they finally parted.

"Tell me about it, Jason," she said.

"What? Tell you about what?" Jason asked, surprised by the unexpected question.

"The parachute leap," Leah said. "Tell me about it."

Jason began telling Leah the story, and the more he

talked, the more aroused she became until finally, unable to hold off any longer, she welcomed him to her bed.

———

About an hour later, Jason lay on the bed beside Leah listening to her deep, even breathing. He raised up on one elbow and looked down at her. The bed-sheet only covered her halfway, leaving her naked from the waist up. Her left arm was raised above her head and that had the effect of flattening the left breast so that rather than a mound of flesh there was only a smoothly rounded torso, topped by a hard, little nipple. The right breast, because of the position of her arm, was somewhat more pronounced. Leah was a beautiful girl and Jason felt enough interest returning that he decided to wake her. As he was about to reach for her, however, he heard someone walking down the hall. Reacting quickly, he rolled off the bed, then slipped under it, reaching out onto the floor and pulling his clothes with him, just as the door to Leah's bedroom opened. From his position under the bed, Jason could see bedroom-slippered feet walking across the floor.

"Why, for heaven's sake," a woman's voice said, gasping. "You are absolutely naked, Leah! Don't you know you could catch your death of cold sleeping like that? To say nothing of it being positively indecent. Thank heavens your father didn't come in here to see you like that. Get your nightgown back on."

"Okay, Mama," Leah replied sleepily.

"Where is it? Under the bed? I'll get it."

Desperately, Jason reached up on the other side of the bed from Leah's mother, and put the nightgown in Leah's hand. Leah was wide awake now and able to react. She grabbed the little piece of silk.

"No, Mama, it's right here," she said, holding the nightgown up.

"Well, put it on for crying out loud. It's a good thing I came in here. You'd be sick in the morning and we wouldn't have the slightest idea why."

Leah began slipping on the nightgown. "Did you want something, Mama?" she asked.

"I just wanted to check on you, that's all. To make sure you were covered up and sleeping okay."

"I'm fine, Mama."

"Dear," her mother started, then she stopped. It was obvious she wanted to say something but couldn't find the way to approach it.

"What is it, Mama?"

"You know that boy you used to see? Jason Vandervort?"

"Yes."

"Your father heard today that he jumped from an airplane. I mean he was actually crazy enough to jump from an airplane."

"He did, Mama. I was there."

"In the airplane?" her mother gasped.

Leah laughed. "No, Mama, on the ground. I picked him up in my car and took him back to the country club."

"Yes, your father heard that too," Mrs. Sherman said. She sighed. "The fact that you admit it at least tells me you are honest. Are you still seeing him?"

"Sometimes," Leah admitted.

"You know, your father doesn't approve of him."

"Yes, ma'am, I know," Leah said.

Mrs. Sherman leaned forward and brushed Leah's hair back from her forehead. "I may as well be as honest with you as you were with me," she said. "I didn't come in here just to see if you were covered up. Your father had the idea that...well, that you might try and slip out of the house to meet him tonight. You aren't going to go somewhere to see him, are you, baby?"

"No, Mama, I'm not going anywhere."

"You promise you won't?"

"I promise, Mama. I will not leave this bedroom tonight."

Mrs. Sherman smiled, then leaned forward to kiss her daughter.

"That's a good girl," she said. She got up from the bed and, once again, Jason found himself staring at her slippers. "You sleep tight now."

"Yes, Mama," Leah replied. "Good night."

"Good night."

Jason watched the bedroom slippers cross the room, then go through the door. After that, he slipped out from under the bed.

"That was close," Leah whispered when Jason sat on the bed beside her.

"I don't know why you put the nightgown back on," Jason said. He put his arms around her and kissed her. "You're just going to have to take it off again."

"Jason, you aren't really going to do it again, are you? My parents are just down the hall. Mama was just in here, for goodness sake."

"I know," Jason said. "That just makes it all the more exciting, don't you think?" He removed her nightgown and got into bed with her again. At that moment, Leah's mother called out to her from down the hall.

"Leah, you are covered now, aren't you?"

"Yes, Mama," Leah answered. "I'm covered."

NEW YORK

Mike took the pins from his mouth and used them to fasten the headline to the wall. This one read:

FEDERAL AGENTS STOP RUM-RUNNING BOAT IN SHOOT-OUT

"Mikey?" Bill said.

"Yeah," Mike answered. He had already pinned the headline up and now he was standing there, admiring his handiwork.

"I've got someone I want you to meet."

Mike turned around. Standing beside Bill was a slender, dark-haired, dark-eyed young man with a prominent nose. He was wearing a policeman's uniform.

"This is Joe Provenzano," Bill said.

"Provenzano?" Mike asked, reaching for Joe's hand.

"Yes," Joe replied, shaking his hand.

Mike frowned. "The Sangremanos have a man working for them..."

"Their consigliore, yes," Joe said. "His name is Al Provenzano. Al Provenzano is my father's brother."

"I see," Mike said. He sat down and leaned back in his chair, with his hands interlocked behind his head. "Look, Provenzano, I don't know what Johnny Sangremano has sent you here to say to me, but you can tell him that I'm not interested."

"Johnny Sangremano? What makes you think I'm bringing a message from him?"

"Aren't you?"

"No, sir."

"Then I don't understand. Why are you here?"

"I'm here because I want to join you."

"Sorry," Mike said. "I'm not using cops anymore."

"I know," Joe said.

"He wants to quit the police force, Mikey," Bill said. "He wants to leave the force and join the Bureau."

"Is that a fact?" Mike asked.

"Yes, sir."

Mike sighed, then pointed to Bill. "Before you rush

into anything, I think you should know that you are looking at the entire force, right now. Other than this office, we get no support from the city. It isn't that they haven't offered it, it's that I don't want to use it. I can't afford to have anyone around me unless I can trust them implicitly."

"And you don't think you can trust a cop, is that it?" Joe asked. "I understand. All of us have to pay for the few."

"He's a clean cop, Mike, if that means anything," Bill said.

"Yeah, that means something. That means a lot. I have nothing but respect and admiration for the cops who keep themselves clean."

"That's good," Joe said. "Because there are a lot more of us who do than there are who don't. It's no great accomplishment for a cop to be clean...that's the way it's supposed to be."

"You have a point," Mike said.

"But it isn't because I'm a cop, is it? That's not what you're talking about."

"No," Mike admitted.

"It's because I'm Italian."

"No, not that either," Mike said. "That is, not exactly. It's because you are a Provenzano, and your uncle works for the Sangremanos."

"My uncle works for the Sangremanos, I don't," Joe said.

"I had a friend who once told me that blood was thicker than water and Italian blood was the thickest of all," Mike said.

Joe sighed. "Look, if you don't think you can trust me, I don't even want to join you. I wouldn't want to have everything I ever did questioned. Thank you, anyway." He started toward the door.

"Joe, wait," Mike called after him. Joe stopped, but he didn't turn around.

"What do you know about the Mafia?" Mike asked.

Joe stiffened noticeably and Mike saw it. "Nothing," he said.

"Come on, Joe. You are Sicilian, aren't you? Are you trying to tell me that a Sicilian like you has never even heard the term 'Mafia'?"

"I don't know what you are talking about."

"Sorry. I can't use you," Mike said, dismissing him out of hand.

Joe turned toward Mike with a pained expression on his face. "Look, can we go somewhere?" he asked. "There is a saying among my people. The walls have ears."

"Your people, my ass." Mike laughed. "The Irish have been saying that for years." He got up and put on his jacket. "Okay, let's take a walk. Bill, you man the fort."

Mike and Joe walked down the polished concrete steps, then out onto the street. A sidewalk vendor was selling hot dogs and they each bought one and began walking as they ate.

"I have to admit, you really caught me off guard with that question," Joe said. "I guess I was just surprised to hear that an Irishman knew about the Mafia. What do you know about it?"

"Other than the fact that it exists, I know nothing," Mike admitted. "I was told that even knowing that much was dangerous."

Joe chuckled. "You were told right. Agent Kelly, you said you weren't sure whether or not you could trust me. Well, you just have, with your very life. If I told the right people I heard that word on your lips, you would be killed, and I would get a reward. A very large reward."

"It's that secretive?"

"It's that secretive," Joe said. "I don't think you

understand the danger you are in. Please, be very, very careful about who you say that word to."

"Well, then I guess I have put myself in the position of having to trust you after all, haven't I?" Mike asked.

"I guess you have." Joe smiled, as if he knew a secret. "But of course, this isn't the first time you have trusted me."

"It isn't?"

Joe used his napkin to wipe a bit of mustard from his lips before he spoke again.

"I was the friend who told you of the whiskey shipment," he said.

"How do I know that?"

"As I recall, there was some question as to whether I might be leading you away from another shipment somewhere else."

"Yeah, that's right," Mike said. He smiled broadly. "Sonofabitch! It was you."

"Yes."

"But I don't understand. Why did you tell me? You're a policeman. Why didn't you just get a few of your own people and make the raid yourself?"

"It didn't look to me like you had been having a whole lot of luck with your operation," Joe said. "I figured you needed a little help."

"Boy, did you ever figure that right," Mike said. "When I called Washington to tell them about it, they confessed that they were seriously considering handing me over to Agent Hoover to help him search for Communists. Do you know what they are?"

"I'm not sure," Joe said.

"I'm not either," Mike replied, laughing. "But, whatever they are, I don't think I want to fight them. I'm very grateful for your tip. It did me good to put Fusco in jail."

"By the way, I'm not telling you any secrets am I

when I tell you that Fusco has already made bail?" Joe asked.

They were, at that moment, approaching a wide concrete fence. The fence was about waist high and Mike, with a sigh, put his hands out and leaned forward on it.

"I didn't know that," he said. "I should have, I guess. The bastard told me he would be back on the street before I could spit."

"That's only half of the bad news," Joe said. "The other half is the liquor. It will be back on the streets as quickly as Fusco."

"The hell it will. That liquor belongs to the federal government," Mike said. "I control what happens to it."

"You have your own warehouse, do you?"

"No."

"Where are you keeping it?"

"Warehouse 101B."

"Uh-huh. Well, I have to tell you, Agent Kelly, no matter who it belongs to, whiskey doesn't even slow down when it goes through Warehouse 101B," Joe said. "Especially the good bonded stuff. They'll be drinking that in the Babylon Gardens by six o'clock tonight, and it won't make any difference whether it was confiscated by the federal government, the state, the county, or the city."

"You sure it's going to the Babylon Gardens?" Mike asked.

"I'm sure."

Suddenly Mike laughed. "I have an idea," he said.

"Am I a part of it?"

"Do you want to be?"

"You're damned right I do."

"Then you are a part of it," Mike said.

From the Los Angeles Times

On the surface, the movie Glory Dust has absolutely nothing to recommend it. It is full of bombast and swirl, with confusing battle and crowd scenes that give the viewer no hint of what is going on or that a story is being told.

There is, however, a redeeming feature to the movie. One should go see it so that one can, in the future, say, "I saw Katie Starr in her very first role."

Who is Katie Starr, you ask?

Katie Starr has only one scene in Glory Dust, but that scene is the salvation of the entire picture. How can one describe the innocent sensuousness of Katie Starr? It is, perhaps, a little like discovering a beautiful young wood nymph at her bath. You feel guilty at invading her privacy...but you enjoy the view.

Every producer in Hollywood would like the opportunity to feature Miss Starr in one of their own films, but the word is that the wily Mr. Solinger has her sewed up tighter than a drum with an exclusive contract to her services.

CHAPTER 8

"Listen," Roger was telling Jason. "This isn't one of your run-of-the-mill, low-down, no-class speaks. I mean Babylon Gardens is really a swank place, with velvet carpets, big chandeliers, and mirrors all over the place."

"It's the cat's pajamas," Joyce, Roger's girlfriend, added.

"And they've got real shows, with big bands, chorus girls, and comedians," Roger continued. "We saw a comedian the other night who was really great. What was his name, Joyce?"

"His name is Jimmy Durante," Joyce said. She laughed. "I don't know if he was really that funny, or just that ugly. He has a nose as big as a toucan."

"Oh, and the booze is good too," Roger added. "It's not that rotgut bathtub gin. I mean there's no chance you're going to go blind or something from drinking it. This is the real stuff. They say all the whiskey comes from Canada. They bring it in on boats or something."

"But it is illegal," Jason said.

"Well, of course it is illegal, Ducks," Joyce quipped. "That's all part of the fun."

"Besides," Roger said. "I thought you were a person who liked to take risks."

"There's a difference between taking risks and breaking the law."

"Oh, come now, Jason," Roger said. "You can't be serious! Everybody knows that Prohibition is a dumb law."

"It may be dumb, but it is the law and when we break it, we put ourselves in league with the criminals who supply it. And if the place gets raided, we'll be going down to the jail, right along with the rest of the lawbreakers."

"That's a lot of banana oil," Roger said. "Maybe at the real low-down speakeasies you might have to worry about things like that. But not at the Babylon Gardens. Trust me, you'll see only the finest people there. I mean the cream of society. And politicians too, like state representatives and senators, aldermen, commissioners, even judges. Now, do you really think a place like that is going to be raided by the cops?"

"What about the feds?"

"The feds don't care about the decent people who go to the nice nightclubs," Roger insisted. "They're only interested in moonshiners and the rough places. Anyway, I know some people who were picked up in a raid one time, and nothing happened to them. They were just sent home, that's all. It's only the gangsters who get into trouble."

"If you don't go, you're going to miss a great time," Joyce said.

"Oh, I didn't say I wasn't going to go," Jason said. He smiled. "I was just telling you all the reasons we shouldn't."

"Then you will go?"

"Yes."

"Good!"

"But I must tell you, I do rather resent those places," Jason added. "Nightclubs are where the underworld and the so-called top level of society come together. We stand around and gawk at the gangsters, titillated by the promise of mystery and excitement, while they play to our fantasies, all the time figuring out ways to fleece us. I'm quite sure that after we are gone, they make jokes about us. I don't enjoy being anyone's stooge."

"Aw, it's not like that," Roger insisted. "It's fun. You can take Leah. She's a real hip girl, she'll go along with it, I'm sure."

"Leah isn't the problem," Joe said. "It's her father, remember?"

"Don't you worry about that. I'll call Leah and ask her for you," Joyce offered. She laughed. "But you are right. If her old man knew you were her sheik, he'd have kittens."

———

The Babylon Gardens was housed in an old but elegantly refurbished mansion. From outside the place, there was no way of telling that it was a nightclub. It looked just like a fine old home, and Leah made that observation as Roger's car glided to a stop at the curb.

"It is," Roger said. "It once belonged to the Touhey family. I can remember visiting here as a child."

The doorman walked down the wide, polished concrete steps to greet them as they stepped out of the car.

"May I help you, sir?" he inquired of Roger. His voice was resonant with the affectation of one who was trying to put on airs.

"Joe sent me," Roger replied, handing the man a ten-dollar bill.

"Very good, sir, I'm sure you will have a wonderful time," the doorman replied, taking the bill. He pulled a bright orange ticket from a book and handed it to Roger. "Here is the claim ticket for your automobile. Let me assure you that it will be quite safe. I'll park it in our private parking lot and you can reclaim it when you leave."

"Thanks," Roger said.

"Who is Joe?" Leah asked as the doorman drove away with the car.

Roger laughed. "The trick is, you can't get into a speak unless someone sends you. I don't know anyone to recommend me, but I'm sure there must be someone named Joe."

At the top of the steps, Roger rapped on the door and when a little slot was opened, he held a ten-dollar bill up, again repeating the formula that he was "sent by Joe."

Just inside the door of the club, there was a raised landing that looked out over the main floor. To the left of the landing, a window opened into the hat-check room. A heavily madeup young woman was leaning on the counter, filing her nails and chewing gum vigorously. She took Jason's and Roger's hats and handed each of them a blue claim check to go with the orange they had already received for the car.

On the main floor itself, there were dozens of tables, occupied by elegantly dressed couples and groups who were not only eating, but drinking liquor in an open, almost challenging defiance of the law. The patrons of the club were laughing and talking at such a level that the long-legged young woman who was sitting on the piano, belting out a blues tune, could scarcely be heard. Girls, in almost indecently short skirts, moved around the room selling cigars and cigarettes from a tray they carried, held in place by a strap that was looped around their neck. In addition to the cigarette girls, waiters darted about, carrying delicately balanced trays of glasses. There were also several "table-hoppers," young men and women who, not content to stay at their own table, were darting madly around to see who and what was going on at all the other tables in the room.

"Oh, look, up there at the bar," Joyce said. "Those two men in dinner jackets. Those dark eyes and that dark, slicked-down hair. Don't they look positively wicked?"

"Those are the Vaglichio brothers," Roger told her, as if he were privy to some inside information. "I suppose you know who they are."

"I've heard of them," Joyce said. "They're...they're gangsters, aren't they?"

"Yes," Jason said. "You might say that."

Roger smiled. "You can also say that they were once our neighbors. They used to own a house out on Long Island but it met with an accident not too long ago."

"Yeah, some accident," Jason said. "The house was bombed from an airplane."

"Oh, I read about that," Leah said. She squinted at the two men who were standing at the bar, trying to get a closer look at them without having to put on the glasses she considered unattractive. "You mean those two men were in that house?"

Roger laughed. "No, my dear," he answered. "If they had been, they wouldn't be here now. Their father, Sam Vaglichio, was in the house."

"What happened to him?"

"He was killed."

"Why, that's awful. Who dropped the bomb? The army?"

"No," Jason said. "The bomb was dropped by

enemies of the Vaglichio brothers. It was a rival group of gangsters. There are gang wars going on all the time. That's almost a part of this business."

"You mean it was crooks who dropped the bomb?" Leah asked in disbelief.

"Yes."

"My. I didn't know they did such things. I mean, I thought only the army had such things as bombs and airplanes and the like."

"These fellows can get very inventive when it comes to violence," Jason said.

"I hope they don't decide to do something 'inventive' while we're in here," Leah said.

"Ooh, me too," Joyce said with a little shiver. "But isn't it exciting to think that they might?"

The maitre d' seated them at a table and a waiter came to take their orders. As soon as they were seated, Leah took out a cigarette and put it into a long holder.

"Isn't this something, though?" she asked as she placed the cigarette holder between her scarlet lips. "I mean, to think of us in a place like this. It's—it's positively scandalous!"

Jason reached for the book of matches in the middle of the table, intending to light Leah's cigarette, but before he could, a strange man leaned over the table to light it for her.

"Thank you," Jason said.

The man looked at Jason with dark eyes that flashed annoyance.

"Who are you, some wise guy, or somethin'?" he asked. "What the hell are you thankin' me for? I wasn't doin' it for you, I was doin' it for the lady."

"Yes," Jason said. "And I appreciate it."

"Look, you, ain't you listenin' to what I said? I wasn't doin' it for you," the man said a little more belligerently.

"And I appreciate it," Leah said quickly.

"My name's Vic," the man said. "Vic Tampino. Ask anyone here, they all heard of me. Anyway, I'd like to ask you to dance."

"Thank you, no," Leah said. "My friends and I have just arrived, and I think I would like to just sit here for a while."

"Whatsamatter?" Tampino asked. "You one of them society dames thinks you're too good to dance with me?"

"No, it isn't that."

"Then dance with me."

"I'd rather not."

"I ain't goin' to leave this table 'til you do," Tampino said.

"Excuse me, Mr. Tampino," Jason interrupted. "The lady said she didn't want to dance, so why don't you just go away and leave us alone?"

"Yeah?" Tampino replied, glaring at Jason. "Well, you want to make me go away?"

Jason stood up. "I would rather it not come to that," he said.

"Yeah, that's what I thought, you society punk," Tampino said. "All you society types, you're all alike. There ain't none of you worth spit on a hot plate."

"If you are so against us, why do you solicit our business?"

Tampino grinned wickedly. "We like your money all right. We just don't like you," he said.

"Tampino!" a stern voice called. The man who called Tampino was one of the two Vaglichio brothers who had been standing at the bar when they came in. When he saw Tampino harassing the customers, he moved from the bar and was now a few feet away from the table.

"Mr. Vaglichio, I was just about to…"

"You were just about to go away and leave these people alone," Vaglichio said.

For a moment a purple vein throbbed in Tampino's temple, then suddenly he broke into a broad grin.

"Yeah," he said. "Yeah, I was just teasin' 'em a little. You know, havin' a little fun?" He looked at Jason. "Listen, society boy, I hope you wasn't scared or nothin' like that," he taunted. "I didn't mean nothin' by it."

"That's all right," Jason said. "I wasn't scared, or nothin' like that," he answered.

Tampino seemed to realize then that Jason was mocking him, and his eyes flickered in sudden anger. However, he got control of himself so quickly that only Jason read his reaction.

"You folks have a nice time, now," Tampino grumbled insincerely as he walked away.

The man who had sent Tampino away now apologized to the little party. "My name is Luca Vaglichio. I want to apologize for my employee. I hope you weren't too disturbed by it."

"He didn't bother us any," Roger said quickly. "He was just having some fun with us, that's all."

"Well, if you are sure," Luca said. "I wouldn't want any of our good customers disturbed."

"In that case, tell your friend that we can do without his fun the next time," Jason added.

Luca smiled. "You can be sure that I will," he said. "Waiter," he called to one of the waiters moving through the room.

"Yes, Mr. Vaglichio?"

"The first round for these good folks here," he said, pointing to the table, "is on me."

"Very good, sir," the waiter replied.

"Thank you, Mr. Vaglichio," Roger said.

Luca smiled. "Think nothin' of it," he said. "We want you folks to have a good time."

"Whew," Roger said a moment later as Vaglichio walked away from the table. "That was close. You probably didn't notice, but our friend Tampino was..."

"Carrying a gun," Jason said. "A forty-five-caliber automatic. It was in a shoulder holster under his left arm."

"My God! You mean you knew that, and you still challenged him?"

"Well, I seriously doubt that he would have attempted to use it here."

"Nevertheless, I'm glad he's gone," Roger said. "Listen, be careful, will you? Don't get us involved in anything."

"I'll be more careful," Jason promised with a little laugh.

Outside the club, about two blocks away, on another street, Mike, Bill, and Joe were sitting in a car, parked along the curb with its lights off. A Ford Roadster pulled up behind them and a man got out. He walked toward them, carrying a camera. When he reached Mike's car, he leaned down and looked in through the window.

"Mr. Kelly?" he asked tentatively. "I'm Tim Peters. You called the newspaper and asked me to meet you here?"

"Get in the back seat, Mr. Peters," Mike replied, starting the engine.

"Yes, sir," Peters said, getting into the seat as directed. Then, almost as an afterthought, he asked, "Where are we going?"

"Do you have film for that camera?" Mike asked, without answering the question.

"Yes, sir, I've got it. I don't know what it's for, but I've got it."

"You are the only member of the press that I called," Mike said. "You get the exclusive right to take pictures of us in action."

"Thanks," Peters said, checking his camera. "But I'm curious. Why? I mean, why was I the only one you called?"

"Let me answer that by asking you a question, Peters. On our first raid, when we hit that laundry, you were the only one who didn't run a picture of the pile of dirty clothes and make cute comments about our 'cleaning up crime.' Why didn't you?"

"Because I knew it really was a bookie joint," Peters answered. "And if I couldn't print a picture confirming what I knew to be true, then I had no intention of running one that would give the wrong impression. That would just be playing into the gangsters' hands."

"Good, I'm glad you feel that way. You stay close to us tonight and I promise you, you'll get something worth running in tomorrow's newspaper." Mike started the car and pulled away from the curb. After a drive of only a couple of blocks, he stopped, right across the street from the Babylon Gardens, then pointed to it. "You know this place?"

"Sure. It's the Babylon Gardens."

"We are going to hit it tonight," Mike said.

"Wow!" Peters said. "This is an uptown joint. All the bigwigs go here. I'm surprised you even got a judge to give you a warrant."

"I didn't," Mike said.

"What? You mean you don't have a warrant?"

"Not exactly," Mike said. "But I do have a letter of authority."

"What is that, a letter of authority? I've never heard of such a thing."

Mike chuckled. "I haven't either, really. I guess we'll

find out tonight whether or not it's going to work. It authorizes me to protect government property."

"What kind of property?"

"Whiskey," Mike said.

"I see," Peters answered in a voice that made it very plain that he didn't see. "So, tell me, are we going to wait right here for the others?"

"What others?" Mike replied. "There's just us."

"What? Just the three of you? That's insane! You don't mean to tell me you're going in all by yourselves?"

"Why not?"

"Why not? Look, Mr. Kelly..." Peters started, but Bill interrupted him.

"We like to be addressed as 'agent,' not 'mister,'" Bill said firmly.

"Agent, mister, whatever you want to be called, you're crazy, all three of you. Do you know that?" Peters asked. "I told you, all the bigwigs come here. If some of them are in there when you raid it tonight, they are going to be plenty upset. You'll be hearing from the folks downtown over this. And if you don't have a bona fide warrant, you are really going to catch hell. Besides which, do you know who owns Babylon Gardens?"

"The Vaglichios own it," Mike said easily.

"Yes, the Vaglichios," Peters said, not wanting to let him get away with it that easily. "And in case you don't know it, the Vaglichios aren't the kind of people who will go down and file a complaint about you if they don't like what you are doing. And they aren't the kind of people who sue either. No, sir. They take care of things themselves. And if you are serious about this raid, they'll take care of you."

"You keep saying 'you.' Does that mean you don't want any pictures?" Mike asked.

Peters took a deep breath, then reached for his

camera. "No," he said. "If you three men are crazy enough to go in there, then I suppose I'm crazy enough to go in there with you. But after this I think all four of us should visit a doctor to have our heads examined."

"Let's go," Mike said, opening the door. All four men got out of the car. Bill and Joe were carrying shotguns, Mike was carrying a baseball bat.

"Hold it! Hold it!" Peters said, pointing to the bat. "What's that?"

"What's it look like?"

"It looks like a bat. Are you going in there with nothing but a baseball bat?"

"Bill and Joe are armed," Mike said. He smiled. "And, of course, we've got you."

"Me? What the hell do you expect from me? I'm a newspaperman, not a cop."

"Never underestimate the power of the press, Mr. Peters," Mike quipped.

As the four men crossed the street, the doorman came down the steps to meet them. When he saw that two of them were carrying guns, he stopped, then started back toward the door.

"Hold it right there!" Joe shouted.

The doorman stopped and put his arms in the air, trembling uncontrollably. "My God, mister, please, don't kill me," the doorman said. "I just work here, I'm not mixed up in the gang wars."

"Take it easy," Bill said. "We're not going to shoot you, we're federal agents."

"Open the door," Mike ordered.

Still shaking, though at least mollified by the fact that he wasn't about to be shot, the doorman walked up to the top of the steps and opened the door.

The guard who was supposed to be watching inside was standing with his back to the door while he watched the show instead. A young woman dressed in a red-sequined dress was singing a song. The sequins sparkled in the long spotlight beam that was cutting through the curling cigarette smoke of the room. All eyes were on the performance so that very few people actually saw Mike and the others come in.

Mike stepped down onto the top step, pulled out his badge folder, and held it up. It caught a flash of light from the same spotlight beam that was pointed toward the singer.

"Federal agents!" Mike called out. "This is a raid! Everybody stay right where you are and no one will be hurt!"

"What the hell?" the guard shouted, surprised that they had gotten in without him seeing them. He started toward Mike as if he were going to throw Mike out, but Mike, using the ball bat like an oversized cue stick, sent a thrusting jab into the guard's stomach, stopping him in his tracks. The blow took away the guard's breath and he fell to the floor, temporarily paralyzed.

There were several screams and shouts of surprise from the club patrons.

"It's all right, folks, it's all right," Luca Vaglichio called out, holding up his hands to quiet them. "Just a little inconvenience, is all. There's nothin' to worry about, somebody didn't get the word. I'll take care of it."

Luca came quickly across the club floor, stepped over the prostrate bouncer who was gasping for breath, then stepped up onto the bottom of the four steps that led from the club floor, up to the entry landing.

"Okay, just what the hell do you guys want?" he asked. "What are you doin' here? You got nothin' better to do than to come out here, harassin' decent people like this? They don't want nothin' but to have a nice evening's entertainment."

"Vaglichio, you wouldn't know a decent person if you saw one," Bill said.

"Gentlemen, maybe I can be of some assistance," a dignified-looking, gray-haired man said as he came up to join the group. He smiled at Mike. "I'm Judge Carter. And you are?"

"This doesn't concern you, Judge Carter," Mike said.

"But of course it does. It happens to be in my circuit and everything that happens in my circuit is of interest to me."

"I have reason to believe that Mr. Vaglichio has something that belongs to me," Mike said. "Or, more properly, to the federal government. I'm here to look into it."

"And what might that be?"

"I confiscated a shipment of whiskey the other night," Mike said. "I think it might be here."

"And you have a warrant?"

"Show him what we have," Mike said.

Bill took a piece of paper from his jacket pocket and gave it to the judge. Judge Carter looked at it for a moment, then smiled and handed it back.

"Why, this isn't a warrant," he said. "This is nothing but a federal letter charging you with the responsibility of safeguarding the whiskey you confiscated the other night. It certainly doesn't give you the right to come into this building on any kind of a raid."

"If you'll notice that bottom paragraph, Judge, it authorizes me to remove the whiskey from any premises, if I think those premises are not conducive to the safeguarding of the whiskey."

"Yes, I see that."

"That's my authority to come in here."

"You must be insane. That's no authority at all."

"Sure it is, Judge. I happen to know that the whiskey that I confiscated the other night is now in this building.

That is the United States Government's whiskey, and I do not believe these premises are conducive to its safeguarding. In fact, if it stays in here, I'm sure someone is going to drink it." Mike smiled. "You might even drink it, Judge. Therefore, I've decided to remove it from these premises."

"I'm sorry, but I'm afraid that's much too narrow a basis for me to allow you in here. Even if it did constitute authority, you would have to be able to positively identify it in order to justify your claim."

"Oh, don't worry about that. I'll know it when I see it," Mike said, dismissing the judge's argument. "Let's look over there," Mike said, pointing to the bar.

"See here, now!" Judge Carter sputtered. "I will not allow this!"

"You can't stop it, Judge," Mike said. "Only a federal judge can tell me my interpretation of this letter of authority is incorrect."

By now, everyone in the club was watching the unfolding drama with curious eyes. This would be the subject of a hundred conversations tomorrow.

"I don't know who you think you are, mister," Luca said angrily. "But if you so much as break one glass, I'll have your ass!"

"You mean like this?" Mike replied. Mike walked over to the bar and swept off a pile of glasses with his baseball bat. They shattered into hundreds of pieces when they hit the floor.

"Hey, go easy with that!" Luca warned. "That stuff costs money." He tried to step in front of Mike, but Mike swept him aside. Angrily, Luca's hand darted toward the inside of his jacket, but Joe cocked his shotgun, the sound reverberating throughout the room. He aimed the gun at Luca.

"When your hand comes out from behind that jacket

lapel, it had better be empty," Joe said in a cold, quiet voice.

"You," Luca said. "I know you." He squinted his eyes as if studying him. "Yeah, I know you. You're an Italian boy, aren't you? What are you doing, mixed up with a bum like this?"

"I'm doing my job," Joe said.

"Your job! Your job! Is it your job to come into a man's place and break it up like this?"

"Bill," Mike said, pointing to several bottles of whiskey. "Doesn't this look like our whiskey?"

"It sure looks like it," Bill said.

"I caution you, Agent Kelly," Judge Carter said. "Unless you have some way of proving it..."

"Oh, but I do have a way," Mike said. He picked up one of the bottles and smashed it across the edge of the bar. With the top broken off, he then held it under his nose and sniffed. He smiled, and held it out to Bill. "Tell me, Bill, doesn't that smell like the whiskey we confiscated?" he asked.

Bill smiled. "Smells like it to me," he said.

"That's what I thought." Mike suddenly took a wide swing with his bat, just as if he were hitting a ball over the centerfield fence. He smashed through half a dozen bottles, sending a shower of whiskey and pieces of glass everywhere. "Get your pictures, Mr. Peters," he shouted back over his shoulder.

As Mike smashed the bottles, Peters began taking the pictures. After the initial shock, most of the club patrons stood around in stunned silence.

Vic Tampino wasn't standing around. Instead, he began creeping up, slowly, behind the bar. Jason caught a glimpse of him out of the corner of his eye, seeing too that Tampino had pulled the forty-five-caliber automatic from the shoulder holster under his left arm. Not only that, he was about to use it, for he had raised up just far enough to rest the pistol on the bar as he took aim at Mike.

"Look out mister!" Jason shouted, while at the same time diving over the bar at Tampino. He hit Tampino just before the gunman could pull the trigger and as the pistol clattered out of Tampino's hand, he and Jason wound up on the floor.

Mike looked around and saw what happened, realizing at once that the young man struggling with the gangster had just saved his life.

"Bill, or Joe, one of you had better get over there," Mike said. "I don't think that young man knows what he's leaped into."

After having knocked the gun away from the gunman, Jason hopped up lightly on his feet. Tampino came up too, only he didn't come up empty-handed. He had a knife in his hand and an evil smile on his face.

"I shoulda taken care of you when you first come in here like I wanted to," Tampino growled. He was holding his knife low and flat, letting it rest easily in the palm of his hand. He weaved the point of the blade around slightly so that it looked like the head of a serpent, watching its prey. Adding to that illusion, Tampino's tongue flicked out across his lips. "I'm going to carve up your ass like a can of kraut," he said. Suddenly he lunged toward Jason, thrusting the knife forward wickedly.

Jason stepped nimbly away as the gangster's hand lunged forward. He sent a chopping blow down on the would-be gunman's wrist and the knife, like the gun before, clattered to the floor.

"You sonofabitch!" Tampino shouted. He reached back to the bar and grabbed one of the smashed bottles, then held it out so that its raw, jagged edges were toward

Jason. "I'll cut your face up so your own mama won't recognize you!"

Again Tampino lunged toward Jason, and again Jason stepped nimbly out of his way. This time, however, instead of sending a chopping blow toward the wrist, Jason reached out to grab it. He pulled Tampino toward him while, at the same time, he fell on his back and put his feet up, catching Tampino in the belly. With a mighty pull, helped along by a shove from his feet, he sent the gangster flying across the room. Tampino fell heavily, but he struggled back to his feet and took a swing at Jason. By now, however, he was so groggy that his swing caught nothing but thin air. Jason returned the punch with more authority and a great deal more accuracy. Tampino went down again, this time to stay.

The crowd who had gathered around to watch the fight now cheered Jason loudly.

"Thanks, Mr..." Mike started to say, pausing in midsentence to get his name.

"Vandervort," Jason said. "Jason Vandervort."

"I appreciate your help, Mr. Vandervort," Mike said, just before he turned to the work of smashing every bottle of whiskey he could find.

ONE HOUR LATER

"Goddamnit!" Luca swore, smashing his fist down on the top of the desk in the office at the rear of the Babylon Gardens. "I'm getting a little tired of those sonofabitchin' feds causin' us trouble all the time. What good is it having half the goddamn police force on the payroll if you're going to get raided every time you turn around?"

"They aren't on the police force," Trapnell explained. "They are federal agents of the Bureau of Investigation."

"I don't give a shit if they belong to the United States

Marine Corps," Luca shouted. "I want them out of my hair!"

"One of them was a policeman," Mario pointed out. "Joe Provenzano isn't a federal agent."

"No, he isn't," Trapnell said. He smiled. "But he is the nephew of Al Provenzano. Maybe that's where you should look."

"What are you saying?" Mario asked. "You saying that Al Provenzano set this deal up?"

"He does work for Vinnie Sangremano," Trapnell said. "You think the Sangremanos didn't like what happened here tonight?"

"He's right, Mario," Luca said. "The Sangremanos are behind this, just as sure as a gun is iron. And sooner or later, we're going to have to deal with it."

"You take care of them and you won't have any problems with the police," Trapnell said, happy now to be off the hook.

"I'll take care of the Sangremanos," Luca said. He pointed his finger at Trapnell. "You take care of the federal agents who have been breathin' down my neck. What's the head man's name?"

"Kelly," Trapnell said. He chuckled. "I already took care of his old man. I may as well finish the job."

———

"G-MEN RAID BABYLON GARDENS," the newspaper headline blared. Mike cut it out and put it on the wall with the others.

"So, they're calling us 'G-men' now, are they?" Joe asked. Mike turned to see the young policeman standing just inside the door. He was surprised to see that Joe wasn't in uniform.

"Us?" Mike asked.

"Us," Joe answered. "That is, if you'll have me. I just resigned from the police force and I'm looking for a job."

Mike reached for the middle drawer of his desk and took out one of the two remaining badges. He held it up, but he didn't give it to Joe. Instead, he said, "Shall we take another walk?"

"All right," Joe agreed.

The two men left the building. The police, of course, knew about the raid Mike had made and though some were embarrassed by it, many were pleased and had been sincere in their congratulations. Some of these officers passed them as they left and they smiled and spoke to them.

"They don't seem too upset by what we did the other night," Joe pointed out.

"No, they're some of the good guys," Mike agreed. He chuckled. "I've run into a few of the other kind though."

"Yeah, I have too," Joe agreed.

"Were they making it rough on you for the part you played in the raid? Is that why you quit?"

"What's rough?" Joe asked. "Don't forget, I was an Italian police officer. I'm not sure you fully appreciate what that means. When I was around the other cops, they never quite trusted me because I'm Italian, and when I was around my own people, they didn't trust me because I was a cop."

"I trust you," Mike said.

"That's good to know. I wouldn't want to work for you if you didn't."

"I trust you enough to tell you what my grand design is," Mike said.

"Your grand design?" Joe asked. He chuckled. "And what would that be?"

"I'm going after the Mafia, Joe," Mike said.

Joe was silent for a long moment.

"Did you hear me?"

"Yeah," Joe replied. "I heard you."

"Are you going to have a problem with that?"

"What do you mean, problem?"

"I mean with loyalties?"

Joe shook his head. "No, nothing like that. I don't belong to the Mafia. I don't sympathize with them either. But that doesn't mean there's no problem. There's a big problem."

"In what way?"

"You ever been to California, Agent Kelly?"

"I guess you'd better call me Mike." Mike said. "After all, we are going to be working together." Mike looked at Joe. "Aren't we?"

"Yes," Joe said.

"Good. And to answer your question, yes, I have been to California. Why?"

"Did you see any of those big trees while you were out there? Those giant redwoods?"

"Yes."

"How far do you think you would get if you tried to cut one of those giant redwood trees down with a pocketknife?"

"Are you saying that's what going after the Mafia is going to be like?"

"Yeah," Joe said. "That's what I'm saying."

"Uh-huh. Tell me, Joe, when you went out to California, how did you go?"

"By train."

"Did you go the southern route, or the northern route?"

Joe laughed. "What difference does it make?"

"I went the southern route," Mike explained. "By the Grand Canyon. You ever see the Grand Canyon?"

"I've seen pictures."

"Nothing like it in the world," Mike said. He looked at Joe. "They say that huge hole out there, more than a mile deep, was cut by the Colorado River."

"I see what you are getting at," Joe said. "But it took that river a long time to cut that hole."

"Yeah, it did. And the first drops of water that went through never saw what the canyon became. Well, we're those first drops of water, Joe. You, Bill, and me. It may take us a long time and the job we start today may be finished by someone else, perhaps a hundred years from now. But it has to start somewhere. "

"All right," Joe said solemnly. "If you are serious about this, count me in."

"We'll have to learn something about them," Mike said. "Will you teach us?"

Joe was silent for a long moment, then he pinched the bridge of his nose as if searching his soul. Finally, he nodded.

"I don't know anything about any of the specific operations. Things like that are kept in layers of secrets so that only those people who need to know, know. I can't even really tell you in great detail how it is organized. But I will tell everything that I do know."

"Good. Let's go back and get Bill."

When the two returned to the office, they saw the young man who had intervened in the raid at Babylon Gardens. Bill had been talking to him and he introduced him.

"You remember this guy, don't you, Mike?" Bill asked.

"Vandervort, wasn't it? Jason Vandervort?"

"Yes, sir," Jason said.

"Jason Vandervort. J. D. Vandervort. Wait a minute, you wouldn't be the J. D. Vandervort, would you?"

"Well, not the J. D. Vandervort," Jason answered.

"Your father?"

"Technically, he isn't either," Jason said. "He is J. D. Vandervort, Jr.," Jason said. "My grandfather was the original J. D., the one who founded the investments company and made the family fortune. I am J. D. the Third."

"I'll be damned," Mike said, his mouth falling open in surprise.

"I've heard of your father. He is a very wealthy man, isn't he?" Joe asked.

"Yes," Jason agreed frankly. He chuckled. "In fact, he is so rich that he likes to joke that when he writes a check the check doesn't bounce, but sometimes the bank will. I'm afraid there's more truth than humor there."

The others laughed, then Mike said, "I'm curious, Mr. Vandervort. What would bring someone like you down here to see us?"

"I'll bet I know," Bill said. "You don't want it known around that you were at that club the other night, do you? It might look bad for someone like you if all the society folks found out you were there. Well, don't worry, we weren't interested in any of the customers, just the guys who were selling the booze."

Jason laughed. "I know," he said. "I heard your explanation to that pompous ass, Judge Carter. You were looking for the government's whiskey. By the way, I got a big kick out of the way you found it. I thought that was funny the way you identified it by smell. But that's not why I'm here."

"Why are you here?"

"I want to join you," Jason said simply.

"You want to join us? What do you mean?" Mike asked.

"I mean, I want to be a federal agent for the Bureau of Investigation," Jason said. "I want a job just like the one you have."

Mike and the others laughed.

"What is it?" Jason asked. "What is so funny?"

"Mr. Vandervort, do you know how much this job pays?" Mike asked.

"Not very much, I suspect," Jason said.

"One hundred and twelve dollars per month," Mike said.

"The money isn't important," Jason said. "In fact, I don't care whether I get paid or not. I just want the job."

"I'm sorry," Mike said. "I can't use you."

"You didn't say that the other night," Jason said.

"You mean when you stopped Tampino from shooting me?" Mike asked.

"Something like that."

"I appreciate what you did, Mr. Vandervort," Mike said. "But that doesn't change my mind."

"May I ask why you are so against letting me come to work with you?"

"May I ask why somebody like you would even want the job?"

"I think the work would be interesting."

"You mean exciting, don't you?" Mike asked. "Like it was the other night?"

"I suppose you could say that."

Mike shook his head. "That's what I thought. Well, I'm sorry, Mr. Vandervort, but, like I said, I can't use you."

"I don't understand this," Jason said. "If someone came in here looking for a job because they needed the money, even though they weren't particularly interested in the work, would you hire them?"

"I don't know. I'd probably come closer to hiring them than I would you," Mike admitted.

"Why?"

"Because I know that, to them, the job would be

important. To you it would never be anything more than a hobby."

"No, it wouldn't be a hobby. But, even so, you shouldn't dismiss it out of hand. Have you no hobbies, Mr. Kelly?"

"No, I..." Mike started, then paused. "Well, I suppose I do," he corrected himself. "You might say flying is a hobby."

"Do you like it?"

"I love it."

"Do you love it to the degree that you can see how a man might be dedicated enough to a hobby to give it his all?" Jason asked.

"Maybe," Mike admitted. "If it isn't merely a way a rich man entertains himself."

"Don't hold it against me because I'm wealthy," Jason pleaded. "It was an accident of birth and it has nothing to do with the kind of person I am."

"What would your father think about you being a law-enforcement officer?" Joe asked.

Jason looked at his questioner. "Let me turn that around," he said. "I heard them question you the other night. They were wondering how a nice Italian boy like you wound up in such a job. What about your father, your peers? What do they think of you being a policeman? More importantly, does what they think have any bearing on what you do?"

"No," Joe said. "I'm my own man, I don't care what..." He paused, smiled, then looked at Mike. "Mike, he has a point," he said.

"It's not the same thing," Mike said.

"Why not?" Jason asked.

"Because," Mike started, then unable to come up with a real reason, he said it again, "because."

"Look, if you're worried about whether or not

someone like me can take orders, the answer is, yes, I can."

"That's part of it," Mike admitted.

"I wish I could make you see that I am quite sincere in my desire to join you," Jason said. "But if you won't have me, I won't belabor the point."

"Believe me, it's better this way," Mike said. "Somebody like you, from your background and all, I don't think you have any idea of what you would be getting into."

"If you say so," Jason said.

"By the way, that was quite a demonstration you put on the other night," Mike said. "I don't think I've ever seen anyone fight quite like that, sort of a combination of wrestling and boxing. In fact, I'm not even sure what you would call something like that."

Jason smiled. "You would call something like that jujitsu."

"You would call it what?"

Jason laughed. "Jujitsu," he said again. "It's an ancient Japanese form of self-defense, based upon the principle of forcing an opponent to use his weight and strength against himself."

"Jujitsu, you say? Where on earth did you ever learn something like that?" Mike asked.

"In Japan," Jason answered. "I spent a year there, living and studying under the great master Saito."

"You say you learned this...jujitsu?" Bill asked.

"Yes."

"Could you teach someone else how to fight that way?" Bill asked.

"It's not that easy," Jason said.

"What do you mean it's not that easy? Don't you think if you can learn it, we could?" Joe snapped.

Jason chuckled. "No, you misunderstand me. I didn't

mean that it would be hard for you to learn. The mechanics of it are quite easy actually. What I meant was, I can't take lightly the trust that was placed in me when I learned the art." When he saw that they didn't understand what he was talking about, he tried to explain.

"Listen, I told you I spent a year there. But there is more to it than that. I wasn't just a pupil, I was a noviotiate. I lived on the grounds of an ancient monastery and I followed a very strict regimen. My room, if you can call it that, was six feet six inches long and three feet wide. I slept very little, and when I did sleep, I slept on a straw mat. I was awake by four o'clock every morning, tending to my chores. By dawn, I had already done as much work as most people do in a full day. I was there for one month before anyone said a word to me. It was three months before I could speak and six months before I had my first lesson. It didn't get any easier once the lessons started. Sometimes I would spend three weeks learning a maneuver that required a hand movement of no more than an inch. I ate rice twice a day and I drank only water."

"Why the hell would anyone do something like that?" Joe asked.

"What you have to realize is that jujitsu is much more than just a form of martial arts. It is a philosophy, a mental and emotional discipline that must be followed. Anyone who studies it, really studies it, must be prepared to adopt that philosophy. And I am bound, by oath, to teach it only to those who so agree."

"You mean for us to learn, we would have to do all that?" Joe asked. "I mean sleep on a straw mat and eat rice twice a day?"

"No," Jason answered. "You wouldn't have to do all that. But you must be prepared to live by the jujitsu code."

"Yeah, well, just how good is this jujitsu, anyway?" Joe asked. "I mean, I know Vic, the guy you roughed up the other night. He's a gunsel, but he's never been much of a fighter."

"Yes, he was quite easy," Jason agreed. He smiled. "I'm afraid he made me look somewhat better than I am."

"Yeah, that's the question I'm asking," Joe said. "How good are you?"

"Rather than speak of my own skills, I would rather tell you something about the art itself. My master..."

"Your what?" Mike asked.

Jason smiled. "My master. I know it sounds strange to you, but that is how you address someone who is sufficiently proficient to teach the art. Just as you are called 'agent.' Anyway, my master was a seventy-two-year-old man, and to look at him, you might think he would need help in crossing the street. However, I once saw him stop a charging two-thousand-pound bull with a single blow."

"Damn! Can you do that?" Bill asked.

Jason smiled. "I wouldn't like to put it to the test," he admitted.

"But stopping a man is no problem, huh?" Joe asked.

"Not when you apply the principles of jujitsu."

"Listen, I'm a pretty good street fighter myself," Joe said. "Why don't you show me a few moves? Not to teach me anything, you understand, just to sort of demonstrate what you can do." Joe raised his fist. "Come on," he said. "Come after me."

"It doesn't work that way," Jason explained.

"What do you mean?"

"Jujitsu is a defensive art, not an offensive one. If you want a demonstration, you'll have to attack me."

Joe lowered his fists. "No," he said. "I wouldn't want to make the first move...I wouldn't want to take advantage of you like that."

"You won't be taking advantage of me."

"Go ahead, Joe," Bill invited.

"No," Joe said. "Like I told you, I'm a street fighter, that means I don't exactly use the Marquis of Queensbury rules or anything like that, if you know what I mean?"

Jason smiled. "I know exactly what you mean. But if you want a demonstration, you are going to have to attack me."

"All right," Joe said. He threw a punch at Jason, but Jason avoided it, just by moving his head to the side, allowing the punch to slip by. It was a halfhearted punch at best, and Jason chided him for it.

"You weren't really trying," he said.

"All right, you asked for it," Joe said. This time he feinted with one hand, then threw the other. There was power behind this punch and as Jason slipped it, he could feel the wind of its passing.

Mike laughed.

"He's showing you up pretty good, Joe."

"You want to take a try at him?" Joe asked after he missed still a third time.

"I'll make you a deal," Jason said. "I'll take on all three of you. If I win, you'll let me join you. If you win, I'll go away and never bother you again."

"Come on, Mike, what do you say?" Bill said. "If he can handle all three of us, he's the kind of man we could use."

"All right," Mike said. "But not here in the office."

"Where, then?"

"Downstairs, in the gym. There's a ring we can use down there. And we can close and lock the door so nobody can see us." He smiled. "I'd feel kind of funny if anyone saw us, three against one. And if he really can beat us and someone saw it, I'd never again be able to hold my head up around here."

"Gentlemen, there is one ground rule," Jason said a few minutes later as the four of them stood in the boxing ring in the middle of the floor in the basement gym.

"So," Bill said, smiling, "here comes the catch. Okay, what is it?"

"Simply this," Jason said. "You must not try and hold back. You must come after me with every intention of doing me bodily harm."

"Doing you bodily harm?" Joe asked.

"He means we're supposed to bash in his head," Bill joked.

Jason smiled. "Something like that, yes," he said. He crouched down a little, bent his knees, and raised up onto the balls of his feet. He held his arms out in front of him, hands open, and palms facing toward his opponents. "I'm ready," he said.

Joe laughed. "You look pretty silly, you know that? You look like you're getting ready to slap us."

"Do I?" Jason replied noncommittally.

Bill and Joe, obviously having worked out something between them, suddenly swung at him at the same time. Jason dropped below their punches, but reached up to grab their wrists. He fell to the mat of the ring, and using the energy they had already put into their punches, he pulled them forward, off-balance, then jerked down. Both Bill and Joe turned a flip and wound up on their backs. Jason was back on his feet in an instant, looking down at them.

Mike, taking advantage of the fact that Jason seemed preoccupied with Bill and Joe, launched his own attack, letting out a shout of triumph as he did so. The triumph changed to frustration as he found his fist punching empty air, then surprise as he found himself being thrown for a flip, to join his two friends on the floor.

The three men tried for the next ten minutes to best

Jason but they were not only unsuccessful, they never even came close. On top of that, Jason seemed to be getting fresher as they were becoming more and more winded. Just before the end, Jason began turning it into a teaching lesson.

"Of course, I'm only defending myself now," he explained after he avoided one of Mike's attacks by leaning to one side. "If it were necessary, however, I could counterattack like this." He stuck out his right hand and touched Mike just behind his ear. He provided several more counterattack demonstrations until, finally, Mike, Bill, and Joe, their chests heaving as they hung on to the ropes, held up their hands in surrender.

"I don't know," Mike said as he gasped for breath. "After seeing how easily you handled us, do you still want to join?"

"Yes," Jason said.

Mike took a couple more deep, rasping breaths, then he smiled and held out his hand. "Welcome to the Bureau, Jason," he said.

CHAPTER 9

GREEN MOUNTAINS, VERMONT

Jason tossed another log into the fireplace, then he, Mike, Bill, and Joe sat in front of the fire. They were contemplative for a few moments, just watching the different colors formed in the flames by the mineral deposits in the wood. Though winter was not yet officially begun, a late fall snowstorm had started early in the afternoon and now the fields and roads were covered with it. Outside the cabin, on the slopes of the Green Mountains, the boughs of the fir trees were bent under their mantle of white.

The fire snapped and roared and threw out a large bubble of heat that warmed the area just around the fireplace. The rest of the cabin ranged from cool to cold, but there were down comforters on all the beds and the walls of the cabin kept out enough of the wind so that the men had no trouble sleeping at night.

It had been Mike's suggestion that the four of them get out of the city for a week and Jason had offered the use of a mountain cabin that belonged to his family. Mike instructed them to tell no one where they were going, other than to say that they "would be out of town for a few days." They had been in this place now for nearly a week.

"Did this house really belong to Ethan Allen?" Mike asked.

"Yes," Jason answered. "My father has a keen sense of history and whenever he finds some historical place that he thinks is not being properly preserved, he buys it. He owns houses and farms that belonged to such people as John Adams, Henry Clay, Millard Filmore, U. S. Grant, and even Grant's adversary Robert E. Lee."

"What's he going to do with all of them?" Bill wanted to know.

"Oh, I imagine he'll eventually give them to the government or the state, or whoever will promise to take care of them. There have been Vandervorts here, you know, since New York was New Amsterdam, so my father is pretty keen on preserving the heritage of our country."

"These old places are fine, I guess," Bill said. "But I wish they had electricity, and maybe a modern furnace."

Jason laughed. "You're too much of a city boy," he said. "There aren't many rural homes with electricity, even the modern ones. And even if electricity was available out here, I doubt if my father would avail himself of it. He likes to keep everything just the way it was." Jason pointed to a rough-hewn table. "Most of them even have their original furniture. That table, for example, is where Ethan Allen and his Green Mountain Boys took a blood oath of loyalty, not to the Continental Congress but to each other." He chuckled. "Before the Revolutionary War, you see, they weren't heroes, they were outlaws, fighting against New York. There was some dispute over who owned the land. Vermonters claimed it for themselves, even though there was no such place as Vermont at that time. New York said it belonged to them and they sent settlers in to homestead. Ethan Allen and his Green Mountain Boys ran the settlers off at the point of a gun and burned their houses and barns, so the governor of New York offered a reward of seven hundred fifty dollars for his arrest."

"You say Ethan Allen and his boys took a blood oath to each other," Joe said. "You sure they weren't Sicilian?"

The others laughed, then Jason said, "Forgive me if I sound patronizing, but the Sicilians do seem to set a great store by such things as blood oaths, don't they?"

"Yes, they do."

"Why?"

"It has to do with honor," Joe explained. "I know you've heard the thing about there being no honor among thieves, but within the clearly defined limits established by the Mafia, there is honor. Honor, loyalty, and secrecy. That's the glue that holds the Mafia together. That's what gives them their *facolta*, their powers. Without it, they are *impotente*, powerless."

Part of the reason Mike had brought the four of them to this retreat was to find a place of absolute privacy where Joe could share with them everything he knew about the Mafia. Bill and Jason had no idea that such a thing even existed until Joe began his impromptu lessons. Mike knew of the existence of the Mafia, because he had been told about it by Johnny. But Mike knew nothing else about it and he was dependent upon Joe for any more information.

Though Mike considered Joe's instruction on the Mafia of vital importance, it wasn't the only reason he had brought them up here. The information Joe provided was important, of course, as was Jason's instruction in jujitsu and Bill's instruction on firearms. However, what was even more important as far as Mike was concerned was the fact that the four men were beginning to know one another, to learn to depend upon one another, and to come together as a team.

"If you stop to think about it," Mike had told them, "each of us brings a unique perspective to the group. Bill is a weapons expert, Jason is skilled in the peculiar art of Japanese fighting, and Joe has an insight into the Mafia as well as the ability to speak the language."

"What do we need you for, Mike?" Bill teased.

"I'm just along for the ride," Mike answered and the others laughed.

"You have something better than any of our skills," Jason suggested. "Much better. You have the ability to lead. And, as Euripides once said, ten men, wisely led, are worth a hundred without a head."

"Who was Euripides?" Joe asked.

"I think he used to manage the Brooklyn Dodgers," Bill joked.

"*Impotente*," Mike said.

"What?"

"*Impotente*," Mike said again. He smiled. "I like that word. I like the idea of it. I like the idea of the Mafia being powerless."

"Yeah, but they're not *impotente*," Bill said.

"Maybe we can make them that way," Mike suggested.

"How?"

"By canceling out their facolta with jujitsu."

"Right," Bill said. "We'll just go down on Mulberry or some such place and say, 'Come on out, boys, let's wrestle.'"

"No, I'm not joking," Mike said. "And you weren't listening when Jason told us about jujitsu. I don't mean just the fighting part, I mean its philosophy of turning strength back upon itself."

"I'm lost," Joe admitted.

"Do you know, Jason?" Mike asked. He smiled. "After all, it was you who gave me the idea."

Jason laughed. "I'm glad I'm so brilliant. I'm so brilliant in fact that I don't even know what you are talking about."

"Then hear me out for a moment or two and I'll try to explain. Now, to begin with, from what Johnny Sangremano told me and from what Joe has verified, the very fact that we are aware of the existence of the Mafia makes us dangerous to them. Therefore we must keep to ourselves the fact that we know of the Mafia. There is a certain advantage to that as I'm sure you can see. If they think nobody is even aware of their existence, it will give them a false sense of security. For the time being, we will let them continue to think that."

"What do you mean, for the time being?" Bill asked. "If it gives us an advantage, why should we ever let them know that we know?"

"Because, under the right circumstances, it may be even more to our advantage for them to realize that they have an enemy...especially if they don't know who that enemy is."

"Go on, we're listening," Jason said.

"We'll have an organization too," Mike said. "As secret as theirs, more so, for we know of their existence, but they won't know of ours. I want us to form a group, composed of the four of us. Membership in this group will bind us more closely together even than the oath of office we took when we joined the Bureau. I want this group to go beyond fraternal, to become more like a sacred order. I want us to gather around this same table that Ethan Allen and his Green Mountain Boys used, and swear a blood oath of honor, loyalty, and secrecy. If we do that, we will turn the strength of the Mafia right back on them."

"Damn!" Joe said. "Damn, that's a great idea."

"Bill, you were the first one to join me. What do you think? Are you willing to take a blood oath, swearing honor, loyalty, and secrecy to the group?"

"Sure," Bill answered. "Actually, you and I took an oath like that a long time ago, remember? We vowed that if we ever joined the police force we would be honest cops. We were only what... twelve or thirteen when we made that oath? But as far as I'm concerned, I'm still bound by it. I would have no problems taking this oath, for as I see it, it would just be a reaffirmation."

"Jason?" Mike asked.

"I have shared with the three of you some of the philosophy I learned, and to which I ascribe. So you know that for me an oath is almost a mystical thing." Jason smiled at Joe. "I guess in that, I'm not too distant from your people, Joe." He looked back at the others before he continued his thought. "I tell you this now so you will understand that if I take this oath, it will be an oath for life. I will be bound by it if I live to the age of one hundred. Now, if you are prepared to have a totally inflexible member of your pact, then I shall take the oath."

"Joe, that leaves only you," Mike said. "Would you be willing to take it?"

"Yes," Joe said solemnly. "I would be proud to take it."

"You have no feelings of ethnic loyalty or anything like that?"

"My loyalty is to the four of us," Joe said.

"Good," Mike said. "Good. You already understand just what I am getting at."

"Mike, let me ask you something. This group we are forming, are we to be its only members?" Jason asked.

"We will be for now," Mike answered. "There will be other members, though as I see it, membership should only be granted to the select few who will meet the ideals that we will set. It is my hope that the group will outlive us and its future members will take up the journey we are starting."

"What do you mean, starting?" Bill asked. "Aren't we going to finish the job?"

Mike smiled. "There will be victories for us, yes," he said. "I feel confident that we will be victorious over the Sangremanos, the Vaglichios, the Nicolos, and other individual families within the Mafia. But I am equally sure that the Mafia as an institution will survive us. We will therefore have to pass the torch to those who follow us if there is to be an ultimate victory."

"What will we call ourselves?" Bill asked.

"I don't know," Mike said. "Anybody have any suggestions?"

"How about the Green Mountain Group?" Jason suggested.

"Yeah," Joe said. "I like that."

"No, it's too narrow," Mike said. "It means something to us...what will it mean to the man who joins fifty years from now? We need something with more punch."

"How about the Blood Oath Gang?" Joe suggested.

"That's closer."

"Blood Oath Society," Jason said.

"Yes!" Mike agreed. He smiled broadly. "Yes, that's it. Gentlemen, the Blood Oath Society it will be."

"Let's take the oath," Bill said.

"Wait a minute," Jason replied. "Mike, if you are serious about this being an organization that is going to last from now on, we need to take the time to come up with an oath that is worthy."

"I agree," Mike said. He put his hand on Jason's shoulder. "You are the most educated one of the lot," he said. "I'd like you to write it if you would."

"I would consider it a distinct privilege and honor," Jason said. "If you'll give me a few minutes I'll see what I can come up with."

"Fine. You work on that, we'll get supper," Mike proposed.

The men had been taking turns preparing the meals. Joe had fixed spaghetti the night before but tonight was Bill's turn. He began by frying thick slices of bacon, then he sliced up several potatoes to cook in the bacon grease. Just before the potatoes were done he broke half a dozen eggs over them so that the end result was a scrambled egg and potato mixture.

"Last night we ate like Italians," Bill said as he brought the meal to the table, the same table where Ethan Allen and his men had no doubt eaten their meals. "So tonight we're eating like the Irish."

"It doesn't look bad," Joe admitted as Bill spooned it onto the plates.

"You're Irish too, Mike. How about it, is this stuff any good?"

Mike grinned and doused his potatoes and eggs liberally with catsup. "Yes, but I have found that it goes down a lot better with this," he suggested.

"Is that Irish?" Jason asked.

"American Irish," Mike replied.

When the supper dishes were cleared away the four men returned to the table to take the oath Jason had written.

"Have you got any idea about how we should do this?" Mike asked.

"Yes," Jason said. "After we take the oath, we will prick our fingers and seal the oath with a drop of our blood. After that, we'll burn the paper so that its elements become a permanent part of the gases of the atmosphere. That way, a thousand years from now, though dispersed by wind and time, these atoms will still exist."

"What about people who join later?" Mike asked. "If we burn this copy, will we remember what we said?"

"Part of the rites will be that we must commit to memory the oath that we take," Jason explained. "That way there will never be anything in writing to point to us. If we truly are to be a secret organization, that's the only way to do it."

"That's a good idea," Mike said. "Why don't you read it aloud once, all the way through?"

"Yeah," Bill agreed. "I'd like to hear it."

"Me too," Joe added.

Jason cleared his throat, then began to read.

"I"—he looked up—"and here, we will say our names," he explained. Then he started again. "I, Jason Daniel Vandervort the Third, in agreeing to become one of the Brethren of the Blood Oath Society, do hereby solemnly swear allegiance to the Society, loyalty to the Brethren, and fidelity to the principles upon which the Society was founded.

"As Brethren of the Blood Oath Society we are sworn enemies to the Mafia and are the true stewards of justice. We vow never to betray these ideals by any act of dishonesty or compromise. We further swear to hold sacred the mystic rites of the Blood Oath Society, keeping secret even its very existence except to those deemed worthy of induction into its mysteries."

"Let's commit it to memory," Mike said.

After all four had memorized the covenant, they extinguished the kerosene lantern, then in the flickering shadows of light from the fireplace, they took the oath. Afterward, each of them pricked the ring finger of their left hand, touched a drop of their blood to the paper, then tossed the paper into the fireplace so that it could be consumed by the fire and its elements returned to the earth's atmosphere.

The Blood Oath Society was born.

CHAPTER 10

When Mike, Bill, Joe, and Jason returned from the Green Mountains, they returned to a city at war. Luca Vaglichio, convinced now that there would be no peace until the Sangremanos were gone and their organization destroyed, struck first, killing Luigi Sarducci and two of his top lieutenants as they sat over wine after a leisurely dinner in an Italian restaurant on Mulberry Street. Vinnie Sangremano retaliated by sending Angelo Cardi and two carloads of gunmen to shoot down Arnie Fusco and Vic Tampino.

After that, both Families "went to the mattresses," meaning that it was necessary for them to move out of their houses and into secret apartments. The term came from the fact that as many as a dozen men would be together in one apartment, so that extra mattresses would be brought in and put down on the floor to give them a place to sleep.

The war raged on throughout the winter and on into spring, during which time the transportation of liquor came to a near halt and all the speakeasies, even the more glamorous ones, had to close for lack of whiskey.

The newspapers were full of a daily account of the battles and every morning anywhere from three to four new victims would be added to the growing list of those killed. The killing reached far down into the ranks of both sides so that not only the capo-regimes and their lieutenants were killed, but many of the little men as well, including bookies, loan sharks, and even the lowly numbers runners. The idea was to bring all revenue-producing operations to a halt, for wars were expensive to conduct and they required a steady source of income. If the whiskey joints were closed, and the bookies, loan sharks, and numbers runners were frightened to the point that they couldn't, or wouldn't, do business, then the entire Family suffered. It was war on a grand scale with every stratagem employed, from psychological terror to economic deprivation.

Unfortunately, it wasn't only the soldiers of warring Families who were being killed. There was also a growing list of innocent victims. An ice man, delivering on Morris Avenue, was shot down in front of his customers. A woman and her little girl were killed on Delancey Street in Little Italy. When someone threw a bomb from a speeding car on Spring Street, three school-children were injured. That was when the mayor of New York decided there had been enough and he called in the heads of all his departments, demanding that something be done immediately. It was shortly after that that Mike had an unexpected visitor, in the person of Lieutenant Herbert Trapnell. The police lieutenant was standing at Mike's desk, playing with a crystal paperweight, turning it over to watch the snowstorm inside, when Mike, Bill, Joe, and Jason came back from a late lunch.

"You can just all go to lunch at the same time, can you?" Trapnell asked. "Is that the way the federal boys do things? Suppose someone really needed you at noon? How would they get you?"

"By coming to the restaurant on the corner," Mike answered. "What is it, Trapnell? What do you want?"

"Come now, Mikey, is that any way for fellow law officers to greet each other?" Trapnell asked.

"So we're fellow law officers now, are we? As I recall, you laughed longest and hardest over the great laundry raid last year," Mike said. He took off his jacket and hung it from a coat rack near the large wall map of the United States. When he did so, his shoulder-holster rig and the forty-five-caliber Colt automatic it contained stood out sharply.

"I did that, to my great shame," Trapnell admitted. "I guess I was just a little jealous. I mean here we were, New York's finest, sitting on our duffs while you were getting all the attention just because you were federal boys. But that's all behind us now. We've done some good work together over the last year, the federal boys and the New York Police. And I'll wager there's good work to be done yet."

"What do you have in mind, Trapnell?"

Trapnell looked at the other three men who, like Mike, had removed their jacket and had revealed their shoulder holsters and pistols. Trapnell cleared his throat and stroked his chin.

"Listen, Mike, is there somewhere we can go?" he asked. "Could we go someplace where we could talk privately?"

"We can talk here," Mike replied. "We have no secrets from each other," he added, taking in the others with a sweep of his hand.

"Is that a fact now? It's too bad we can't say that in the police department. You never know who you can trust. Your own father was an example of that."

"Are you saying my father was guilty?" Mike bristled.

"Now don't get yourself all in a huff," Trapnell said quickly, holding his hands out. "All I'm saying is, if your father was guilty, then that's a clear example of police corruption. And if he wasn't guilty, then he had to be set up by another policeman and that's an example too. Either way, lad, your father getting killed as he did is an example of not being able to trust the police department."

"We have no such problems," Mike said.

"Good, good," Trapnell said. "Then I've come to the right place."

"You've come to the right place for what?"

"Mike, how would you like to round up the Sangremano gang? Or at least enough of them to put them out of business, once and for all."

"I'd like that," Mike replied.

Trapnell smiled broadly. "I can help you do it," he said.

"Why would you want to do us a favor?" Mike asked.

"Call it for old time's sake," Trapnell answered. "Your father and I walked the beat together when we started."

"You're going to have to try something else," Mike said. "I don't believe that bullshit for a minute."

Trapnell chuckled. "You don't?"

"No."

Trapnell sighed. "Well, you're right, kid. Your old man and I hated each other's guts. You see, we both took a payoff every now and again. The only difference, I wasn't a hypocrite about it—your old man was."

"Get out, Trapnell."

"Wait! Don't you at least want to hear what I have to say? I think you're going to find it to your liking. Unless..." he let the word hang for a moment.

"Unless what?"

"Unless it's true what the Vaglichios say, that the

Sangremanos have you guys in their pockets. You and Johnny Sangremano are big friends, I hear, and that one" —Trapnell pointed to Joe—"is the nephew of Al Provenzano, one of Vinnie Sangremano's top men. Maybe you aren't really interested in arresting them."

"You sonofabitch," Mike growled. "You know that isn't true."

Trapnell smiled victoriously. "No, it probably isn't true," he said. "But you are worried enough about what other people might think about it so you are going to listen to my plan."

"You haven't told me yet why you are doing this," Mike said.

"It's simple," Trapnell replied. "I'm going to make captain out of this. Do you have any idea how much power a police captain has?"

"Your pockets will get deeper," Mike said.

"And fuller," Trapnell agreed. "But what do you care? You'll get Sangremano, the mayor is made happy, and I'll get promoted."

"All right, what do you have in mind?"

"A joint operation between your men and mine," Trapnell said. "I'm using you instead of another police task force so that I won't have to share the credit with anyone."

"You'll have to share it with us," Mike told him.

"You don't count. When this is over, the mayor is going to be looking for people to reward. He can't reward you, so he'll have to reward the police who were involved. That will be me and my men."

"All right," Mike said. "What do you have in mind?"

"Have you ever heard of something called the Trojan Horse?" Trapnell asked.

"Yes, of course I have," Mike said.

Trapnell laughed. "Well, tonight you are going to use

a Trojan Horse. Or at least the same principal. There's a warehouse down on Orchard Street, just off Broome. I know that the Sangremanos are expecting a truckload of booze there tonight. I also know where the booze is coming from, and what route it is taking. All you have to do is stop the truck. I'll have another truck there, ready to confiscate the booze and take it down to the police warehouse. After the booze is pulled off the truck, put your men into the rear of the truck and continue on to the warehouse as if nothing has happened. I'll be waiting a couple of blocks away with two carloads of police officers. We'll give you time to get into position inside, then we'll come in. Sangremano can't get away."

"No," Mike said.

"What's the matter, don't you like the plan?" Trapnell asked. "Or is it too dangerous for you?" he chided.

"You're damned right it's too dangerous for me," Mike said. "Especially if you come in like you said. There's bound to be shooting and we'll be caught right in the middle."

"Do you have a better idea?"

"Yeah," Mike said. "You surround the building from outside. Like you say, they can't get away. But you have to figure that they aren't going to have a lot of armed men down there, just a bunch of strong backs. After all, they are expecting to receive a truckload of whiskey, not fight a battle. When we jump down out of the back of that truck, we'll be armed. We can get the drop on them."

"And make the arrest all by yourself?" Trapnell complained. "Where does that leave me?"

"We'll turn them over to you," Mike said. "And the arrest will be a joint arrest."

Trapnell stroked his chin for a moment, then nodded. "All right," he said. "I don't like just standing by and letting you hand them over to us like that. But if that's the way it has to be..."

"That's the way it has to be," Mike said.

Trapnell pulled a piece of paper from his pocket and handed it to Mike. "Be at this intersection at eight o'clock tonight," he said. "The whiskey will be in a red REO, New Jersey license number 5618."

"We'll be there," Mike promised.

"Mike, you know that guy is as dirty as they come, don't you?" Bill said after Trapnell left.

"Yeah, I know."

"Well, do you believe him?"

"If you mean, do I believe the Sangremanos will be receiving a load of whiskey tonight, the answer is yes. But if you are asking me if I really think he is doing this for the mayor, then the answer is no. He's a Vaglichio man. What I figure is he's using his position to get rid of the Sangremanos, not for the police, but for the Vaglichios."

"And we're going to help him?"

"Sure," Mike said. "What do we care why he wants to help? The only thing important to us is that it gets done. The way I look at it, if we take care of the Sangremanos now, that's one down."

"Yeah," Bill said. "I guess you're right. It's just that it sticks in my craw to do anything that might help that low-assed sonofabitch."

"Mike, what about the booze?" Joe asked.

"What about it?"

"Chances are that the truck we load the booze into will take it straight to Vaglichio," Joe said. "With the war going on, it's worth more than ever, now."

"Yeah," Mike said. "Yeah, you're probably right. Okay, we'll contact a couple of Treasury men and have them get a truck over there. Instead of putting the booze in the police truck, we'll put it in the Treasury truck."

Bill laughed. "Trapnell isn't going to like that," he said.

———

Trapnell wasn't there when the REO was stopped, so he couldn't complain. The two policemen who were driving the truck Trapnell had in position to receive the confiscated liquor did complain, but there was nothing they could do about it. There were only two of them, there were six with Mike, counting the two Treasury agents who were with the truck Mike had brought up.

Working quickly, the REO was off-loaded, then Joe took the coat and hat of the driver and got behind the wheel. Mike, Bill, and Jason got into the back of the truck.

Just as Joe was about to start the truck, he saw a piece of paper taped to the instrument panel. On the paper was the word "tradimento."

"Mike!" he said. "Something might be wrong. They may be on to us."

"Why?"

"There's a word here, written on a piece of paper. Tradimento."

"What does that mean?"

"It means treachery."

"Shit," Bill said. "They must've found out. What do we do now?"

"If they know about it, they could be waiting on us," Mike said.

"I've got an idea," Jason said. "I'll ride under the truck. If they suspect anything at all, it would be that we're all back here."

"What do you mean, ride under the truck? There's no place to ride down there."

"I'll find something to hang on to," Jason said, grinning broadly as he hopped down, then crawled up underneath. "Okay!" he shouted a moment later. "Let's go!"

It was about a mile from where the truck had been stopped to the warehouse on Orchard. Jason had to hang on by his hands and feet for the whole way, with the pavement just inches below his body, and the twisting driveshaft less than an inch above his gripping fingers. When they finally got there, Joe turned off the street and headed for the warehouse itself. Mike felt the turn and stood up to pull the canvas aside and look ahead to see where they were. He could see the headlights playing upon the warehouse door.

Joe honked the horn and the small door beside the large warehouse door opened. A man stuck his head out.

"*Morte*," the man said.

What did he mean by that? Joe wondered.

"*Morte*," the man said again, more insistently this time.

Morte. Death. Treachery. Death for treachery, Joe thought. It must be a sign and countersign.

"*Tradimento*," Joe answered.

The man in the door smiled, then in Italian shouted, "I was beginning to think I was going to have to shoot you."

"I wouldn't like that," Joe answered in Italian.

The man went back inside and closed the little door. A moment later the big door came open and someone waved the truck on. Joe put it in gear and drove on inside the building.

"No one is armed," Mike whispered as he looked through the canvas. "We can take them now."

Mike and Bill jumped down from the back of the

truck with pistols drawn. Joe came out of the cab of the truck, and Jason rolled out from underneath. The surprise was complete and all the men in the building, most of whom were muscular dockworkers, threw up their hands in fear and confusion.

"We're federal agents," Mike shouted, holding up his badge. "You are all under arrest for violation of the Volstead Act."

"Hello, Mike," Johnny said, holding his hands up in the air with the others. "I can't say that I'm happy to see you."

"Hello, Johnny," Mike replied.

"Vinnie," Johnny said. "This is my friend, Mike Kelly."

"Some friends you pick, Johnny," Vinnie said.

"Who are the others?" Mike asked.

"That's Angelo Cardi," Joe said, pointing to Angelo. "I don't know who the boy is."

"He's nobody," Johnny said. "We call him Weasel. He's just a kid. How about you let him go? And those fellas over there too. They are just day laborers looking for work where they can. They didn't know what was coming in on the truck. Do you have to arrest them?"

Mike looked at the men, and at the fear in their faces.

"They got families to support," Johnny said. "You got us," he added, "you don't want them."

"Take a look, Joe," Mike said. "Are we letting anyone get away if we let these guys go?"

Joe looked closely at all of them, then shook his head.

"All right," Mike said. "We'll get statements from you men, then we'll turn you loose. Jason, cuff Johnny, his brother, and Angelo Cardi."

"What about the kid?"

"Let the kid go," Mike said.

Johnny, Vinnie, and Angelo Cardi, now handcuffed, moved to the front of the truck as directed.

The front door opened then and half a dozen uniformed policemen came in.

"Come on in, Trapnell," Mike called over his shoulder. "I've got them all ready for you."

"Thanks, sucker," Trapnell said. The tone of his voice caused Mike to look around in surprise.

"Mike, it's Sal Croce!" Joe suddenly shouted. "They aren't policemen! They're Vaglichio's men!"

The six uniformed men opened fire.

"Get down!" Mike shouted, for the firing was indiscriminate, the uniformed "policemen" were shooting at everyone, Vinnie and Johnny, the unarmed dockhands, and Mike and his men.

Mike saw Vinnie and Angelo Cardi go down under a hail of fire. A couple of the dockworkers also grabbed at wounds in their stomach or chest as they crumpled to the concrete floor.

The federal agents reacted quickly and were already firing back. The machine guns being wielded by Vaglichio's men were spitting out a much higher rate of fire, but the bullets came out like water from the end of a hose, with volume having to make up for accuracy. Mike and his men were firing pistols. They were slower, but much more accurate. Mike saw the back of Sal Croce's head burst open in a spray of blood and brain matter as Bill hit him right between the eyes with a particularly well-placed shot.

Vaglichio's men were depending upon surprise and volume of fire to get the job done so none of them had taken cover. Instead, they were all standing their ground, firing from the hip, moving their guns back and forth as they sprayed bullets. Bullets struck orange sparks as they hit concrete, or ricocheted off steel girders and tubing. A few bullets penetrated the gas tank of the truck and the fuel began dripping out to form a stream that spread across the floor.

Mike's men were now well positioned. One was behind a stack of tires, another behind a barrel, Mike was on the ground behind the concrete base of a supporting girder, and Jason was behind a stack of wooden boxes. One by one their marksmanship began paying off as Vaglichio's men went down. Trapnell, suddenly discovering that he was the last one standing, threw up his hands and shouted.

"Kelly! Kelly! I give it up! I quit!"

"Cease fire!" Mike called, and the shooting stopped. Slowly, Mike and his men got up and started advancing toward Trapnell. The building, which had reverberated with the crash of gunfire a moment earlier, was now quiet, except for the moans of the wounded.

"Joe, Bill, Jason," Mike said. "Are any of you hit?"

"I'm okay," Bill said.

"Me too," Joe replied.

"I wasn't hit," Jason added. "But if you want my advice we'd better get out of here. There's gasoline all over the place."

"That ain't all you got to worry about," one of the dockworkers said. "There's quite a few barrels of raw alcohol in here too. That stuff would burn like all the fires of hell if it was to get started."

"Okay," Mike said. "Let's get everyone outside." He leaned down to help one of the dockworkers to his feet.

"Mike, look out!" Johnny suddenly shouted.

Reacting to Johnny's shout, Mike looked toward Trapnell and saw that the police lieutenant had pulled a hidden gun from somewhere. Mike and Trapnell fired at the same time. Mike's bullet caught Trapnell in the neck and he went down with his throat and windpipe destroyed by the bullet. Trapnell's bullet missed Mike, but it wound up doing even more damage, for the spark of it striking concrete ignited the little stream of gas. The fire raced across the floor to the fuel tank in the truck where it went up with a mighty whoosh. Instantly, the entire building was engulfed in flame.

"Get out of here!" Mike shouted. "Everyone out!"

"Mike!" Joe called. "Bill's trapped under the tires! Help me get him out!"

"I'll go!" Jason shouted. Jason was already dragging one of the wounded men out.

"No, you get these guys! I'll go," Mike said.

Covering his face with his arm, Mike leaped through a wall of flames. Just on the other side of the flames, he saw Joe frantically tossing burning tires aside. Mike rushed to his aide, and within seconds the two men were able to reach down and help Bill to his feet.

"Can you walk?" Mike shouted. Shouting was necessary now because the fire was roaring loudly.

"Yes!"

"Then let's get the hell out of here!"

The three men ran toward the same wall of flame that Mike had just come through. They managed to get back through even though it was larger now, though not without paying the price of singed hair and smoldering clothes. They slapped at their clothes to put out the fire when they got outside.

A little pile of wounded and rescued was lying just outside the burning building, looked over by Jason. He shouted happily and ran over to greet his three friends when he saw them emerge. From somewhere in the distance they could hear the sound of an approaching fire engine.

"Where's Johnny?" Mike asked, coughing and gasping for breath. "Did he get out?"

Jason shook his head. "No," he said. "I'm sorry, Mike. He was your friend, wasn't he?"

Mike shut his eyes tightly, and he could see Johnny, naked on the top wing of the biplane, his arms outstretched into the wind.

"Yeah," he said. "He was."

"Mike, look!" Joe said, pointing toward the front of the building. There were two people coming out of the burning building. One of the two was Weasel. He was struggling hard under the load, for he was half carrying and half dragging the other man. The other man was Johnny Sangremano.

"Johnny!" Mike shouted, surprised at how happy he was to see that Johnny had survived the fire. He ran over to help Weasel pull Johnny the rest of the way to safety.

Johnny coughed hard, then looked up at Mike. His face was blackened with soot and his eyes red-rimmed from the smoke.

"Now, you didn't really think you would get rid of me that easily, did you?" he asked.

Mike smiled. "No, not really," he said. "You're like a bad penny."

Johnny looked up at Weasel. "I owe this kid my life," he said. "And I'm never going to forget it."

"It was my privilege, padrone," Weasel said.

"So," Johnny said to Mike. "Are you going to arrest me now?"

"For what?" Mike asked, looking at the burning building. By now the first fire engine had arrived and the firemen were rushing through the crowd to get their hoses in position to play water upon the roaring inferno. "All the evidence has gone up in smoke."

"You mean you aren't going to arrest me?"

"That's what I mean," Mike said.

"You won't regret it," Johnny said.

"What do you mean by that?" Mike asked sharply. "Because if you mean you are going to make it worth my while, I'll…"

"No!" Johnny said quickly. "No, I didn't mean that at all. Mike, I know how you feel about things like that. But listen to me for a moment, will you?"

"All right. What do you have to say?"

"My brother is in that building."

"I'm sorry," Mike said.

"That means I am now the head of the Family," Johnny went on. "I'm going legit, Mike. I promise you."

"I wish I could believe you."

"I don't expect you to believe my words," Johnny said. "But a year from now, you can believe my action."

"What kind of business can you do that is legitimate?" Mike asked. "The only thing you've got going is prostitution, gambling, loan-sharking, extortion, and bootlegging. Which one of those businesses are you going to make legitimate?"

"I'll find a way," Johnny said. "You know me, Mike. I didn't want to get into this in the first place, but I had no choice. I did it because of my family. Now, the only family I have left is my mother and sister. My sister is a movie star. How would it look if the public knew that Katie Starr's brother was in the rackets? Don't you see, the same family obligation that got me into the rackets in the first place is now going to get me out. I owe it to Katherine."

Mike smiled. "Johnny, if that's true, nothing in this world would make me happier."

"It's true," Johnny said. "You can take it to the bank."

The newspapers, the same ones who once belittled Mike's efforts, now praised the success of the federal agents of the Bureau of Investigation. Headlines blared that the war had been stopped and the rackets busted up.

The mayor of the city, though embarrassed that the city police had not responded to the task, was nevertheless generous with his own praise. The Washington headquarters of the Bureau of Investigation sent J. Edgar Hoover up to New York to personally represent Chief of the Bureau William J. Flynn, and to extend the congratulations of the Bureau, and to inform them that money had been allocated to provide them with their own New York office.

"You won't have to depend upon the generosity of the local police for a place to stay anymore," Hoover told them.

"Good," Mike said. "That way we will never again have to worry about the wrong ears hearing our plans."

"You have put together quite an impressive group of young men," Hoover said. "You work remarkably well together. I'll remember you when I am made Chief of the Bureau."

"Are you going to be Chief of the Bureau?" Mike asked.

"Someday," Hoover replied without false modesty. "And when I do, I will make the FBI the greatest law-enforcement agency the world has ever seen." He smiled. "That is, as long as I can count on people like you and your group."

"What is the FBI?" Bill asked.

"We are," Hoover said. He laughed. "Actually, that's just what I call us. Federal Bureau of Investigation, get it? That's just to let people know that we have the power of the federal government behind us. Of course, FBI isn't the official title. But it will be one day."

"FBI," Mike said. "Yeah, I like that. I like that a lot."

EPILOGUE

ONE YEAR LATER: HOLLYWOOD, CALIFORNIA

Johnny Sangremano stood on the depot platform in his dark, pin-striped suit. He stood out like a lump of coal on a snowbank. There were several other people on the platform, some entraining, some detraining, others telling them goodbye or hello, but most of them weren't even wearing suits and those who were, wore suits in various light colors, blues, grays, or tans. There weren't that many wearing hats either, and the ones who were, wore straw hats.

"Are you Mr. Starr?"

The man who asked the question was shorter than Johnny and wearing a chauffeur's uniform.

"No," Johnny said.

The chauffeur smiled. "I'm sorry. Mr. Solinger told me I would be picking up Miss Starr's brother. That's why I called you that. I forgot your name would be different."

"My name isn't different. Her name isn't Starr,"

Johnny said. "It's Sangremano, just like mine. Katherine Sangremano."

"Yes, sir, I know. But you know how it is with these movie stars. They all got to change their name. The car's over there. Mr. Solinger says I'm to bring you straight to his house for lunch."

The car, like everything else he had seen in California, was a blaze of color. In this case, a bright yellow Lincoln. The driver's seat was open but Johnny rode in the closed part of the car. The inside of the car was rich with red leather and burled wood.

"Mr. Sangremano." Johnny was surprised to hear a voice until he realized that the driver was talking into a speaking tube and the sound was coming through a little acoustical vent especially designed for that purpose. "If you'll let down the panel in front of you, you'll find a bar. Help yourself. It's good liquor."

Johnny lowered the panel and looked at the selection of liquor. "Thanks," Johnny said. "But I promised a friend I was going straight. It wouldn't do for me to get caught drinking."

"Yes, sir," the chauffeur replied. "Whatever you say."

Solinger's house was in Beverly Hills. It was a huge spreading mansion sitting in the middle of a large, manicured estate and surrounded by a high stone fence. A uniformed guard opened the steel gate at the entrance of the driveway and the Lincoln rolled across crushed marble chips and under flowering trees as it maneuvered through the garden up to the house. Sammy Solinger met the car personally, showing his capped teeth in a smile that split his evenly tanned and meticulously barbered face.

"Johnny, Johnny, it is so good of you to come out here to see me," Solinger said.

"It's nice of you to receive me, Mr. Solinger."

"Please, please, call me Sammy. I mean, after all, we're business partners, aren't we? Haven't we made money on our pictures? We have had tremendous runs in New York, and I credit that to you and your marketing genius in handling the distribution there."

"It was my brother Tony's idea," Johnny said. "And my other brother, Vinnie, put it into place. All I've been doing is keeping an eye on it."

"Yeah, well, it's going great, just great. Come around back to the pool. I think Sidney has lunch set up for us. How was it when you left New York? Cold, I'll bet. You wouldn't think of sitting alongside a swimming pool eating lunch, would you?"

"No, I guess not," Johnny said.

"Yeah, well, today, we're going to sit alongside the pool and enjoy a nice meal on the patio." He laughed. "Patio, that's probably a word you've never heard. It's like an outside porch, only it's not attached. It's all part of living in California. You can't beat it, Johnny. You really can't beat it. Ah, here is Sidney."

Sidney was a tall, dignified-looking man dressed in a morning coat and striped trousers. He was standing stiffly by the table.

"This is Sidney Whitehouse, my manservant," Solinger said. "What a goddamned Englishman is doing using as a last name the place where the American president lives, I'll never know. He's a cultured sonofabitch, though. Listen to the sonofabitch talk. Sidney, this is my friend, Johnny Sangremano."

"Pleased to make your acquaintance, sir."

"Listen to that," Solinger said. "Listen to those tones. Goddamn, I'm just like you, I grew up in New York over on Hester Street, probably not too far from where you grew up. I mean someone can listen to me talk and he'll think, goddamn, this fella ought to be workin' in the garment trade, you know what I mean? But here I am, livin' like this in California, with a cultured sonofabitch like Sidney Whitehouse as my manservant. Sidney's royalty, did you know that?"

"Not royalty, sir," Sidney said.

"Well you're somethin' like that. What are you now?"

"I am the illegitimate son of an earl, sir."

"Goddamn, can you imagine that?" Solinger said. "I got the son of an earl workin' for me. Of course, he's the illegitimate son and I tell him the only thing that means is he is a bastard, right?" Solinger laughed loudly at his joke. "He doesn't like me much. You don't like me, do you, Sidney?"

"Not very much, sir," Sidney said.

"Not very much, sir," Solinger mimicked. "Yeah, but he likes my money. Everyone likes my money. I'll tell you a secret you probably already know, Johnny. When you got money, you got everything.

You're sittin' on top of the world and there can't nobody touch you. Look at that. Look at this backyard, at the pool. Sonofabitch, there ain't nothin' like this on Hester Street."

The pool was kidney-shaped, held in place by pink coping, surrounded by pale green ceramic tiles. The meal Sidney had set up for them was laid out on a glass table.

"Sit, eat," Solinger invited. "Just for you, Sidney had Ramon prepare a nice veal parmigiana. Ramon is my chef. We may as well eat Italian. If you are a good Jew and you want to eat kosher, ah, forget it," he said with a shrug of his shoulders. "So, I do what I can do."

"It looks good," Johnny said. "Thank you, Sidney."

"Enjoy, sir," Sidney said as he withdrew to allow the two men to talk in private.

"Have you seen your sister yet?" Solinger asked as he rolled linguine onto his fork.

"No," Johnny said.

"You will not recognize her. She is a beautiful young woman," he said. "Not that she wasn't always beautiful," he added quickly.

"I liked her more before," Johnny said. "I have seen her in the movies, and in the movies she looks like a *puttana*."

"*Puttana*? What is that?"

"Whore."

"But no! How can you say that?" Solinger asked.

"She has played beautiful roles in the movies. She has a certain sensuality about her, yes, but it is a very innocent sensuality."

"She has made a lot of money for you, hasn't she?"

Solinger cleared his throat. "Well, she is coming along nicely, yes," he said. "In fact, I would even go so far as to say that she is paying her own way. Most movie stars don't do that for several years, you know. That she has done it in just three movies is really quite amazing. But, as far as making me a lot of money? No, I wouldn't say so. Not yet, anyway. You see, it is costing a lot to develop her, to bring her along." Solinger smiled. "But it will all be worth it in the end, you'll see."

"Worth it to who?"

"Why, to Katie Starr, of course."

"We're talking about Katherine Sangremano."

"Of course we are," Solinger said. "Katie Starr is just a screen name, that's all. She is still known as Katherine to all her friends."

Johnny finished eating, then pushed his plate away and dabbed at his lips with the bright red napkin. "Mr. Solinger, I've had Al look into a few things for me," he said.

"Al. Let's see now. That would be Mr. Provenzano?"

"Yes. Al says that Katherine is one of the, I believe the term is, 'hottest properties' in Hollywood now."

"I see. And Mr. Provenzano, in addition to his other talents, is now an expert in movie production, is he?"

"What he is, Mr. Solinger, is an expert in money matters. He tells me that Katherine's last two pictures grossed more than any other picture produced by Redwood Studios. In fact, they grossed more than all the rest of Redwood's pictures, combined."

"That's gross," Solinger pointed out. "The bottom line is net."

Johnny smiled. "You don't have to talk to me about gross and net, Mr. Solinger. Most of the family business is in the difference between gross and net so I know how the figures can be manipulated."

"What are you getting at, Sangremano?" Gone was the California joviality. Solinger sensed some serious business discussion coming and he was going to be ready for it. He didn't have the reputation of being a tough businessman without reason.

"We've looked at the contract you have with Katherine and we don't like it. She's been offered a much better deal by another studio."

"I can't be responsible for what another studio has offered," Solinger said. "I have a business to run."

"Yes, well, we thought you might let her out of her contract."

"And just what made you think that?"

"We thought you might listen to reason."

There was that expression again. In New York, on Sangremano's home territory, the expression had had a certain ominous sound to it. Here, it took on an almost pathetic quality. Solinger dabbed at his own lips with his napkin, then folded it and put it on his plate.

"Mr. Sangremano," he said. "Perhaps it is time we got something straight. In New York, your brothers thought they were King Shit. But they are both dead now, and the Sangremanos got no power anymore, not in New York, and sure as hell not out here. Out here, I am the King of the Jungle. People cringe when I roar. You want me to listen to reason? Come with me. I want to show you something. I want to show you just how tight my hold is on this contract."

Solinger stood up and looked across the table at Sangremano.

"Come with me, please," he said. "I want you to see a little piece of film that I think you might find very interesting."

Curious as to what Solinger had in mind, Johnny followed him across the patio and into the house. The inside of the house duplicated the California lifestyle Solinger had shown off so opulently outside. There was a good deal of chrome and glass, and overstuffed furniture in tans and beiges scattered around in large airy rooms. Johnny followed Solinger down a hallway and into a smaller room that was set up as a projection studio.

"Sit there, Mr. Sangremano," Solinger invited. "I want you to see a piece of film that the entire world will see if you try any of your dago shit on me to get Katie Starr's contract nullified."

Johnny sat down and watched the screen.

The movie opened with a picture of Katherine lying on her side on a couch, looking into the camera with what the newspapers and magazines now called the "Katie sizzle," a smoldering, wide-eyed, pouted-lip look that seduced the camera. The camera then panned around the back so that it was shooting over Katherine's shoulder to see the man she was looking at.

The man was returning Katherine's smoldering look

with one of his own. Then Johnny was shocked to near insensibility by what happened next. The man suddenly dropped his trousers to reveal a tremendous erection! He walked over to the couch where Katherine, now nude, was waiting for him. *He put his hands in her long, black hair and pulled her face toward his groin so that she took his penis into her mouth.*

The entire scene was shot from just behind Katherine's shoulder so that nothing was missed. The camera moved in for an extreme close-up on the action itself so that the throbbing penis and the lips filled the entire screen.

After several moments of intercourse, the camera pulled away so that the smooth, bare skin of a nude Katherine's back could be seen once more.. When the screen wasn't full of the male and female genitalia, it was full of Katherine's face, with her eyes large and smoldering, and her lips pouting, as if she were really enjoying it.

"I've seen enough," Johnny said quietly.

Solinger turned on the lights, then stopped the projector.

"I thought, perhaps, you might find this interesting," he said.

"I can't believe it," Johnny said. "I can't believe my sister would do such a thing."

Solinger laughed, a high, thin cackling laugh. "You dumb dago shit," he said. "Do you really think that was Katie?"

Johnny looked up in surprise and Solinger laughed again.

"I did that," Solinger said, pointing to his chest. "I hired some hooker who had about the same build and color hair as Katie, then I paid some well-hung stud to ball her. I opened with a scene of Katie on the sofa, then when the camera came around behind, it was the hooker. Didn't you notice that I never showed the naked girl's face? Whenever I did show a face, it was full screen of Katie. I spliced it in, every time."

"That wasn't my sister?"

"Hell no, it wasn't your sister," Solinger said. "But there won't be one person in a hundred who won't believe it if they saw this film. Do you understand what I'm telling you, guinea? I've got ways you've never even heard of to protect my interest. You mess with me and I'll ruin your sister and disgrace your entire family, what there is left of it. Now, get out of my house, you wop bastard. And get out of my town."

Johnny stood up. "I am sorry to have disturbed you, Mr. Solinger," he said calmly. "And I am sorry I couldn't make you listen to reason."

Solinger smiled, magnanimous now in his victory. "Yeah, well, listen, don't take it so hard," he said. "Leave your sister's career in the hands of someone who knows what he's doing. Trust me, I'll do right by her." He took the reel of film off the projector and handed it to Johnny. "Here, to show you there is no hard feelings, I'll give you this film." He laughed. "I could always put together another one if I needed. But of course, now that you know I can do it, I won't really have to, will I?"

"No," Johnny said contritely. "You won't have to do that. I won't be talking to you again."

"I'll have my driver drop you off anywhere you want to go," Solinger said. "And don't feel bad about losing to me, my friend. This is a different world out here. It's hard for any outsider to come in and start throwing his weight around."

Solinger walked Johnny to the front drive of his house, put him in the car, then waved goodbye as he left.

"Mr. Sangremano won't be staying for dinner, sir?" Sidney asked from behind Solinger.

"No," Solinger said. He laughed. "I think he just lost

his appetite." He waved again as the car disappeared from view, though as Johnny was sitting very still and very stiff in the back seat, staring straight ahead, Solinger's wave wasn't returned.

Solinger looked at his watch. "My goodness, look at the time. I promised Fatty Arbuckle I'd play a round of golf with him this afternoon," he said. "I should be back around six. I'll have an early dinner by the pool...tell Ramon to make it something light, then I'm going to bed to catch up on some reading. I have several script offers for Katie Starr and I want to make certain I pick the one that will make the most money."

"As opposed to the one that would be best for Miss Starr's career?" Sidney asked.

Solinger laughed. "So who are you? Her dutch uncle or something? To hell with Katie Starr's career. You know how this business is. Everyone loves you today, nobody has ever heard of you tomorrow. I'm going to get every cent out of her as fast as I can. But that's none of your concern, is it?"

"No sir, I suppose not."

"I suppose not," Solinger mimicked. "Just have the goddamn dinner set up by six o'clock like I told you."

"Very good, sir," Sidney said.

Solinger chuckled. "You should have seen that guinea bastard's face when I turned the lights on after that film," he said. He laughed again. "Goddamn, I feel good!"

At exactly five minutes of six, Sidney went into the kitchen to see what Ramon had prepared for Solinger's dinner. Ramon, who was once the head chef for Delmonico's in San Francisco, had arranged on a large silver tray an artistic display of cold cuts, cheeses, and hard rolls along with condiments of mustard and horseradish. A bed of bib lettuce, cherry tomatoes, and pickles completed the tray. Sidney protected the food with a large silver cover, then took it out onto the patio and placed it on the table to be ready at exactly six o'clock when Solinger returned from his golf. As he was setting the table, he noticed that the cut flowers in the vase were somewhat wilted, so he removed them and took the vase around to the garden where he changed the water, then cut a fresh new bouquet, arranged it carefully, and brought it back to put on the table. He stepped back to study the table in order to see it in the same perspective Solinger would when he arrived. It gave him pleasure to be perfectly correct all the time because he knew that it just pointed out Solinger's own inadequacies. It was a quiet way of getting back at Solinger, but a satisfying one. After admiring the table for a moment, he walked over and lifted the silver cover, then he staggered back in shock at what he saw there. His knees grew weak and he had to grab the back of the chair to keep from fainting. Then the well-bred English reserve took hold and he calmed himself. He replaced the silver cover so that he wouldn't have to look at the gruesome display, then he walked over to the nearest telephone to call the police.

"Yes," he said when the police answered. "My name is Sidney Whitehouse. I am the butler…that is, I was the butler for Mr. Sammy Solinger. I think you had better send a few officers out to Mr. Solinger's estate. He seems to have lost his head."

As the train pulled out of Los Angeles, Johnny heard a quiet knock on the door of his bedroom compartment. He had been reading a book and he lay it aside to open the door. Weasel was standing just on the other side.

"Hello, Weasel," Johnny said. "How did everything go?"

"It went fine, Don Sangremano," Weasel said. "We won't be hearing from Mr. Solinger again."

"Good, good. Now, come in and have a seat. We've

been quiet long enough. It's time to put things to right. I have several things I want you to do for me when we return to New York."

"*Sí*, padrone. It will be my great honor to serve you," Weasel said respectfully.

A LOOK AT: BLOOD OATH

WHEN HONOR DIES BOOK TWO

There's only one way to escape the Mafia... bloodshed.

Johnny Sangremano and Mike Kelly were inseparable as kids, bound by loyalty and shared dreams. But now, the paths they've chosen pit them against each other. Johnny, born into one of the most powerful Mafia families, is destined to rise through the ranks. Mike, determined to uphold justice, has followed his father's footsteps to become a federal agent. His mission: take down the very Mafia that Johnny calls family.

As tension escalates, both men must decide how far they're willing to go to protect those they love. Can Mike uphold the law without betraying his oldest friend? Will Johnny sacrifice everything to protect his family's legacy?

Dive into the second book of the *When Honor Dies* series today and experience the ultimate showdown between loyalty and justice.

AVAILABLE NOVEMBER 2024

ABOUT THE AUTHOR

Robert Vaughan sold his first book when he was nineteen. That was several years and nearly three-hundred books ago. Since then, he wrote the novelization for the mini-series Andersonville, as well as written, produced, and appeared in the History Channel documentary Vietnam Homecoming.

Vaughan's books have hit the *New York Times* bestseller list seven times. He won the Spur Award, the Porgie Award in Best Paperback Original, the Western Fictioneers Lifetime Achievement Award, the Will Rogers Medallion Award, the Readwest President's Award for Excellence in Western Fiction, and is a member of the American Writers Hall of Fame and a Pulitzer Prize nominee.

Vaughan was also a retired army officer, helicopter pilot with three tours in Vietnam, who has received the Distinguished Flying Cross, the Purple Heart, the Bronze Star with three oak leaf clusters, the Air Medal for valor with 35 oak leaf clusters, the Army Commendation Medal, the Meritorious Service Medal, and the Vietnamese Cross of Gallantry.